OUT OF ASHES

CARRIE VIXENHART

CONTENT NOTE

Please be advised that this book contains explicit content that may not be suitable for all readers. Dark themes include violence, death, grief, mature subjects, substance abuse, addiction, supernatural elements, and explicit sexual activities that are shown on the page. Readers sensitive to these topics are encouraged to proceed with caution. For more details, visit Vixenhart's website at vixenhart.com/books or scan the QR code.

DEDICATION

To the creators of online dating apps & all the people I met there: Your chaos was...a gift. You provided endless plot twists and an unending well of inspiration. Your legacy lives on in these pages— and likely in my stories—for years to come.

OUT OF ASHES

CHAPTER

ONE

Ophelia felt a shiver of loneliness as she realized the bartender was staring at her. Knocking back the earthy drink, she scrunched her nose against the putrid scent of agave and desert that clung in the air long after the liquid scorched a path down her throat. Good. No lime and salt for her. She wanted it to burn. Swirling her glass, she looked down at its emptiness, a frown of recognition tugging at the edges of her lips.

"Another?" The man's voice wavered with a mix of desperation and ill-placed hope. His scrawny frame hunched awkwardly behind the dark mahogany bar as he clutched the cheapest tequila bottle he could find.

She squinted at him through the haze of alcohol. Wrong. His voice, his stature, his everything—wrong. Nothing like Luka. But maybe this shadow of a man could distract her. Just for a few minutes.

"Sure," she said, slurring as she swayed on the creaky barstool. Her skirt hiked up another inch, revealing long legs she didn't bother to adjust for modesty. Midnight-black hair spilled around her face in a tangled mess.

At some point, she'd switched from vodka to tequila, desperate for something to pierce the numbness. She barely noticed the empty bar now cloaked in the sickly sweet scent of stale vape fumes. Glancing at her phone, she struggled to focus on the screen. Time blurred.

What did it matter anyway?

Sighing, she lifted her eyes to the bartender, giving a half-nod that might have resembled a bobblehead on a bumpy ride. "Only if you'll join me," she said, stumbling over the words as they spilled out.

The man grinned, his eagerness radiating neediness. He poured her another drink, then grabbed a shot glass for himself, practically skipping to her side of the bar. She suppressed a shudder when his clammy hand grazed her thigh, moving up to linger below the hem of her crop top.

Well, at least that was feeling something.

He leaned in, all teeth and tongue, his mouth darting like a whack-a-mole searching for a target.

No. She turned her head sharply, pulling back just as he asked, "Can I take you to my place?"

She blinked at him. In no world would she allow herself to be surrounded by this man's belongings. This fragile illusion couldn't survive it.

"How about the alley?" she said, low and breathy from the alcohol. Maybe there she could pretend, just for a moment, that it was Luka's hands on her body, his mouth on hers.

The man giggled—a high-pitched, grating sound. "You're a freaky slut, huh?"

Flinching, she didn't bother to hide her disgust. He didn't notice—or didn't care. Sliding off the barstool, she tugged her skirt down with shaky hands, catching herself on the wall as her balance wavered.

He grabbed her wrist and tugged her toward the back exit. His grip was slick, his nails rough against her skin. She followed, her fire dulled by the alcohol coursing through her veins. Good. No magic. No freak show.

As they stumbled into the alley, the stench hit her first—rotting food and vomit mingled with the grease of bar food discarded hours ago. She gagged.

Before she could rethink her decision, he shoved her against a peeling blue dumpster, his wiry frame pressing into hers. She felt his breath on her neck, stale with liquor and something sour.

Bile rose in her throat.

"No," she whispered, the word barely audible.

"You wanted this," he said, pawing at her hip. His lips moved toward hers again, his weight trapping her against the metal.

"No," she said louder, shoving weakly against his chest. "No, no, no."

Her head spun, thoughts tangled in a fog of alcohol and shame. What was she doing here? Luka was gone. He wasn't coming back. And this man—this thing—would never come close to what she'd lost. She couldn't remember her training. Couldn't call any magic. She'd dulled her power to oblivion. *What an idiot*, she berated herself. Letting herself get to this place. Yet again.

"Relax," the man said, voice dripping with false reassurance. "You'll love it."

Ophelia braced herself, clenching her jaw as he reached for the hem of her skirt. But he froze, his movements halted by a low voice that sliced through the night.

"I suggest you take your hands off her. Now." The rumbling

timbre of his voice wasn't loud, but it sliced with precision. It was the kind of voice that commanded attention and obedience.

Her stomach twisted. That demanding voice grated on her. Damn it. Gabriel. Always rescuing her.

The man turned, his Adam's apple bobbing as he swallowed hard. "Man, fuck off. What's it to you?"

Ophelia sighed, already knowing how this would go.

Before she could warn him, the bartender made the mistake of clamping a hand over her mouth. His palm smelled like a damp bar rag soaked in mildew and regret.

The bartender flew backward before Ophelia even registered Gabriel moving. One moment he was in front of her, the next, the man was crumpled against the wall. Gabriel stood between them, his body tense with restrained force, every inch of him screaming danger. He radiated control—everything she'd been losing, drowning in the tequila that was still on her tongue. Gabriel's broad shoulders blocked her view of the man crumpled on the ground.

She leaned to the side, trying to peek around him, but stumbled into his back instead, her balance faltering as she lost a shoe. Grabbing a fistful of his leather jacket, she caught herself, steadying her swaying frame against him.

The bartender groaned, struggling to his feet. "What the hell, man?"

Gabriel adjusted his sleeves, covering the tattoos that crawled from his hands up his arms. His expression was calm, almost bored. "I told you to take your hands off her," he said, his tone slow and deliberate. "I don't like to repeat myself. You think this is about you? It's not. She's mine to protect. Now, leave before I change my mind."

The man muttered something incoherent before slinking back into the bar, his pride and courage left behind in the alley.

Ophelia snorted, a mix of laughter and disgust bubbling up. "As if I'd want him."

Gabriel turned to face her, his eyes dark and unyielding. His proximity made her head spin faster, though this time, it wasn't the alcohol.

"What?" she said, grinning up at him. Her giggles returned, her body rocking with the force of her hiccups. She giggled again when she realized her breasts were bouncing against him. He wouldn't like that.

His growl rumbled low in his chest, and she felt the heat of his frustration radiating between them. Without a word, he grabbed her around the waist and threw her over his shoulder.

"Gabriel!" she shrieked, pounding weakly on his back. "That was too fast!"

He deposited her in the deeper shadows of the alley, his hands on her shoulders as he steadied her against the wall. "Ophelia, I was getting you away from that trash and smell."

"Oh." She crossed her arms over her chest, pouting. "Well, I was having fun. You scared my date away."

"Date?" he said, voice clipped with lethal anger. "That wasn't a date, Ophelia. That was a bartender you tried to screw in an alley."

Her face burned, but she refused to let the shame settle. She jabbed a finger into his chest. "You don't get to judge me, Gabriel. You don't know what it's like to lose everything."

His eyes darkened further, but she pressed on, her magic sparking at her fingertips as her anger flared. "Or are you jealous, Gabriel? Do you want to be the one to fuck the sadness out of me?"

His hand shot out, wrapping around her wrist, the fire of her magic flickering against his skin. He didn't flinch. Instead, he stepped closer, their bodies almost flush.

"Ophelia," he said, voice low and steady, "when I fuck you,

it won't be because you're running from someone else. It won't be because you are thinking of some other male. It will be because you've begged me to make you come. And it certainly won't be in an alley surrounded by the insides of humans who couldn't hold their liquor."

Her breath caught, her body betraying her even as her mind screamed at her to back away. That raw and unfiltered bluntness made her uncomfortable and exhilarated at the same time. Heat rose to her cheeks, and not of embarrassment. Of longing. Of desire. She felt it between them. She always felt it between them. But she ignored it. She just couldn't go there with another vampire. Luka had been it for her, and there would be no other. But this man—vampire—made her ache.

She shifted uncomfortably, and he smirked down at her. He knew. Of course, he knew. As a vampire, he had superior senses. He could smell it on her.

But then the tension shattered as her stomach heaved. She folded at the waist, emptying the contents of her stomach onto his shoes.

He sighed, stepping to the side. Without a word, he held her hair back, his movements careful and deliberate.

When she finally straightened, her face flushed with embarrassment, he reached out, wiping a tear mixed with mascara from her cheek.

"I can walk," she muttered, refusing to meet his eyes.

He arched a brow, waiting until she relented with an eye roll.

"Fine," she said.

His dark smile returned, and in a blur of preternatural speed, he carried her out of the alley and into the waiting night. He didn't ask if she wanted to leave or wait for her resistance. He simply acted, cradling her as though he could mend her broken pieces with his bare hands.

CHAPTER

TWO

The shrill, incessant ringing sent needles through Ophelia's pounding head. She groaned, every sound a jagged edge carving through her skull.

Sunlight sliced through the curtains, cruel and unrelenting, causing nausea to twist and knot in her stomach. She buried herself deeper under the blanket, tugging it over her head as if that could silence the world. Then she threw a pillow on top for good measure.

It didn't help.

The ringing only grew louder, a discordant clash with the drumming behind her eyes. It wasn't the kind of noise she could ignore—because it wasn't in her head.

With a muffled growl of frustration, she shoved the pillow away and flung the blanket back, her disheveled hair tangling around her face. "What the—" Her voice croaked like she hadn't spoken in days.

The room came into disjointed focus—mostly because her cousin, Brisa, stood dead center, an infuriating smirk pulling at her painted lips. With a lazy flick of her tattooed hand, books, knickknacks, and empty wine bottles floated in mid-air around her, clashing together in an orchestral disaster.

Ophelia's jaw tightened. "Brisa," she growled, the name a threat.

Brisa's expression didn't waver, the corners of her mouth twitching like she was suppressing laughter. "Morning, sunshine. You smell like vomit."

Ophelia rolled her eyes and forced her magic to react, her palm twitching as invisible threads of fire flicked through the room. Her belongings stuttered in the air, then dropped with a chaotic crash—shattering glass, thudding books, and a satisfying finality as the last liquor bottle hit the floor.

"Was that really necessary?" Ophelia grumbled, flopping back onto the bed. She groaned and tried to yank the blanket back over her head—only to find that it wouldn't budge.

Her eyes shot open, narrowing at her cousin. Brisa, looking perfectly unbothered, now held the other end of the blanket in an invisible tug-of-war.

"Dammit, Brisa!"

Brisa didn't move, didn't falter. She just kept staring at Ophelia with that maddening mix of boredom and expectation. "It's time."

Ophelia blinked, her sluggish brain finally registering the words. "For?"

"You know what for." Brisa's gaze swept the room with undisguised disdain—empty bottles, dirty clothes, half-eaten takeout containers, and the general mess of someone who'd stopped giving a damn. Her nose wrinkled. "Gods, Ophy, you smell worse than you look."

"Not true," Ophelia mumbled, ignoring the nickname and turning her face toward the window in protest.

The bed creaked as Brisa sat down on the edge. The mattress groaned beneath her, and Ophelia felt the weight shift—a physical reminder that Brisa wasn't leaving until she said what she'd come to say.

"Ophelia," Brisa said softly.

There was something in her cousin's voice—sharp yet tinged with an edge of worry. Ophelia hated it. She hated the pity, the care, the attempt to peel back the layers she'd so carefully wrapped around herself.

"Don't," Ophelia snapped as she stared hard at the ceiling.

Brisa let out a long-suffering sigh. "Fine. Let's skip the niceties, then. You're making an ass of yourself. You're drunk all the time. You smell disgusting. You're sleeping in the same clothes you wore last night. And dulling your powers is dangerous. Get it together."

There it was. Brutal honesty, Brisa-style.

Ophelia turned her head, glaring at her cousin's sharp, angular face. The fiery red streaks in Brisa's black hair caught the light, almost mocking her as if even her appearance said *I have my shit together and you don't.*

"Fuck off," Ophelia muttered, but the words carried no real venom.

Brisa didn't. Instead, she stood abruptly and rummaged in her pocket. "You're stubborn as hell, you know that?" Her tone had shifted again, softer now—too soft. It made Ophelia's chest constrict.

Brisa drew a plain white envelope from her pocket and held it out, her expression unreadable. "Elijah wanted you to have this."

The blanket fell from Ophelia's hands. The room tilted slightly, her hungover brain struggling to process what Brisa had just said.

"What?" she asked, the word trembling out of her.

Brisa didn't repeat herself. She simply held the envelope out further. The smirk was gone now, her dark eyes searching

Ophelia's face for something—maybe understanding, maybe strength.

Ophelia stared at the envelope as if it might burst into flames. Her fingers trembled when she reached for it, the handwriting sending an immediate ache through her chest.

Elijah. The man who'd raised her after her mom—his best friend—disappeared when she was six. Despite no blood relation, he'd taken on the role of dad with ease.

"Where is he?" Ophelia asked, the edge in her tone undercut by the tremble she couldn't quite suppress.

Brisa hesitated, her gaze flicking away for the briefest second. "Gone."

"Gone where?" Ophelia asked.

"He didn't say." Brisa's shoulders slumped slightly, as if she knew the answer wouldn't satisfy. "Just that he needed to step away. He said you'd understand when you read the letter."

Ophelia couldn't breathe. She couldn't think. The envelope shook in her grip as her mind churned. Elijah wouldn't just leave. He wouldn't do that.

Brisa moved toward the door, pausing at the threshold. "We miss him, too, Ophy. You don't get a monopoly on grief."

The nickname pierced something inside Ophelia—something raw and fragile. She watched Brisa disappear, leaving behind silence and the smell of lingering magic. Of course, they all missed Luka. But he'd been her person. The love of her life. Didn't she deserve to be sadder than them?

Ophelia slumped back into the bed, the envelope clutched against her chest. For a long moment, she just lay there, staring at the ceiling as the tears pricked her eyes.

Two people in the world had been allowed to call her Ophy. One of them—Sebastian—was dead, and the other one —her best friend, Alex—barely spoke to her. The term of endearment reminded her of a time before she knew about vampires and witches and supernaturals. Before she'd fallen in love with Luka and lost him.

The silence stretched after Brisa left, thick and suffocating, as though the air itself had grown heavier. Ophelia sat up on the edge of the bed, the crumpled blanket pooling at her feet, the envelope still clutched in her trembling hands. The sunlight pouring through the window no longer burned; instead, it pressed against her like an accusation.

She hesitated.

Opening that envelope felt like a line she couldn't uncross, a confirmation that Elijah was truly gone. That this house— their house—was now just hers, a monument to memories and ghosts. But the familiar ache in her chest wouldn't let her ignore it. Not forever.

Her fingers brushed over the paper, tracing Elijah's neat, elegant handwriting. He'd always had that careful way about him—his words deliberate, his letters precise.

"Just open it, Ophelia," she muttered to herself. Her voice sounded small and fragile, even to her own ears.

With a shaky breath, she tore the flap open and pulled the letter free. The parchment was thick beneath her fingers, carrying the smell of cedar and ink—just like Elijah. It was too much, that familiar scent, and it took everything in her to steady her shaking hands as she began to read.

Dearest Ophelia,

I've loved you as my own daughter for more than twenty years, and I will always love you. But the time has come for me to step away. Losing Sebastian shattered me in ways I can't explain, and I've realized that I can no longer be the person you need right now. You've grown into a fierce and capable woman, even if *you don't see it yet. With your mother back in your life, it feels like the universe is telling me that it's time to let go. Just a little.*

I need to heal, Ophy. To find a way to live in a world without Sebastian. But please don't think for a second that I'm abandoning you. I'll always be here if you need me, even if it's from a distance. This house, these memories—they're all yours now. Build a life here, or leave it behind if you must. Just know that you have my blessing either way.

You are my greatest pride, and I know you'll overcome whatever challenges lie ahead. I just wish I could have protected you from more of them.

With all my love,

Elijah

The letter shook in her hands as her vision blurred with tears she refused to shed. She read it again and again, the words digging into her chest like shards of glass.

This wasn't abandonment, she told herself, even as the thought lodged in her heart like a splinter. He just missed Sebastian, the man he'd married when Ophelia was eleven. It'd seemed like fate that Sebastian had come into their lives. He'd been a teacher at Ophelia's elementary school. Elijah and Sebastian fell in love, and Sebastian brought light back into their lives after Ophelia's mom disappeared.

Then Sebastian died. Killed by a member of the vampires' governing body, the Concilium. Because he'd been a plant in her home. A low-level witch sent to watch her powers grow. And she still didn't know why.

Elijah didn't know any of that, because she was shielding

him from the supernatural world. All he knew was that Sebastian had died on a trip, and Celeste had reappeared out of nowhere with no explanation after twenty years. And Ophelia was a disappointment because she just couldn't seem to move on from Luka's death.

She crumpled the letter in her fists, anger bubbling over. How could he leave now? After everything? Elijah had been her constant. And now the house felt emptier than ever, like a hollow shell echoing with ghosts.

The smell of bacon and coffee pulled Ophelia from her room like a thread tugging her forward, even as her emotions lingered in the space between grief and anger. She padded downstairs barefoot, her limbs heavy with the weight of the letter still crumpled in her hand.

The kitchen was a mismatch of memories. Sebastian's handiwork was everywhere, from the copper pots hanging over the stove to the worn butcher block counters. It looked unchanged, yet it felt so different now, as if his absence had drained it of its warmth.

Brisa was perched on a stool at the counter, scrolling on her phone with a steaming mug of coffee in one hand. She didn't look up as Ophelia entered, posture casual as ever.

Behind the stove stood Marcello—Mo—Brisa's father, a man she didn't know existed until recently. Celeste's older half brother—a warlock with command of earth and the ability to speak every language—had a calming effect on everyone.

His shoulders hunched as he flipped bacon in a cast-iron skillet. The scent of it filled the air, mingling with the bitterness of brewed coffee. It should have been comforting, but it only irked Ophelia further. Mo had been in her life for barely more than six months, yet here he was, cooking in Sebastian's kitchen like he belonged.

And then there was the apron—the one Sebastian had

worn every Sunday morning when he made pancakes. Thankfully, it hung untouched on its hook near the pantry. Ophelia didn't think she could stomach the sight of someone else wearing it.

Mo turned at her approach, his cavernous dark brown eyes sweeping over her face as his lined face softened with a small smile. He held out a mug of tea, its steam curling in the air between them. "This will help," he said, his tone gentle.

Ophelia hesitated, her first instinct to reject the gesture. But she knew what he meant—the tea wasn't just tea. It was laced with herbs, something to steady her nerves and restore the magic she'd dulled with alcohol.

Reluctantly, she took the mug and sipped. The warm liquid slid down her throat, and almost instantly, she felt the familiar hum of her power roaring back to life. Her hangover ebbed away, but it was replaced by her magic, coiled tightly in her chest like a restless animal.

"Better?" Mo asked, his bushy eyebrows drawn together in concern. His curly brown hair reminded her of her mother. She tried not to hold that against him.

She nodded, though she avoided his gaze.

Brisa snorted from her stool, finally looking up. "At least you don't smell like a bar mat anymore."

Ophelia shot her a glare, but the jab lacked its usual sting. She crossed her arms, leaning against the counter as she watched Mo expertly maneuver around the kitchen.

"How are you so chipper this early?" Ophelia asked, still hoarse.

Brisa raised an eyebrow, her smirk firmly in place. "It's called 'not drinking yourself into a coma every night.'"

Ophelia rolled her eyes, but before she could retort, the distinct thrum of magic prickled along her skin, a presence she felt before she even saw him.

In the living room, Gabriel sprawled in an oversized armchair, looking far too relaxed for someone his size. The sight of him sent a flicker of annoyance through her. Why was he always here?

He was dressed in his typical casual attire—sweatpants and a black T-shirt that did little to hide the breadth of his shoulders. His long legs stretched out in front of him, one foot crossed over the other, as if the chair barely contained him.

Why did men always sit like that, as if it was too uncomfortable to sit properly with their legs together? And then she couldn't help but think that it probably *was* too uncomfortable for Gabriel to sit with his legs together. Because his body was so big, which probably meant that his—

Brisa snorted and spat out her coffee as she laughed.

Scowling, Ophelia jerked her attention back to her cousin. "Get out of my head, Brisa." She'd forgotten to shield like Luka had taught her, one of the many lessons she'd tried to forget over the last six months. And she'd let her guard down around her cousin, one of the few supernaturals with the power to read minds without touch or tasting blood.

"But how could I when you think such *big* thoughts?" Brisa winked and then laughed when Ophelia's scowl deepened.

Ophelia snapped a mental shield into place and stomped into the small living room, sitting in the chair across from Gabriel. She was still confused as to why he was always around. He'd guarded her and rescued her more times over the last several months than she wanted to admit. He'd seen her at her ugliest. And it had been—and still was—really ugly. But he kept coming back, no matter how mean or sloppy she was.

"Why are you staring?" he asked, without opening his eyes.

"Why are you always here?" she asked, tucking her long legs underneath her and turning to stare at the fire he must have started. It was spring in New York and unseasonably warm, but the flames always brought her comfort. She refused to acknowledge that the comfort stemmed from her lineage as one of the last fire witches. But not *the* last, since her mom was, after all, still alive.

"Why are you always hungover?" he shot back, still not opening his eyes.

Heat flushed her cheeks. "I don't need your lectures," she said.

He finally opened his eyes and turned his head to stare at her, those intense deep brown eyes seeing through her. "No, but you need to train. And you need to stop running from yourself. Ignoring your training won't make you less of a supernatural. It'll just make you a reckless and unpredictable," he said, still lounging in that annoyingly unbothered posture.

His words struck a nerve, but she refused to show it. "Why do you even care?" she asked, harsher than intended.

Gabriel leaned closer, his intense gaze holding hers. "Because someone has to," he said, unyielding. "And because I'd rather burn the world down than see you destroy yourself."

He seemed to thrive on her defiance, his eyes daring her to push back as they roamed her body. She wondered if he saw that the muscles had softened from lack of use. When his eyes found hers again, her cheeks stained a darker shade of red. From the way he was looking at her, her softer form didn't seem to bother him at all.

Stifling the attraction she always felt around him, she let loose a fake yawn. "Pass," she said.

His dark gaze pinned her in place. "You want to drink yourself into oblivion? Fine. You want to sleep your way through New York? Go for it. But you can't erase who and what you are. You're a powerful supernatural. Ignoring your training will only make you a threat—to yourself and everyone around you," he said.

Feeling anger bubble to the surface, she clenched her teeth to keep from lashing out.

But that didn't stop him as he leaned in closer to her, his eyes dropping to her pursed lips as the corner of his mouth lifted. "Finally feeling something, Cinis?" he asked, the question so low only she could hear.

Her temper flared, and flames burst to life in her palm, annoyed he was using a nickname she didn't understand. She pressed her fiery hand against his chest.

"Showing some fight," Gabriel said, his grin widening as the flames danced in her palm. "About time."

He didn't budge. "You can keep pushing me away, Ophelia, but I'm not going anywhere." Ophelia kept her palm in place, even as she smelled burnt hair when the flames reached the light dusting on his chest. She would not give in on this one.

Their standoff was interrupted by Brisa's sarcastic drawl. "Children, children. Do I need to dump a bucket of water on you two?"

Ophelia reluctantly extinguished her flames, turning her attention to the plate of food Brisa shoved into her hands. The flavors were rich, the bacon crisp, the eggs perfectly seasoned. But everything tasted hollow, like ash on her tongue. Across the room, Brisa continued scrolling through her phone, her occasional snickers grating on Ophelia's nerves.

Gabriel, still lounging in the chair, seemed utterly at ease, though she could feel his eyes on her. His gaze was both comforting and vexing, a constant reminder that he saw too much. She focused on her plate, willing herself to eat.

The thrum of magic hit her first, a ripple of energy crawling up her spine and sparking in her veins. She froze mid-bite, her fork clattering against the plate. The air shifted, heavy with the unmistakable presence of another supernatural.

"Someone's here," she said, tense and clipped.

Gabriel was already on his feet, moving with the kind of fluid grace that only vampires possessed. His hand hovered protectively at Ophelia's back as she stood.

"Stay here," he said, voice low and commanding.

"Not a chance," Ophelia said.

Brisa followed them to the front door, her movements less hurried but no less alert. The three of them formed a line, their magic charging the space with an almost tangible tension. Ophelia's flames licked at her fingertips, ready to ignite at a moment's notice.

When she flung the door open, the sight that greeted her made her breath catch.

The woman's unruly dark brown curls circled her face, and though her features had aged, they were unmistakable. The lines around her eyes and mouth hinted at years of hardship, but there was a sharpness in her gaze that hadn't dulled.

"Good morning, darling," the woman said, her tone almost saccharine.

Ophelia's flames extinguished as she stepped back, her heart pounding against the walls of her chest. She hadn't realized how deeply she'd buried this memory, how much effort it had taken to suppress the pain.

"Celeste," she said coldly, refusing to address her as anything else. The word felt foreign on her tongue, weighted with resentment and mistrust.

"Is that any way to greet your mother?" Celeste asked.

THREE

Celeste's body tensed, the only visible sign that Ophelia's refusal to call her "mother" had struck a nerve. But like always, the tension melted away in seconds, replaced by that infuriating mask of calm indifference. She lifted her chin, her posture perfectly composed, her gray-streaked curly brown hair falling like a veil down her back.

"We need to talk," she said, her deep brown eyes locking onto Ophelia's shrewd, yellow-green gaze.

That voice—calm, composed, and utterly self-assured—sent a new spark of anger through Ophelia's veins. Once, as a child, she had clung to the sound in her dreams, imagining it whispering lullabies and gentle reassurances. Now, it grated against her like steel scraping bone.

The woman standing before her was a stranger, all hard lines and lean muscle honed from hours of training. Her hands bore scars and calluses; her body was bruised more often than not. Celeste rarely explained her injuries or her absences, reappearing unannounced and demanding Ophelia's full attention.

"Oh, good. Talking. My favorite," Ophelia muttered, her words dripping with sarcasm. She shoved off the wall where she'd been leaning and stalked across the room, the scuff of her boots echoing as she dropped heavily into the oversized chair by the fire. Sparks crackled to life at her fingertips, flickering across her knuckles as she lazily traced circles in the air.

Celeste remained standing, poised like a commander waiting for her soldiers to fall into line. "This must be reminiscent of the adolescent years I missed," she said dryly.

Ophelia's lip curled, her flames flaring brighter. "Oh, you want the full experience? Fine. Where were you during those adolescent years, *Mother*?" She spat the last word like it burned her tongue. "Too busy gallivanting across the globe while I sat at home trying to convince myself you hadn't just disappeared? Or did it just not occur to you to write a letter, send a smoke signal—hell, even a pigeon?"

Celeste's lips thinned, her gaze flickering briefly to the flames before settling back on Ophelia. For a split second, something else flashed across her face—perhaps regret or guilt—but it was gone too fast to be sure.

In the dining room, Brisa snorted loudly, the sound breaking the tension like a bubble popping. "Ophy, you've gotta warn a girl when you're about to go off like that," Brisa called, doubled over with laughter. She leaned against the table for support, her platform boots barely touching the floor.

Ophelia shot her cousin an exasperated look, but the edges of her mouth twitched, threatening a smile. She'd barely thought the words before Brisa picked up on them, her mind-reading power ever at work. *Maybe I should've singed Celeste's perfect hair for good measure.* Brisa snorted again, likely hearing that thought, too.

A huff of laughter slipped out, and Ophelia shook her head.

For a moment—just a fleeting, fragile moment—she wondered what it might have been like to grow up with family like Brisa. To laugh at stupid things together. To share a home instead of a haunted shell.

The firelight caught Gabriel's face as he leaned silently against the kitchen counter, posture anything but casual. His broad shoulders seemed to fill the room, his dark, unreadable gaze fixed on her. He didn't say a word, but Ophelia felt the heat of his attention, heavy and undeniable. That unnerved her more than Celeste.

"What?" she snapped, suddenly defensive.

Gabriel tilted his head slightly, his expression softening. "I haven't seen you smile like that in months."

Her faint smile vanished as if he'd snuffed out the flames with his words. The guilt slammed into her chest like a battering ram. How could she smile—how dare she smile—when Luka was gone? When Sebastian was buried six feet under?

Her gaze dropped to the fire again, the embers mimicking the ache in her chest. "Don't," she said softly. "Don't say things like that."

The room went still, the silence pressing down on Ophelia like an invisible weight. She couldn't bear it—the watching, the judgment, the unspoken demands. She shoved herself up from the chair, ignoring the way her magic flared in response to her frustration, and moved to the bay windows.

Pulling the heavy curtains aside, she scanned the street outside out of habit. For weeks after Luka's death, she'd paced these very windows at night, waiting for something— anything—to appear. Now it was second nature, an instinct she couldn't shake. She let the curtains fall back into place and turned to find the entire room staring at her.

"What?" she asked, the irritation creeping back into her tone.

Celeste stepped forward, her arms crossed and expression steely. "No more stalling. We need to go to Trieste."

Ophelia froze, her pulse spiking. She took an unconscious step back, her shoulders hitting the window frame. "I've told you—I want nothing to do with those people. With supernaturals."

"*You* are a supernatural, Ophelia," Celeste said firmly, taking another step closer.

Ophelia's laugh was resentful and humorless. "Wouldn't that have been helpful to know when I was a child, Celeste? Or should I thank you for leaving me with Elijah to explain the 'episodes' while you disappeared off the face of the planet? To be one of his psychology experiments?"

Elijah hadn't understood what was happening to Ophelia as a child. Her magic manifested immediately after Celeste disappeared. She'd tried to explain the warnings to him. At first, he didn't believe her. But then he witnessed it time and again—her ability to sense danger or impending change.

Those physical warnings had been just the beginning. Now, she understood that she was a fire witch with the command of all elemental power. And her magic was still manifesting and revealing itself to her and others. But, as a child, she and Elijah hadn't understood. They referred to magical elements as "episodes." Convinced he could cure her, he'd become a child psychologist, looking for any scientific reason to explain what was happening to her.

"I made mistakes," Celeste said, the words quiet, almost pleading.

"Mistakes?" Ophelia's temper flared, and the fire in the hearth roared in response. "You abandoned me. Elijah spent years trying to fix what he thought was broken in me—

because of you. And now you show up here with your cryptic bullshit and want me to play nice? No explanation of where you've been?"

The flames crackled, casting shadows across Celeste's face as she squared her shoulders. "Try to hurt me all you want, Ophelia. It doesn't change the fact that you have responsibilities now. You can't deny what you are."

Ophelia's magic answered her mother before she did. A breeze swirled around Celeste, tugging a curl into her face. Celeste blew it back absentmindedly, narrowing her eyes.

"You did that on purpose," she said, her lips thinning further. "I'm still your mother."

"Since when?" Ophelia shot back, the wind dying as her magic withdrew.

Celeste's mask slipped, just for a heartbeat. A pink hue dotted her cheeks, and her voice hardened. "Since I brought you into this world."

But her next words cut too deep. "The last time I checked, you stopped being a mother to me when you left me at six years old. You disappeared without a word. You let Elijah raise me—and Sebastian die—because of your selfishness." The words should've landed like a boulder, but they felt hollow. Ophelia didn't miss the shimmer of guilt—or regret—that passed over Celeste's face, quickly buried beneath her usual stoicism. For a split second, Ophelia felt a cruel satisfaction at seeing her mother flinch.

Celeste recoiled, her composure cracking like glass. She didn't speak, didn't even move, and for the first time, Ophelia thought her mother might actually be at a loss for words. But that frustratingly calm composure returned. "The Alliance has called a meeting in Trieste. They want you there. You have no choice," she said, her shoulders pulled back and chin raised.

"Enough," Gabriel's voice rumbled, commanding as he

stepped between them. "You think she owes you?" He growled as he turned his dark gaze to Celeste. "She doesn't owe you anything. Not her time, not her trust. And definitely not her help."

"I don't know why you're always here," Celeste said, crossing her muscular arms over her chest as her shrewd gaze turned to meet his. "But you've been around long enough to know that you can't ignore the Alleanza, especially if a meeting of all supernaturals is called. Something big is happening. And she was specifically requested."

Gabriel turned toward Ophelia and placed his hands on her shoulders, his steady warmth a grounding force. "I know this is the last thing you want. If the Alliance has called a meeting so soon after the Lunula Amulet was destroyed, it means something big is happening. Something dangerous. But I'll take you away from here if you want. Try to help you escape it. But it could be bad for your family," he said, jerking his head toward her cousin and uncle, who still stood in the kitchen.

Ophelia's shoulders sagged, the fire dimming to a soft, sullen glow behind them. She was still learning so much about the supernatural world. But she at least knew that the majority of supernaturals—witches, vampires, fae—had an alliance formally referred to as the Alleanza, with a neutral meeting place in Trieste. She didn't want to return to the city where she'd met Luka and had started to learn about her lineage. She wanted it to all disappear.

Shoving Gabriel's hands away, sparks of magic flared at her fingertips as she stepped back. "Dangerous? Big? You think I care about them? They didn't care when my world was crumbling. When I lost Sebastian. Luk—" She cut off the word and turned away, her hands shaking as she raked them through her midnight-black hair.

Her mother's calm voice sliced through the tension. "You think this is about you?"

Ophelia froze, her back still turned. The words hit her like a slap, but she couldn't bring herself to face Celeste.

"It's not," Celeste continued, her tone stern but steady. "This is bigger than your grief, bigger than any of us. You might not want to hear that, but it's the truth. You have a responsibility—to yourself, to this family, to the world you belong to."

"Don't lecture me about responsibility," Ophelia snapped, whirling around, her face flushed with fury. "You don't get to show up after twenty years and start spouting bullshit about duty and destiny. I didn't choose this life."

"No one chooses it, Ophelia," Celeste replied, unflinching.

Ophelia's laughter was scathing and bitter, echoing off the walls of the old brownstone. "How comforting. Thank you, Mother. I feel so much better."

Brisa leaned against the dining table, inspecting her black-painted nails as if utterly bored, though the slight curl of her lips betrayed her amusement. "You're exhausting when you're like this," she muttered. "And I mean that lovingly."

"Don't start with me, Brisa," Ophelia said, pointing a finger at her cousin.

Brisa raised both hands in faux surrender, her eyes twinkling. "Fine, fine. I'm just saying, throwing a tantrum won't get you anywhere."

"I'm not throwing a tantrum," Ophelia growled.

Brisa grinned. "You literally blew wind into Celeste's face two minutes ago. That's tantrum territory, Ophy."

Ophelia's temper flared at the nickname, and flames flickered briefly at her fingertips. Brisa only snorted in response, completely unfazed.

"Enough," Mo said quietly, stepping into the space

between them. His steady demeanor seemed to settle the air, defusing the tension as always. "Brisa, stop antagonizing her. Ophelia, listen to what we're saying."

"I *am* listening," Ophelia said, the fire dimming slightly. Her gaze shifted from Mo's steady expression, to Celeste's intense stare, and finally to Gabriel, who watched her with a mix of patience and resolve. "You just don't like my answers."

Mo folded his arms across his broad chest, the movement slow and deliberate. "You're angry, and you have every right to be. But anger doesn't change what's coming. You can't avoid this forever, Ophelia. None of us can."

"I don't care what's coming," she shot back, though the words rang hollow even to her own ears.

Mo didn't waver. "Then care about the people who will be caught in the crossfire. You've seen the consequences of ignoring the supernatural world. You know what's at stake."

Ophelia clenched her jaw, refusing to let his words take root. But it was too late. Images of the devastation from the battle over the Lunula Amulet surged through her mind—the blood, the fire, the bodies. Luka. The grief that had nearly consumed her. Destroying the amulet hadn't just ended the fight; it had shattered her in the process.

"Don't," she said hoarsely, pressing the heels of her palms to her eyes.

Brisa's voice broke the silence, softer this time. "We're not asking you to save the world, Ophy. We're asking you to help us keep it from falling apart."

Ophelia dropped her hands and glared at Brisa. "That sounds like two different ways of saying the same thing. And don't call me that."

Brisa smirked, but her words were uncharacteristically gentle. "We need you back. *I* need you back."

The words cut deep, and Ophelia hated how much they

affected her. She turned her back to them all, staring into the dying fire, her shoulders tense. The room was quiet for a beat too long, expectation pressing down on her.

Then Celeste spoke again, firm but no longer cold. "You're one of the last descendants of the Wildes Witch bloodline, Ophelia. And a half vampire. Like it or not, you carry power that no one else does. If you don't take your place—if you don't learn to control it—others will exploit it. And the cost will be far greater than you realize."

Ophelia flinched. "Is that what this is about? My power? You only care because I'm useful to you?"

Celeste's expression softened just a fraction. "No. I care because you're my daughter. And because I know what happens when power goes unchecked."

The truth in her mother's voice disarmed Ophelia more than she wanted to admit. She stared at the fire for a long moment, the silence stretching between them all. Finally, she muttered, "And what exactly is this meeting about?"

Celeste's shoulders relaxed slightly, though her tone remained serious. "We don't know exactly. The Alliance is fractured. Old rivalries are reemerging. If we don't act soon, it could spiral into war."

Gabriel, who had been silent for far too long, finally spoke. "It's bigger than the Alliance. Something's wrong, Ophelia. There's a shift in the balance of power. If we don't figure out what's causing it..." He didn't finish, but the unspoken words hung in the air.

Ophelia turned to face them all, her eyes blazing. "And you think I can fix that?"

Mo nodded solemnly. "We think you can help. And apparently the Alliance does, as well, if they're asking for your presence."

Ophelia scoffed, crossing her arms over her chest as if

trying to shield herself. "Fine. But don't expect me to be a hero."

Brisa grinned, lifting her coffee cup in salute. "Wouldn't dream of it."

Gabriel's gaze lingered on Ophelia, his dark expression cold and unreadable. "We'll leave in the morning," he said.

"Great. Can't wait," Ophelia muttered, walking away from her family and retreating to the kitchen. Her sanctuary. Or what had been her sanctuary before Sebastian's death. The shelves, once filled with his beloved spices and ingredients, were now stocked with liquor bottles.

Grabbing the nearest bottle of vodka off the counter—the most expensive she could buy with the money Luka had left her after his death—she ignored the looks her family exchanged. Deep down, she knew they were right. But agreeing to go didn't mean she had to forgive. Or forget. And it sure as hell didn't mean she trusted them.

She poured a glass of the vodka and downed it in one go. The burn in her throat was nothing compared to the one in her chest, the one that whispered she'd failed them all—Sebastian, Luka, Elijah. And now they expected her to save the rest.

"Ophelia." Mo's quiet voice carried across the room.

She ignored him and reached for another bottle, but a gust of wind held her hand in place with powerful air magic.

"Don't fight me, Brisa," Ophelia said, practically growling as flames licked up her fingertips, displeased with her cousin's interference.

Brisa remained unfazed, inspecting her nails with deliberate disinterest. "You haven't trained in months. And you numb every emotion and power with your favorite crutch. You'd barely last a minute," she said, finally looking up and staring at Ophelia's hand.

The bottle fell and fractured on the floor as Brisa suddenly released her hold on Ophelia's hand. Using her air magic, Brisa swept up the mess and deposited it into the trash without so much as a glance.

Mo stepped forward, calm and steady. Perhaps it was his similarity to Elijah, but it seemed that he'd been the only one over the last few weeks who could talk sense into Ophelia. "Ophelia, we understand your pain. But this meeting isn't about the Alliance. It's about the survival of our kind. Whether you like it or not, you are one of the most powerful witches alive."

"I'm not *just* a witch," Ophelia said, never letting anyone forget that half of her was a vampire. It was another thing that had come as a complete shock. She looked at her mom, who looked down quickly, apparently finding her feet suddenly fascinating. Despite their conflict over the last six months, Ophelia hadn't brought herself to ask her mom what she really wanted to know now. *Who is my father? And why won't you tell me about him?* Celeste had more secrets than a treasure vault, and Ophelia knew this was one she wouldn't be getting out of her. But like it or not, Ophelia's mixed witch and vampire blood was likely the source of her immense power and the reason she could command all the elements.

Mo moved closer to Ophelia, standing on the other side of the counter from her. "That's another reason you should come. You are the only known supernatural hybrid. You could be the one to help mend divisions and prevent other senseless deaths," Mo said.

"A unifier," she muttered under her breath, the word tasting bitter. All it meant was she didn't belong anywhere—not with the witches, not with the vampires, and certainly not with the mortals she was supposed to protect.

She squeezed her eyes shut, his words sinking in. She

didn't want to care. But deep down, she knew she couldn't let more people suffer the way she had.

"Fine," she muttered, grabbing a fresh bottle and stomping toward the stairs. "I'll go. I guess it's better than rotting here."

"Oh, Ophy," Brisa called after her, voice dripping with sarcasm. "You have the best ideas."

Ophelia shot a vulgar gesture over her shoulder. Her magic followed, carrying the bottles as she disappeared upstairs.

FOUR

Ophelia felt every ounce of her inadequacy in the heavy pounding of her feet against the dirt path. Brisa's taunting voice cut through the crisp morning air.

"What's wrong, hybrid? Can't keep up?" Brisa asked, her long black braid bouncing against her leather-clad back as she darted ahead, her platform shoes somehow managing to glide effortlessly over the uneven terrain.

Ophelia clenched her jaw, refusing to take the bait. Her lungs scorched like fire, her legs felt like lead, and each labored breath was a cruel reminder of how far she'd fallen. Once, on this very trail, she'd been a force of nature, her magic thrumming in harmony with her body, propelling her forward as though the wind itself was carrying her. But now? Now every step felt like penance.

"Stop thinking about it," Brisa said, invading her mind.

"Get out of my head, Brisa!" Ophelia snapped aloud, her breath coming in shallow, angry bursts.

Ahead of her, Alex's melodic laughter rang out. "Don't fight it, Ophelia. You'll just make it worse." She tossed Brisa a water bottle as they ran, their ease grating against Ophelia's raw nerves.

Jealousy flared, hot and unwelcome, in her chest. Alex, once her closest confidante, now felt like a stranger. She never spent time alone with Ophelia anymore, always needing Brisa as a buffer. It stung more than she cared to admit. The sight of their camaraderie—a shared glance, a knowing smile—felt like salt rubbed into an already raw wound.

Ophelia slowed her pace slightly, letting them pull ahead. The sunlight filtering through the trees dappled the trail, annoying her with its warmth and cheerfulness. She closed her eyes briefly, focusing on the earth beneath her feet and the steady thrum of her pulse. She wanted to snap back, to defend herself, but she couldn't ignore the truth: She couldn't keep up.

Her body protested every step, each labored breath a cruel echo of who she used to be. She could almost hear Luka's steady, teasing voice in her mind: *"Pace yourself, love. You'll need energy for the climb back."*

The memory cut deep. She hated thinking about Luka—hated how the thought of him still comforted her even as it reopened wounds that refused to heal. She could still picture him, running beside her with that calm, relentless stride. Always pushing her but never tearing her down. Just believing in her, even when she didn't believe in herself.

Now she could barely keep pace with Brisa and Alex, her legs straining to carry her forward under the added weight she'd put on in recent months. Drinking, hooking up with strangers, and drowning in guilt had left her endurance dulled and her body softer. It wasn't the physical weight that bothered her; it was what it symbolized—a tangible reminder of how far she'd let herself spiral.

"What a ridiculous thought," Brisa said out loud, light and

teasing after she'd apparently slipped into Ophelia's mind again. "As a connoisseur of the female body, I can tell you the extra padding suits you. And by the way, Gabriel's definitely noticed."

"Goddammit, Brisa!" Ophelia hissed aloud, warmth flooding her cheeks.

Alex burst into laughter, her silver-streaked ponytail swaying as she glanced back with a grin. "She's not wrong, you know." Alex's hair had once been golden-blonde, but the trauma at the Eye of the Earth had changed her in more ways than one. Her hair's gradual shift to silver was a visible reminder of what she'd endured.

Ophelia flicked a wisp of wind toward Brisa's feet, hoping to trip her up. Brisa, ever the show-off, used the momentum to vault into the air, landing with a smug grin.

"Stop being such a lush and work on your shields," Brisa said, her tone almost sing-song. "Then you won't have to ask me to stay out of your head." She cocked her head before continuing. "Oh, and by the way, I know you're wondering what it'd be like for Gabriel to use those big hands to grab your—"

"Dammit, Brisa!" Ophelia interrupted, her voice rising as her cheeks flamed. "Get out of my mind. And stop repeating everything you hear."

Alex doubled over, laughing so hard she had to clutch her side. Tears streamed from her cerulean eyes.

The commotion was enough to summon Gabriel, who appeared on the trail ahead of them, his long strides effortlessly catching up.

"What are you two arguing about now?" he asked, his tone laced with amusement.

Her pulse quickened for reasons she refused to analyze. She'd been so distracted that she hadn't even noticed Gabriel's approach until he was directly in front of her, impossible to ignore. His dark eyes glinted with mischief, his expression hovering somewhere between amusement and exasperation.

"Nothing," Ophelia said quickly, tight with frustration.

"Well, Ophelia—" Brisa began, her tone laced with feigned innocence.

"I said nothing," Ophelia snapped, her glare sharp enough to cut steel.

Gabriel chuckled, his deep voice vibrating through the air. "Right. Nothing at all."

The fact that he'd almost certainly overheard Brisa's commentary sent a fresh wave of irritation coursing through her. Of course, he'd heard. Damn vampire hearing.

Brisa tossed Alex the water bottle before surging ahead, leaving Ophelia to bring up the rear. She wanted to care, wanted to be angry, but all she felt was tired. Tired of trying to keep up. Tired of always falling behind.

Her gaze followed Brisa and Alex as they vanished around a bend in the trail. She caught the small, almost imperceptible glance Alex gave Brisa as their fingers brushed during the handoff. It wasn't just familiarity; it was connection. And it was something Ophelia hadn't felt in months—not with Alex, not with anyone.

"Ophelia," Gabriel said, splintering her thoughts, steady and grounding in a way she hated to admit.

"What?" she snapped, not bothering to hide the bitterness in her tone. Her pace slowed further, and she turned to face him. She stopped short when she saw the way he was looking at her. It wasn't pity, but it wasn't far off. His dark eyes were steady, almost probing, as though he could see through the cracks in her armor to the raw mess beneath.

He tilted his head slightly, his gaze sweeping over her. "Pick up the pace. You're slowing us down."

The words sparked something in her, a mix of anger and determination that made her legs move again. Her muscles screamed in protest, but she pushed through it, letting the burn in her body drown out the ache in her chest.

She didn't respond to him, but her thoughts drifted back to Luka, to the way he'd run beside her with that quiet, unrelenting pace. He'd always believed in her, always seen the strength she didn't recognize in herself. Gabriel was different. He didn't just see her; he challenged her. Sometimes, she hated him for it.

But as she picked up her pace, closing the distance between her and the others, she couldn't deny that part of her didn't hate it at all.

"Hey." Gabriel's voice pulled her back to the present. He had fallen into step beside her, his dark eyes scanning her face. "You okay?"

"I'm fine," she said quickly, brushing past him. Her tone was biting, but it wasn't directed at him. It was meant for the ghost of Luka that still haunted her, the lingering pull of his memory that refused to release its grip on her.

Gabriel didn't press her, though his presence remained steady, like a storm on the horizon she couldn't quite outrun. The rhythmic pounding of their steps on the trail faded as Gabriel emerged ahead of them, his towering frame cutting an imposing silhouette against the dappled sunlight. He moved with an ease that mocked the effort she was putting in, every stride a reminder of just how dangerous he could be. The air around him seemed heavier, charged with a quiet menace.

Ahead, Brisa and Alex were still locked in conversation, their knowing laughter cutting through the quiet of the trail. Brisa's braid swayed, and Alex's hand brushed hers as they passed the water bottle back and forth. The scar across Alex's hand—imprinted when they'd destroyed the Lunula Amulet and Alex had almost died—was clearly visible. It was a mirror to her own scar.

Ophelia's chest constricted at the closeness between her cousin and former best friend, jealousy clawing at her throat. She wasn't sure what she envied more—the ease of their bond or the fact that it had nothing to do with her.

"Pick it up, Wildes," Gabriel said, low but insistent. "You're not done yet."

Ophelia scowled at him, but she didn't slow down. If anything, she pushed herself harder, her breaths coming faster as she forced her body to comply. Pain lanced through her calves, but she welcomed it. It was better than the hollowness, better than the grief that threatened to crush her every time she let herself stop.

Gabriel effortlessly matched her pace, his broad shoulders brushing against hers as he leaned in slightly. "If you keep up the drinking, you'll be crawling to Trieste. And we both know they'll rip you apart if you show up like that," he said.

By the time they rounded the final bend in the trail, her entire body was screaming for rest. Sweat trickled down her spine, her shirt clinging uncomfortably to her back. Brisa and Alex slowed to a stop ahead of her, their conversation halting as they turned to wait.

Gabriel stayed beside her, his pace slowing just enough to keep them aligned. When they finally stopped, Ophelia bent over, hands on her knees, gasping for air.

"You survived," Brisa said, her grin infuriatingly smug. "Barely."

"Shut up," Ophelia muttered between gasps, straightening to glower at her cousin.

Brisa winked. "I'm just saying, hybrid. Maybe you're not as out of shape as you think. Gabriel didn't seem to mind the view."

"Brisa, would you give it a rest?" Ophelia snapped, heat rushing to her face as she turned away from her cousin's knowing grin.

Gabriel chuckled. "For what it's worth, I think you did just fine."

His words shouldn't have mattered. They shouldn't have sent a spark of something warm and unwelcome racing through her chest. But they did, and she hated it.

As the group slowed to a walk, the tension in Ophelia's shoulders began to ease, though her legs throbbed with every step. The four of them followed the dirt trail toward the edge of the park, the canopy of trees thinning as they neared the city streets. The morning sunlight broke through in patches, dappling the ground and casting long shadows.

Gabriel flanked Ophelia, while Brisa and Alex walked ahead, their heads tilted close in conversation. Ophelia tried not to let the sight bother her, but it was like an itch she couldn't scratch.

They'd discovered Alex's fae heritage when she was attacked by another vampire. At first, Alex refused to believe in supernaturals and had rejected Ophelia's displays of magic. But now she was spending her time with Brisa, learning about supernaturals?

The silence between her and Gabriel stretched, heavy and loaded. She could feel his gaze on her, sharp and assessing. Finally, unable to take it any longer, she snapped, "What? You've been staring at me since we started."

Gabriel raised an eyebrow, unbothered by her tone. "You're out of practice," he said.

Ophelia scowled. "No shit."

"I'm not criticizing," he continued, calm but firm. "But if you're going to Trieste, you can't go like this."

Ophelia stopped in her tracks, turning to face him. "What's that supposed to mean?"

He met her stare without flinching, his expression unyielding. "It means you're not ready. Physically, mentally, emotionally—you're running on fumes. You think the Alliance won't notice?"

Her teeth clenched. "I didn't ask for your opinion, Gabriel."

"You didn't have to," he said, stepping closer. His voice softened, but his intensity didn't waver. "You're not just walking into a meeting, Ophelia. You're walking into a den of supernaturals who will smell your weakness from a mile away. You need to be at your best, or they'll eat you alive."

Brisa and Alex paused up ahead, glancing back at the tension radiating between them. Brisa's smile faded, and Alex shifted uncomfortably, clearly debating whether to intervene.

Ophelia's magic simmered beneath her skin, her frustration bubbling over. "What do you care? Why are you always here, Gabriel? Why do you keep pushing me?"

"Because someone has to," he said evenly. "And because you're worth it, whether you see that or not."

The words hit her like a punch to the gut. She opened her mouth to retort, but no sound came out.

Gabriel's gaze softened just a fraction. "You can't keep running yourself into the ground and expect to win. You're better than this, Ophelia. Start acting like it."

A pang of something aching rippled through her, her breathing uneven as she fought to process the flood of emotions his words stirred. She hated how much they resonated, how much she wanted to believe him. But she couldn't—not yet.

Gabriel's expression didn't change, but he took a deliberate step back, giving Ophelia space. She turned away, her cheeks burning as she fell into step with the group again.

Ahead, her cousin nudged Alex with her elbow. "Think they'll ever admit it?" Brisa asked in a stage whisper.

Ophelia groaned. "I heard that, Brisa."

Her cousin laughed, throwing an arm around Alex's shoulders as they veered off toward a nearby café. Gabriel lingered beside Ophelia, his silence speaking volumes.

She didn't look at him, didn't acknowledge his presence. But as they walked, her thoughts raced.

Gabriel's words lingered like a brand searing into her thoughts, impossible to ignore.

CHAPTER

FIVE

LUKA

The cold had become a constant companion, threading through every muscle and bone until Luka could barely feel the shivering anymore. His skin clung tightly to his frame, pale and almost translucent, the veins beneath spiderwebbing in sharp relief. The hunger for blood was an inferno, roaring in his chest and surging through his veins, leaving behind only ash. It devoured him from the inside out, gnawing at his sanity and eroding everything he used to be.

He curled tighter against the rough stone wall, the grit biting into his bare back. Dampness seeped into his skin as if the walls themselves were conspiring to drain what little strength he had left. The air was thick and fetid, carrying the stench of decay, mildew, and despair. Somewhere in the distance, water dripped steadily—a maddening rhythm that amplified the silence.

His lips cracked as he whispered, raw and barely audible, "Loukas Angelos. Loukas Angelos. Loukas Angelos."

The words were a tether, anchoring him to the man he had

been. To the centuries he had walked the earth with power and confidence. But with every repetition, they sounded less like a name and more like a plea. He forced them past the dryness of his throat again and again, as if saying them enough times would remind his body to hold on, to keep existing.

Memories of who he had been clawed at him, fragmented and fleeting. He had been a predator once—a prince among vampires, unmatched in strength and cunning. Now, he was a hollowed-out shell, his body trembling with need, his mind fraying at the edges. The chains around his wrists and ankles bit into his flesh, the metal cold and unyielding. He couldn't feel the blood anymore; it had dried long ago.

And then there was her. Ophelia.

He didn't dare speak her name aloud, not here, not in this place where her existence could be twisted into a weapon. But in the fractured corners of his mind, her name echoed. *Ophelia.* It was the only light in the suffocating darkness. The memory of her laugh pierced through the agony. The way she had looked at him, her fiery spirit challenging and disarming him in equal measure. For a moment, the hunger retreated, replaced by something just as painful: longing.

He had orchestrated her path, nudged her toward her power with careful precision. But the truth, if she ever learned it, would turn her fire on him. And rightly so. She was never meant to be his salvation. She was a force of nature, and he was a man desperate enough to harness it.

A fresh wave of pain surged through him, lancing and unrelenting. His hands curled into fists, the manacles biting deeper into his wrists. He couldn't afford to think about that now. The witch would return soon, and she would sense his weakness, his doubts. She always did.

The hunger roared back, more insistent than ever, a feral thing inside him. It scraped at his mind, urging him to beg for blood, to surrender to the primal need that ruled his kind. He refused. He wouldn't give her that satisfaction. He would hold on, even if it killed him.

Somewhere in the depths of the dungeon, a door groaned open. Its sound reverberated through the cavern like a warning. Luka's body stiffened, his muscles coiling instinctively despite their depletion. The air shifted, growing colder, heavier, as if the witch had poisoned it. She never announced her arrival, but her magic seeped into the room before she did—an invasive, icy force that wrapped around his mind like a vise.

The iron bindings rattled as he tried to sit up, his movements sluggish and jerky. His vision blurred, and for a moment, he thought he was hallucinating again. But then her silhouette appeared in the doorway, tall and slender, her dark hair almost luminescent in the dim torchlight.

Luka slumped back against the wall, his body too weak to hold itself upright. He closed his eyes, bracing himself for the familiar game of torment she seemed to relish. Her slow, deliberate footsteps echoed, each one a reminder of her control. When she finally stopped in front of him, the silence was deafening.

"Still clinging to life, Loukas?" she purred, voice soft and venomous. "I must say, I'm impressed. Most would have begged by now."

He didn't answer. He had learned early on that silence was his only weapon, his only act of defiance. The hunger might consume his body, but his mind—his mind was a fortress she could not breach. But it didn't stop her from pushing, from prodding at the cracks in his resolve.

She crouched in front of him, her movements graceful and predatory. The pale light of the torches flickered across her face, illuminating high cheekbones and a cruel smile. "What keeps you going, I wonder?" she mused, tilting her head. "Is it her? Is she the one keeping you tethered, stopping you from drifting too far into the void?"

Luka's jaw tightened, but he kept his gaze fixed on the floor. Her words were needles, each one aimed at the rawest parts of him.

She leaned closer, her breath cold against his face. "You think she's pining for you? Mourning the loss of her perfect, devoted twin flame?" She chuckled, low and mocking. "You're a fool if you believe that."

The words burrowed into him, stirring the doubts he tried so desperately to suppress. He forced his lips to remain pressed together, his silence a fragile shield.

Her laughter ricocheted through the chamber, echoing off the stone walls. She stood, her shadow stretching over him like a shroud. "Ah, Loukas. You amuse me. But let's see how long you can keep up this charade."

She turned away, her footsteps receding into the darkness. Luka exhaled shakily, his body trembling with the effort of holding himself together. The door groaned shut, leaving him with the cold, the hunger, and the echo of her taunts.

"Ophelia," he whispered. Her fire burned fierce and untamed. If only she knew the lengths he'd gone to ignite it, to prepare her for the battles she didn't yet see on the horizon.

CHAPTER
SIX

Luka's apartment no longer smelled like him.

That was the first thing Ophelia noticed. The faint trace of night-blooming jasmine that always clung to his presence was gone, replaced by the sterile emptiness of a space long untouched. The air was heavy with stillness, dust hanging like a shroud. The apartment felt smaller than she remembered, suffocating in its silence. She used to find comfort here. Now it felt like a tomb.

The realization hit her like a punch to the chest, a splintering pang of longing and anger tangling together.

Her eyes fell on the decanter of amber liquid that sat on the low table in the corner. It had been abandoned, an artifact of a life stolen from them both. She crossed the room, her black combat boots soft against the wooden floor, and hovered over it. Her fingers brushed the glass lid as temptation pulled her closer.

Don't do it, she told herself. *You're better than this.*

But was she?

Her hand lingered, the cool glass grounding her in a way

that nothing else could. Her throat ached with the need to feel that familiar burn, to let the liquid dissolve the pain and numb the memories clawing their way to the surface.

"Thirsty, Ophy?" Brisa's voice broke through the silence, sharp and teasing as always. She flopped onto the couch, her leather boots dangling off the armrest, the picture of casual irreverence.

"Brisa," Alex scolded as she entered the apartment, setting down the grocery bag she'd carried in. "At least pretend to be helpful."

Brisa stared at her orange-hued nails, unapologetic. "What? I'm the comic relief."

Ophelia hated that they were openly discussing her. And, worse, she knew they had a reason to.

Alex sighed but didn't press further. She pulled out fresh bread and cheese, placing them on the counter.

Gabriel stepped into the apartment behind her, his broad shoulders nearly brushing the doorway, making the room feel even smaller. His scent—cedarwood and sea salt—drifted through the room, grounding and inescapable. He carried himself with the same ease as always, his dark eyes sweeping the space before landing on Ophelia.

"Don't start," Ophelia muttered before he could say anything. She sank onto the couch beside Brisa, her head falling into her hands.

Gabriel said nothing, but his presence filled the room, solid and steady.

"Maybe we should stay somewhere else," Alex offered gently. She crossed to Ophelia, sitting on the edge of the coffee table and resting a hand on her friend's knee.

Ophelia hesitated, glancing at Alex's hand. The warmth of the touch surprised her; it was the first time Alex had reached out to her like this in months. A pang of guilt settled in Ophelia's chest, the strain of their fractured friendship impossible to ignore.

"No," she said softly. "We have a job to do here. After that, I'm leaving." Her voice hardened. "This city...is too much."

Alex didn't push. Instead, she shifted her focus. "Why Miramare Castle for the meeting with the Alliance?" she asked, looking back and forth between Gabriel and Brisa.

Brisa sat up, clearly amused. "You don't know?"

"Not everyone grew up with supernatural bedtime stories," Ophelia said, a hint of irritation in her tone at the reminder of her childhood in the dark, not knowing who or what she was. Elijah did the best he could, but he knew nothing of the supernatural world. And still didn't. She'd only learned the year before when she went searching for her mother. And after yearning for that woman for over twenty years, she was disappointed with what she found.

Gabriel leaned against the wall, arms crossed, his dark eyes steady on her. He didn't say anything, didn't try to fill the silence with meaningless words. He was just there, solid and unyielding, like a rock standing firm against the tide she couldn't stop.

"Trieste has been neutral territory for centuries, declared so by the Alliance. Supernaturals took control of Miramare Castle in the early twentieth century because it is protected by layers of wards, shielding it from humans and safeguarding supernaturals who meet there," he said.

"It's more than just wards," Brisa said, kicking her platform boots off. "The locals say it's cursed. Unexplained deaths, shipwrecks near the shore, weird whispers on the wind."

Alex tilted her head, intrigued. "Cursed? How?" she asked.

Brisa smirked, sitting up slightly. "The most popular legend is about Maximilian of Austria, the old guy who built the place. He declared himself Emperor of Mexico, but—plot twist—he was executed. The locals claim it's because he spent the night in the castle. Anyone who stays there is doomed to die tragically."

Gabriel rolled his eyes. "Propaganda. The curse is an invention to keep humans away. Supernaturals spread the rumors ages ago. It worked."

"But humans still visit, don't they?" Alex asked, her cerulean eyes widening, ever the pragmatist.

"Some do," Gabriel admitted. "And when they stray too far...we make sure the stories stay alive. A widow who went mad. An explorer who died young. You get the idea."

Ophelia raised a brow, voice dripping with dry amusement. "Let me guess. Some of those untimely deaths had your fingerprints on them?"

Gabriel's smirk deepened, but he didn't answer as his dark eyes held hers.

Brisa leaned back, her arms behind her head. "It's quite the cheery place for a supernatural summit. Really sets the tone."

Ophelia glanced at the decanter again. The pull was stronger this time. She wasn't ready for another round of their jokes, their camaraderie. She wasn't ready to face Alex's tentative kindness or Gabriel's steady gaze or Brisa's refusal to just let her be.

Before she could stop herself, she crossed the room and poured a drink. The liquid burned as it slid down her throat, scorching and unforgiving.

The conversation stopped, the silence reverberating around the room.

Brisa raised a brow but said nothing. Alex shifted uncomfortably, her mouth opening as if to say something before she thought better of it. Gabriel's expression didn't change, but Ophelia could feel his intense eyes on her, heavy and suffocating.

She poured another.

The second drink blunted their silence and softened the taut corners of their disapproval. Ophelia felt herself slipping into that familiar numbness, the one place where the grief and guilt couldn't reach her. And where her magic was dulled, almost a whisper.

Brisa spoke first, breaking the tension. "Are we going to keep standing around, or are we figuring out the sleeping arrangements? I call the bed," she declared, stretching dramatically.

Alex sighed. "You mean we're sharing the bed."

Brisa grinned. "Unless you're offering it to Gabriel?"

Gabriel's lips twitched in amusement as he shook his head. "I'll find a place to stay. Don't worry about me."

Brisa feigned offense, raising a hand to her chest. "What? You don't want to stay in the coffin I was going to set up for you?"

Alex smothered a laugh, and Gabriel didn't miss a beat. "Comfortable as that sounds, I think I'll pass," he said before disappearing into the kitchen.

Ophelia sighed, standing. "I'll take the couch. I'm not going to sleep much anyway."

"Suit yourself," Brisa said, tugging Alex toward the bedroom. "Let's go, roomie. Sweet dreams, Ophy."

Alex hesitated, her gaze flicking toward her best friend of nearly twenty years. But when Ophelia didn't respond, she followed Brisa, leaving the door slightly ajar and Ophelia alone with the painful memories.

THE APARTMENT WAS silent except for the soft hum of the refrigerator and Brisa's muffled laughter from the bedroom.

Ophelia slipped from the couch, careful not to disturb the fragile quiet, and stepped out onto the large terrace. It was as she remembered: completely private from all sides with a panoramic view of the ocean, illuminated by the full moon overhead.

The night air was crisp, carrying the scent of the Adriatic. She gripped the wrought-iron railing, eyes fixed on the shimmering lights reflecting off the water. The view was beautiful, serene even, but it did little to still the restless energy knotting in her chest. She closed her eyes, leaning forward with her hands resting on the railing, her breaths shaky and uneven. Despite her best efforts to numb the magic, she felt his approach via that familiar vibration before she saw him.

Gabriel appeared without a sound, filling the space around her like a shadow. His scent was the first thing she noticed, grounding and familiar.

"You're good at sneaking up on people," she said, not looking at him.

He leaned against the railing beside her, his body too close. "Not that good. You always notice."

She huffed a quiet laugh, her breath lingering in the balmy air. "We always seem to meet in the dark," she said, remembering the last time she met him in Trieste, searching for clues about the Lunula Amulet. And look how that turned out.

"Maybe it's where we belong," he replied.

For a moment, silence stretched between them, comfortable yet heavy.

"Why are you always here?" she asked, barely above a whisper as she finally turned her face to look at him. "Why do you care?"

Gabriel's gaze fixed on the horizon. He answered her slowly, "We both know there's a pull between us," he said finally.

Ophelia swallowed, her throat tight. "I feel a lot of things," she admitted, her voice trembling. "But I can't—"

Gabriel turned to her, his dark eyes steady. "I'm not asking you for anything, Cinis."

Turning her face away, she stared at the water below, gripping the railing tighter. She ignored the nickname—again. It lingered between them like a challenge, unspoken but ever-present. She refused to ask what it meant, refused to give him the satisfaction. But dammit, every time he said it, it stuck, like an ember burning under her skin. He'd started calling her the name months ago, and she refused to rise to the bait.

"You don't need to fix me," she said. "I'm not some puzzle you can solve."

"I'm not trying to fix you," he said, voice soft but firm. "I'm just...here."

The simplicity of his words disarmed her, and she hated it. She hated that he could be so steady, so unwavering, while she felt like she was crumbling.

Finally she straightened, forcing a grimace to mask the turmoil inside her. "Think you can beat me to the bottom?"

Gabriel arched a brow, a slow, knowing smile spreading across his lips. "There's no question," he said, vaulting over the railing without hesitation, his descent almost predatory in its grace, in spite of his massive frame.

Following him, Ophelia vaulted over the railing, too, using her air and earth magic to control her descent—but not too much—as she soared toward the jagged rocks below. The adrenaline rushed through her, and she forced her magic at bay until *just* before she was about to hit the surface.

They landed on the rocky shore in near unison, her boots skidding slightly as she found her footing.

"You've been holding back," he teased, voice light for the first time that night.

"Maybe," she replied, brushing invisible dirt from her hands against the black leggings she'd worn to bed. "Or maybe you've been underestimating me."

They walked along the rocky shore in silence, the sound of waves filling the space between them. The city lights reflected off the water, casting shadows across the ground. Gabriel finally stopped, sitting down and stretching out on some small pebbles, his long legs crossed at the ankles. He leaned back on one arm, the other stretching toward her in a quiet invitation.

Ophelia hesitated before settling beside him. They leaned back, gazing at the stars, his arm offering support beneath her neck. For the first time in months, she allowed herself to feel the comfort of someone else. Even as the first light of dawn broke over the horizon, they stayed silent together, a quiet comfort to Ophelia as they watched the world slowly brighten. Gabriel remained steady next to her, his touch grounding her in a way nothing else could these days.

Finally, as the day brightened around him, he spoke softly. "I'm here, Cinis, for whatever you need. And I'm not going anywhere."

She didn't respond, didn't look at him. But as the first rays of sunlight spilled over the horizon, she didn't move away either.

CHAPTER

SEVEN

Miramare Castle stood like a sentinel above the Gulf of Trieste, its white limestone walls gleaming under the pale glow of the moon. The waves crashed against the rocky shore below, their rhythmic sound a counterpoint to the hum of magic radiating from the castle itself. The structure was imposing, a stark blend of historical grandeur and supernatural mystique. Its silhouette was etched against the inky sky like a forgotten relic from another world.

Ophelia slowed her steps as they approached the castle, the gravel crunching beneath her boots muted as if the wards around the property absorbed the sound. The faint shimmer of enchantments layered over the grounds was visible to her trained eye, a slight ripple in the air, like heat waves distorting a distant horizon.

"This place is stifling," she muttered, wrapping her arms around herself as a breeze carried the salty tang of the Adriatic Sea to her senses.

Gabriel stepped beside her, his frame towering and solid.

The wards pressed down on her magic, an unrelenting

weight constricting her chest. Gabriel moved through it without hesitation, steady as stone, while Ophelia's magic rebelled against the suffocating constraints.

"It's the wards," he said, his tone even, gaze fixed ahead. "They're designed to suppress power and prevent conflict."

"Great," she replied dryly. "A supernatural peacekeeping force."

A rare flicker of amusement passed over Gabriel's face, but he didn't respond. Instead, his attention shifted to the castle's looming spires, their spear-like tips pointing accusingly at the heavens.

Behind them, Brisa let out a low whistle. "Well, this is cheerful. Nothing says 'welcome' like walls drenched in doom and magic."

Alex glanced nervously at Brisa, her steps faltering. "Are we sure this is safe? I mean, I know it's supposed to be neutral ground, but—"

"It's fine," Mo interjected from behind them. "The wards are ancient and potent. No one's going to start anything here."

"Unless someone really wants to die," Brisa added with a smirk.

As they reached the arched doorway, Ophelia paused, her breath hitching as the first wave of magic brushed against her skin. It was suffocating, an oppressive force pressing down on her, making her feel exposed in ways she hated.

The heavy oak doors swung open with a groan, revealing an entrance hall that seemed untouched by time. The air inside was cool and perfumed with aged wood and sea salt, a combination both inviting and eerie.

The grandeur of the space was overwhelming. Elaborate frescoes stretched across the vaulted ceiling, depicting epic battles between mythical creatures and supernatural beings. Dragons curled around mountains, fae warriors wielded weapons of light, and witches cast spells that seemed to ripple and shift when viewed from different angles. Ophelia couldn't tell if it was a trick of the light or if the artwork itself was alive.

Ornate chandeliers hung from iron chains, their flames flickering with an unnatural, bluish hue that cast long, ghostly shadows across the polished marble floor. The reflective surface gave the illusion of walking on water, and Ophelia's boots echoed in the cavernous space.

"Impressive," Brisa said, her words breaking the reverent silence. "But I liked the spooky vibe better outside."

Ophelia shot her a warning look, but Brisa only grinned and shrugged.

They moved deeper into the castle, guided by the hum of voices emanating from the grand hall. As they entered, Ophelia felt swallowed by the majesty around her, the sheer scale leaving her breathless.

The grand hall was even more magnificent than the entrance, with towering arched windows that framed the moonlit Adriatic. The sea shimmered in the distance, the silver waves a stark contrast to the dark, intricate carvings etched into the black marble walls. Each carving told a story—a fae queen's triumph, a vampire lord's sacrifice, and a witch's tragic rebellion. The room thrummed with centuries of history, secrets etched into every surface.

At the center of the room stood a circular obsidian table, its surface carved with glowing runes. The light from the runes pulsed as if the table itself were breathing.

The room was already occupied.

To the right, the witches had claimed their space. High Priestess Sofija stood at the center of her coven, exuding authority. Her white balding hair hung in patches over her hunched shoulders, and her robes of black and green shimmered with enchantments. Deep grooves were etched into the lines on her face, showing all 200 of her years, but her aqua-blue eyes were as shrewd as ever, watching the scene unfold in front of her.

Ingrid, Sofija's neophyte, hovered behind her in a ready stance, her angled jaw framed by short-cropped black hair. Ophelia noted the way Ingrid's gaze flitted around the room, absorbing every detail at once. She was one of the coven's most powerful neophytes, fiercely loyal, and capable of summoning ancient spells.

For reasons Ophelia still didn't understand, Ingrid had helped her destroy the Lunula Amulet at the Eye of the Earth. She doubted Sofija knew about Ingrid's involvement.

Nearby, Mo and Brisa stood slightly apart from the witches, their casual stances marking them as outsiders even among their own kind. Mo caught Ophelia's eye and gave her a small nod, his expression unreadable. Brisa, however, looked anything but neutral. She smirked at the tension in the room, clearly relishing the undercurrent of unease. Celeste lingered behind them, taking in the scene without being part of it.

To the left, the vampires exuded their typical cold intensity. Ophelia was disappointed to see that the two other members of the Council had survived when she'd destroyed the Council headquarters in San Marino.

The oldest known vampire, Leander, stood at the forefront. He had graying salt-and-pepper hair and deep grooves reminiscent of crow's feet set around his eyes. His impeccably tailored suit emphasized his regal bearing, and his eyes swept the room with calculated precision. Beside him, Zeon—the only other living member of the Council—was a study in contrasts, silent and brooding, his dark eyes scanning the crowd as though searching for weakness. The vampires around them were eerily beautiful, portraying an almost otherworldly quality.

And then there were the fae, ethereal and arresting. Their leader, Aelirian, was a vision of unearthly beauty, his silver hair flowing down his back like liquid starlight. His teal eyes glowed, their depth hinting at an age and wisdom far beyond human comprehension. He moved with grace, his every gesture fluid and deliberate. The air around him seemed to hum with energy, a subtle vibration that made the hairs on Ophelia's arms stand on end.

Alex, standing near Ophelia, couldn't hide her fascination. Her gaze lingered on the fae, her curiosity almost tangible.

"They're unsettling, aren't they?" Brisa whispered to Alex, her tone dry.

Alex nodded but didn't take her eyes off Aelirian. "They're...mesmerizing. I've never seen anything like them."

Ophelia resisted the urge to roll her eyes. She couldn't deny the fae's allure, but their aura set her teeth on edge. All of the supernaturals were too perfect, too polished—a reminder of just how far removed they were from the messy, chaotic humanity she'd grown up with.

Refusing to align herself with any group, Ophelia lingered near the entrance, her arms crossed. Her posture was defiant, but her heart pounded against her ribs as she felt the collective tension in the room settle over her. She could feel their eyes— measuring, judging, waiting.

As the factions started to mingle, Brisa approached her and muttered, "Welcome to the circus. Just missing the popcorn."

Ophelia snorted, but her gaze remained alert, taking in every detail. Whatever the Alliance had planned, it was clear they weren't here to waste time as the supernaturals sorted themselves by standing with their own kind.

Sofija raised her hand, and the room fell silent. With a subtle flick of her wrist, an illusion materialized above the obsidian table. It showed a massive golden bell, its surface covered in intricate, swirling runes that shifted and shimmered as the light caught them. The glowing edges of the runes pulsed, capturing the attention of everyone in the room.

"This is the Kala Ghanta," Sofija began. "The Bell of Time."

The illusion shifted, showing the bell being lowered into a river, its golden surface gleaming even as it disappeared beneath the water. Wisps of magic curled around it, unveiling the wards placed to conceal it.

"It was forged centuries ago," Sofija continued. "A creation of immense power, designed to manipulate the fabric of time itself. It can halt time entirely or even reverse it. Such power, if wielded irresponsibly, could unravel the delicate balance that sustains our world."

A murmur rippled through the room as her words settled. Even the fae, who rarely displayed overt emotion, exchanged glances.

Leander stepped forward, his aura magnetic. He gestured to the illusion, and the image shifted again, showing the bell encased in thick vegetation, overrun by centuries of nature reclaiming it. "Recent intelligence suggests the bell has resurfaced. It is believed to be on or near Nivara Island, a remote landmass in the Indian Ocean. The island's dense magic may have shielded it for centuries, but those barriers are weakening."

Ophelia furrowed her brow. "Nivara Island? I've never heard of it," she said.

"You wouldn't, having grown up with humans," Leander replied smoothly. "Nivara is a land steeped in ancient magic, older than the factions represented here. The natural magic of the island has kept it hidden from mortal and unwelcome supernatural eyes. Only supernaturals who mean no harm are welcomed by the Island," he said.

"Why would it be on Nivara Island?" Brisa asked, studying

her purple-hued nails with boredom. "One vision shows it in water, and another vision shows it overrun by a jungle. Which is it?"

Sofija answered her. "We don't know for sure where it is. Something—or someone—is confusing any locator spell we could use to find it," Sofija said.

"And if someone claims the bell? What happens then?" Aelirian asked, as the glow of his eyes intensified. His calm tone belied the gravity of his words.

"The consequences would be catastrophic," Leander replied, his gaze sweeping across the room. "Temporal distortions could collapse alliances, reignite old wars, and undo everything we've built to maintain peace."

His eyes flicked momentarily toward Celeste. The brief exchange was fleeting, but Ophelia caught it. There was something unspoken in their shared look, a thread of understanding that seemed to pass between them. Ophelia furrowed her brow, uncertain of what she had just witnessed.

Mo cleared his throat, voice steady as he broke the growing silence. "You're saying this bell can rewrite history? Just like that?" he asked, snapping his fingers.

"Absolutely," Sofija answered, her expression grim. "But such actions are never without cost. The threads of time are fragile. One small change could have devastating repercussions, rippling through every timeline, every reality."

A murmur rose among the gathered factions. Whispers of concern and suspicion filled the air as her words settled over them.

Brisa leaned toward Mo, whispering just loud enough for Ophelia to hear, "I knew this was going to be a disaster."

Mo gave her a pointed look, but she shrugged.

"The question is," Zeon said, his deep voice carrying authority, "who else knows about this?"

Leander's expression shifted, his forest-green eyes darkening. "A rogue faction has been working against the Alliance, seeking to harness the bell's power for their own purposes. We believe they have infiltrated our networks, compromising critical information. It's only a matter of time before they locate the bell."

"And why am I here?" Ophelia's voice rang out, acidic and defiant.

All eyes turned to her.

Sofija's gaze was cool, measured. "Powerful magic calls to you. That was obvious with the Lunula Amulet. Perhaps if you had not destroyed it…"

"What? You would have it to use for yourself?" Ophelia asked, her disdain for the high priestess on display.

Sofija shrugged a hunched shoulder, but she didn't respond.

Leander looked at Ophelia thoughtfully before speaking. "We believe you have a unique ability to find supernatural artifacts, that these artifacts call to you when you are near them. If we can get you near Nivara, we believe the Kala Ghanta could reveal itself to you," he said, studying her face as he spoke.

"But you don't know that, do you?" Ophelia asked, remembering how Leander allowed Sebastian to die and had not intervened. Even if Sebastian had been a plant in her home, he didn't deserve to be murdered with his hands tied behind his back.

"You expect me to fix this?" she asked.

Sofija answered, her tone firm and blue eyes piercing. "Whether you like it or not, your bloodline makes you invaluable to this mission. Your gifts—"

"Are a burden," Ophelia interrupted. "A curse, not a calling."

Leander's stark features were unreadable, but there was

something in his gaze—an intensity that made Ophelia's skin crawl. "This isn't about what you want. It's about what's necessary," he said.

"And that's why you need me?" she challenged, refusing to back down. "Because it's convenient?"

Aelirian, who had remained silent until now, finally spoke. His voice was soft, but it carried a weight that drew everyone's attention. "The bell is older than any of us. Its existence predates even the Alliance. If it falls into the wrong hands, it won't matter which faction is strongest. We will all be undone."

Ophelia turned to him, her eyes narrowing. "Why do you care? The fae don't seem to get involved in the messy politics of the vampires and witches. I barely know anything about the fae," she said.

Aelirian's gaze was steady, unblinking. "And that is the way we prefer our kind to stay. But time binds us all, mortal and immortal alike. It is the one force that cannot be controlled—until now. If the bell is wielded by someone with nefarious intent, it will be the end of everything we know."

"You speak as if you've seen it before," Gabriel said.

Aelirian inclined his head. "The fae have long memories. We know what happens when balance is disrupted. We will not let it happen again."

Gabriel nodded, his expression grim.

"And what about this rogue faction? If they've infiltrated the Alliance, how do we know they're not already in this room?" Brisa asked the question they'd all been thinking.

The tension in the room spiked. Sofija's eyes narrowed, and Leander's jaw tightened.

"We've been monitoring the situation closely," Leander said coldly. "But our priority is securing the bell. Once it is out of reach, we can deal with those who would seek to undermine us."

"How convenient," Brisa muttered under her breath, earning a withering look from Sofija and Ingrid.

Ophelia crossed her arms, her gaze hard. "So you want me to wade into this mess and trust that you'll handle everything else? Forgive me if I'm not feeling particularly cooperative," she said.

"You don't have to trust us," Leander said, his tone cutting. "But if you refuse to act, you're as much a threat as the rogue faction."

Ophelia opened her mouth to retort, but a subtle movement caught her eye. Celeste, who had been silent until now, stepped forward. Her expression was calm, but there was something in her eyes—a flicker of emotion that Ophelia couldn't quite place.

"Enough," Celeste said, firm but quiet. "This isn't about trust. It's about survival. The bell must be destroyed before it's too late."

Leander shifted as she spoke, his unyielding eyes resting on her for a moment longer than necessary. Ophelia's stomach churned at the silent communication she couldn't decipher. A part of her wanted to demand answers, but the sheer weight of the room's tension kept her silent.

"And you're just so sure of that, aren't you?" Ophelia shot back, her frustration bubbling over.

Celeste met her gaze, unflinching. "I am."

The room fell silent again, Celeste's words hanging in the air.

"Your unique heritage makes you indispensable," Sofija said, her steely gaze locking on to Ophelia.

"Of course," Sofija continued, looking at Celeste, "your parents must be punished for breaking the Alliance rules.

Perhaps helping us could allow them some leniency, once your mother discloses the identity of your father."

Out of the corner of her eye, Ophelia noticed Celeste stiffen ever so slightly, her hands folding in front of her as though bracing for something. Leander's expression didn't falter, but there was an almost imperceptible tension in his jaw. *What weren't they saying, and what did they know?*

Ophelia crossed her arms tighter, her jaw clenched. "I don't want to be part of this supernatural world or any so-called Alliance, which seems precarious at best."

Leander's expression darkened, his chiseled features hardening into something cold. "You already are part of our world. Whether you like it or not."

The air in the room grew heavier, tension radiating from every corner. The witches shifted uncomfortably, their silence thick with disapproval. The vampires stood still as statues, their expressions betraying nothing, but the flicker of movement in Zeon's jaw suggested irritation. Even the fae, typically inscrutable, exuded an unease, their glowing eyes dimming as if reflecting the conflict brewing.

"I don't care what you think I am," Ophelia said, her voice rising, "I've already lost too much because of this world. I'm not going to lose myself, too."

"No one is asking you to lose yourself, girl," Sofija replied, her tone annoyed as the edge of frustration bled through. "We are asking you to step into the role you were born for. To protect what you've already sacrificed so much for."

Ophelia's laugh was brittle, bitter. "Born for? Don't make this sound like destiny. This is manipulation, plain and simple."

Leander stepped forward, his towering presence suddenly menacing. "This is survival," he said, his deep voice cutting through the tension. "You would turn your back on this? On all of us?"

"Yes," Ophelia said, firm and unwavering. "And don't try to stop me."

Her boots echoed against the polished marble as she turned on her heel, the sound cutting through the stunned silence like a knife. With a flick of her wrist, the heavy doors to the hall slammed shut behind her, the force of the gesture reverberating through the room.

Outside, the cool night air was a harsh contrast to the heated tension within the castle. The moonlight bathed the grounds in silver, illuminating the intricate gardens that stretched toward the cliffs. Ophelia stood alone near the edge, her chest heaving as she tried to calm the emotions that were threatening to rage inside her.

The memory of the bell's illusion lingered in her mind, its glowing runes and immense power both terrifying and inescapable. She hated the Alliance for dragging her into this, for expecting her to carry their mistakes. But deep down, a small, nagging voice whispered that she couldn't ignore the danger.

She clenched her fists, her nails biting into her palms. The shadow of the Kala Ghanta loomed large in her thoughts, its power threatening to consume everything she had fought to protect.

"I didn't sign up for this," she muttered to herself.

"No one does," Gabriel's voice came from behind her, quiet but steady.

Ophelia didn't turn around, though her shoulders tensed. "You following me now?"

"Always," he said simply.

For a moment, neither of them spoke. The sound of the

waves crashing against the rocks below filled the silence, their rhythmic cadence oddly soothing.

"You don't have to do this alone," Gabriel said. "But you do have to do it." His words weren't comforting. They weren't meant to be. They were the hard truth, unyielding as the cliff beneath their feet.

Ophelia let out a bitter laugh. "Take on the impossible because no one else can or will?"

"They're asking because they believe you can," Gabriel replied.

"And you?" she asked, turning to face him at last. "What do you believe?"

Gabriel held her gaze, his dark eyes unreadable. "If anyone can stop this, it's you."

His words struck something deep within her, a flicker of warmth amidst the cold anger she clung to. But she pushed it aside, unwilling to let herself feel anything but defiance.

"I didn't want any of this," she said, voice cracking slightly.

"No," Gabriel agreed. "But you've never run from a fight before."

Ophelia turned back to the sea, the moonlight shimmering on the waves below. The memory of the bell loomed in her mind, its power as inescapable as the tide. She hated the Alliance for what they were asking of her, but she hated the thought of doing nothing even more.

CHAPTER

EIGHT

The bar looked almost exactly as it had that night—dimly lit, smoky, and vibrating with an energy that seemed to pulse from its very walls. The soft glow of candles flickered against the exposed stone, the warm light doing little to dispel the shadows that clung stubbornly to the corners of the room. The hum of conversation was a low, constant murmur, blending with the strains of music. The ever-present tang of magic lingered in the air, subtle yet unmistakable.

Ophelia hesitated at the entrance, her fingers tightening around her biceps as she crossed her arms. Her gaze swept over the familiar space. It hadn't changed, but she felt like a different person. The hum of magic in the walls felt different this time, sharper, more insistent. She wasn't the naïve young woman who had walked in here all those months ago. She was something else now, fractured and raw.

The memories rose unbidden, biting and vivid. She could see him sitting in the shadows, his calculating eyes watching her with quiet intensity. She remembered the way he had seemed reluctant to engage, as though every word and gesture was calculated, deliberate. He hadn't wanted to tell her his name, and yet, when she'd asked, he'd finally answered, his deep voice tinged with an accent she couldn't quite place. And then there had been the dance—the way his hand had burned against her lower back, the way he'd moved with a predator's grace, every step measured and unyielding. She could still feel the ghost of his touch if she let herself.

Brisa's voice cut through the haze of memory. "Are we just going to stand here, or are we getting drinks?" she asked, brisk and impatient. Without waiting for a response, her cousin pushed past her, leather boots clicking on the stone as she made her way inside.

Alex followed, glancing back at Ophelia as she stepped over the threshold. Her silver-streaked hair caught the candlelight, and her eyes darted around the room, taking in the details with a curiosity Ophelia recognized all too well. Alex paused, her brows furrowing slightly. "This place feels...strange," she murmured, voice low.

"Strange how?" Ophelia asked, though she already suspected the answer.

Alex hesitated, searching for the right words. "It's like...I don't know, unnatural."

Ophelia nodded grimly. She'd felt the same thing the first time they'd come here.

Mo brought up the rear, his steadiness a welcome counterpoint to Brisa's restlessness. "Don't let it get to you," he said softly. "It's just magic." He placed a reassuring hand on Alex's shoulder before gesturing toward the tables.

The group descended into the small bar, where the air grew heavier, charged with energy that seemed to vibrate beneath their feet. The low ceiling and rough stone walls gave the space an almost cavernous feel, the dim light creating pockets of shadow where figures moved and whispered. A bar lined one wall, its surface worn smooth by countless hands, while the dance floor occupied the center of the room, surrounded by small wooden tables that formed a crescent moon shape. The music thumped softly in the background, a steady rhythm that seemed to echo the room's pulse.

Brisa made a beeline for the bar, but Alex hesitated, glancing at Ophelia. "We don't have to drink," she said gently.

Brisa turned back, rolling her eyes. "She's not a nun, Alex. I'll grab her something if she promises not to overdo it."

Ophelia sighed, running a hand through her hair. "I'm fine," she muttered. "I don't need anything."

Brisa shrugged, unbothered. "Suit yourself."

They occupied a group of tables near the rock wall. Ophelia glanced at the bar and could almost see Luka there, leaning against a stool with his long legs stretched out and his hands resting loosely on his thighs. She'd thought he was relaxed, but now she recognized the tension in his posture, the way he'd been ready to spring into action at a moment's notice.

Brisa dropped into the seat across from her, tapping her nails against the table. "You're brooding again," she said lightly, though her eyes were penetrating.

"I'm not brooding," Ophelia snapped, though the words felt hollow even as she said them.

"Sure you're not," Brisa said with a smirk. She leaned back, folding her arms behind her head.

Ophelia's jaw tightened, but she didn't respond. She didn't owe Brisa an explanation.

Mo returned with drinks, setting several glasses of grappa in front of the group and a glass of water in front of Ophelia. She stared at the water for a long moment and then at the grappa, her fingers itching to pick it up. She could already imagine the warmth spreading through her chest, dulling the edges of her pain. But she didn't trust herself. Not tonight.

"Not in the mood?" Brisa asked, her tone casual.

Ophelia shook her head, pushing the glass away. "I'm good."

Alex glanced at her, concern flickering across her face. "You don't have to do this alone," she said softly.

Ophelia's lips twitched into something that wasn't quite a smile, annoyed that everyone was fussing over her and trying to control her. "I'm fine," she said again, though she wasn't sure who she was trying to convince.

The conversation at the table flowed around her, voices blending with the background hum of the bar. She wasn't paying attention, her thoughts spiraling as the memories of Luka tightened their grip on her. Eventually, though, the pull became too much. She reached for a glass of grappa, her fingers tightening around it.

She didn't drink to forget Luka, not entirely. She drank to drown out everyone's expectations—to silence Gabriel's steady gaze, Brisa's smirking judgment, and her own nagging doubts. The first sip was fire; the second was freedom. The warmth spread through her chest, dulling the jagged edges of her grief. She took another sip, then another.

The drink worked its way through her system, loosening her limbs and numbing her mind. The ache in her chest was still there, but it felt distant now, like a faint hum at the edge of her awareness.

Brisa raised her glass in a silent toast, her eyes sparkling with amusement. "Here's to forgetting," she said.

Ophelia didn't reply. She lifted her glass and drained the rest of her drink, letting the liquor burn away the last of her resistance. It felt like sweet freedom.

Ophelia downed four more glasses—this time whiskey—in

rapid succession, letting the burn smother anything she might have felt. When the world around her softened into a blur, she slowed, cradling the next drink instead of drowning in it. Leaning back on her stool, her gaze drifted over the room, caught between detachment and curiosity. The thrumming energy from her first night here still pulsed beneath the surface, an unseen current of magic stitched into the very bones of this place.

As her eyes adjusted to the dim light, she noticed details she'd missed during her first visit. The candles that lined the walls burned unnaturally steady, their flames flickering toward certain patrons in a way that seemed purposeful, almost sentient. The air was heavy with whispers, some too low for even her heightened senses to decipher. There was an order to it all—an underlying rhythm hidden within the disorder.

She turned to Gabriel, who stood at the edge of their group, his arms crossed as he surveyed the room. "This place," she said, low, "it feels different."

Gabriel's eyes flicked to her, his expression unreadable. "It should. This bar wasn't made for humans. It's a sanctuary for supernaturals."

Ophelia's breath hitched, his words settling on her like a stone. "What are you talking about? Alex and I came here last time. We're—" She stopped herself, the word sticking in her throat.

"Human?" Gabriel finished for her, his tone dry. "Not entirely. Even if you didn't know it then, you were always one of us. That's why you were drawn here. Why you felt the pull."

Ophelia's stomach twisted. The realization hit her with the force of a wave. She had felt the pull that night—an undeniable thrumming that had led her down the stairs and into this hidden world. And now, knowing what she was, it all made sense.

Alex, who had been quietly sipping her drink, looked up with a jolt. "Wait. Are you saying we came here because of magic?"

Gabriel's gaze softened slightly as he looked at Alex. "Not magic. Instinct. Places like this are designed to attract our kind. Humans with supernatural bloodlines, even dormant ones, feel the draw. It's subtle, but it's there."

Alex blinked, her mouth opening and closing as she struggled to process his words. "But I'm not—"

"You might not be a full-blooded supernatural," Gabriel interrupted gently, "but there's something in you. A spark of fae. Enough to lead you here."

Ophelia stared into her glass, the amber liquid catching the flickering candlelight. "So, this place...it's a trap?"

Gabriel shook his head. "Not a trap. A haven. Supernaturals come here to mingle, to be themselves without fear of exposure. It's protected, warded against human detection. Even the staff are supernatural. Watchers, mostly, here to ensure the peace is kept."

She thought back to the silent, attentive servers, the way they had seemed to appear and disappear without a sound. "And the bartender?"

"A vampire," Gabriel said simply.

Ophelia's grip on the glass tightened. She glanced around the room again, her eyes lingering on the dance floor where couples moved in perfect rhythm, their bodies too graceful, their movements too fluid to be entirely natural.

The thought sent a pang through her chest, and she pushed it away, focusing instead on the present. "Why didn't I see it before?"

"You weren't ready to," Gabriel said, shrugging.

A sudden commotion near the dance floor shattered her thoughts. A man with pale skin and severe features was arguing with a group of witches, voice rising above the music. Ingrid, Sofija's neophyte, was standing with them. The tension in the room shifted, the air growing heavier as power crackled between them.

Gabriel's posture stiffened, his eyes narrowing as he watched the scene unfold. "Stay here," he said.

Ophelia ignored him, sliding off her seat and making her way toward the disturbance.

"Ophelia," Gabriel called after her, his tone a warning.

But she didn't stop. The whiskey in her veins made her bold, reckless. She wasn't going to sit back and watch while the past threatened to pull her under. She was done being a bystander. Weaving her way through the crowded bar, the pulsing music vibrated in her chest. The alcohol buzzed in her veins, softening the edges of her frustration.

Ahead, the tension hung heavy in the air. The pale vampire stood rigid, his defined features twisted in anger as he argued with the group of witches. Ingrid met his anger with icy calm.

"You've overstepped," Ingrid said, her words a dangerous drawl. "This is neutral ground. You know the rules."

"Rules?" the vampire spat. "Your kind always hide behind rules. But you don't follow them yourselves."

Ingrid's lips curled into a sly smile and her usual air of cold authority. "Careful, Vincent. You're dangerously close to making this personal."

The vampire sneered but fell silent as Ophelia approached, her steps steady despite the tension thick in the air. She couldn't pinpoint why she was interfering, but something about the scene tugged at the frayed edges of her power.

"What's going on?" she asked, her words slurred, but still cutting through the noise.

Before anyone could answer, Ophelia stumbled slightly, bumping into someone. She turned to see a young girl—barely more than a teenager—with wide, startled eyes. The witchling clutched a drink in her hand, now spilling down the front of her robe. Ophelia's apology died in her throat as the girl's hand shot out to steady herself. Instinctively, Ophelia raised her own hand. The magic surged before she could stop it, her power reacting instinctively to the witchling's challenge. The crackle of energy split the air, and the girl crumpled to the floor, clutching her side and gasping for breath. Ophelia's heart plummeted. She hadn't meant to strike so hard.

The bar fell silent. All eyes turned to Ophelia, who stood frozen, her chest heaving as she stared at the girl.

"What the hell?" Brisa's voice broke the silence, tight and panicked. For once, she didn't sound disinterested. She pushed through the crowd to reach Ophelia, gripping her cousin's arms.

"I didn't—" Ophelia began, but the words caught in her throat.

Gabriel's hand was firm on Ophelia's shoulder as he turned to Ingrid. "It was an accident," he said. There was no apology in his tone, only fact. Ingrid's gaze lingered on him, her lips curling slightly as if testing the limits of his patience.

"I didn't mean to hurt her," Ophelia said, trembling.

"I know," Gabriel said. "But this isn't the place to explain. Come on."

As he tried to guide her toward the exit, Ingrid stepped into their path, blocking them. Her gaze flicked to the witchling, who was being helped to her feet by another member of the coven, before settling on Ophelia.

"You've really outdone yourself this time," Ingrid said, smooth and condescending.

"It was an accident," Gabriel said again, his tone curt.

"Was it?" Ingrid raised a brow, her gaze never leaving

Ophelia. "You've hurt one of ours, and that's not something we take lightly."

"Get lost," Ophelia snapped, her fraying temper snapping with it.

"Ophelia," Gabriel warned, his grip on her arm tightening.

Ingrid's expression didn't change, but there was a glint of satisfaction in her eyes. "This isn't a matter of choice, Ophelia. You've created a problem, and now we want a favor: Help find the Kala Ghanta."

"I'm not fixing anything for you," Ophelia said. "I don't owe you—"

Ingrid cut her off with a caustic laugh. "Oh, but you do. And we both know it. I helped you destroy the Amulet. But this..." She gestured to the witchling. "This is different. We are owed a favor."

Brisa stepped in, her words steady but laced with urgency. "Look, Ingrid, she'll help, okay? You know her history with you counts for something."

"I won't," Ophelia snapped, louder this time. She whirled on Brisa, her glare molten. "You can't just decide that for me!"

"Yes, we can," Gabriel said, his calm voice cutting through the rising tension. "Because if you don't agree, this won't end here."

Ophelia turned on him, her fists clenched. "You don't get to tell me what to do. You don't get to make choices for me," she spat, trembling with more than just rage.

Gabriel's expression didn't waver, his calm infuriating. "I'm making this one," he said quietly, "because if I don't, this will spiral out of control."

"You think you can control me?" she demanded, stepping closer to him, her anger spilling over. "You don't know me."

"I'm not here to control you," Gabriel said, quieter now, but no less firm. "I'm here to keep you alive, even if you hate me for it."

"Don't patronize me," she said. "You're not my keeper."

Gabriel's jaw tightened, his patience clearly wearing thin. He turned to Ingrid. "You'll get your help. I promise," he said.

Ingrid regarded him for a moment before nodding. "I'll hold you to that," she said.

Ophelia's head snapped back to Gabriel. "You can't promise for me. I'm not your problem to solve!"

Gabriel sighed, his resolve settling heavily in his shoulders. The world blurred as Gabriel's hand found the back of her neck. His grip was firm, his magic pressing against hers—not a force to overpower, but to calm. The last thing she heard as the darkness closed around her was his voice, low and steady: "I've got you."

NINE

LUKA

The door slammed shut, the sound reverberating through the damp chamber, and Luka allowed himself a single, measured breath. Even now, battered and broken, his mind raced—analyzing and calculating. He refused to let despair claim him. Despair was for those without purpose, and Luka had one: to survive, to see her again.

The blood hunger clawed at him, vicious and unrelenting, but he refused to let it dominate his thoughts. Pain was a distraction, a weapon wielded against him. He closed his eyes, summoning the memory of her voice—the steel in her defiance, the fire in her laughter. Ophelia was his anchor, even now, though he had tied her to him with chains she hadn't seen.

The other witch's voice crept into his thoughts, louder, sharper, twisting the memories into something unrecognizable.

She doesn't need you anymore.

He wanted to scream, to tear the chains from the walls and

obliterate the illusion of her control. But he had no strength left. His limbs hung uselessly, the manacles biting into his wrists. His body had become a prison of its own, refusing to obey him, worn down by starvation and torment.

The witch had been right about one thing: he'd lied to Ophelia. He hadn't corrected her misunderstanding of twin flames and life mates. Because he needed her. Not just for her power, though that had played its part, but for the way she had made him feel almost human again.

He couldn't regret binding her to him. Not entirely. But the truth of it burned in his chest now, searing and unforgiving. He'd made her believe in him, in a connection that was never hers to choose. Or his. She had been drawn to him by magic she hadn't understood, a blood ritual he'd never fully explained. And he had let her. He'd let her love him despite his deception.

The door creaked open again, and Luka stiffened. When the witch entered, her midnight hair shimmering like a living shadow, Luka didn't flinch. He let his head hang, his eyes half-lidded, presenting the illusion of defeat. If she believed him broken, she might grow careless. Careless enemies were the easiest to destroy.

She carried a small silver goblet, its contents swirling with a thick, dark liquid. Luka's stomach twisted violently at the sight of it. Blood. Fresh blood. Human blood. The scent hit him like a wave, his fangs aching in response, the hunger roaring back to life with renewed fury.

She knelt before him, holding the drink just out of reach. Her shrewd eyes glittered with amusement as she tilted her head. "You look terrible, Loukas," she said sardonically. "Barely more than a corpse. I wonder how long you can survive without feeding."

Luka turned his head away, his jaw clenched tightly. He wouldn't give her the satisfaction of begging.

She laughed softly, the sound like ice. "Still holding on to your pride? How quaint." She swirled the goblet, the liquid catching the dim light. "This could ease your suffering. All you have to do is ask."

His throat burned, his body screaming at him to take what she offered. But he stayed silent.

Her voice was silk and poison, weaving doubts into his mind like a master craftsman. "She doesn't need you, Loukas. Not now. Not ever," she purred.

"You sound jealous," he rasped. "Does it sting to know you'll never hold what she does?"

The witch's smile faltered for a fraction of a second, but she recovered quickly, her laughter like shards of glass. "Oh, Loukas. Always deflecting. But tell me, does she know what you've done?"

Luka flinched, the chains rattling with the movement.

Her laughter rang out again, echoing off the stone walls. "Ah, so there is still some fight left in you. Good. You'll need it when she learns the truth." She leaned in closer, her breath cold against his ear. "What do you think she'll say when she finds out how you bound her? How you used her for your own gain?"

"I didn't—" Luka's voice cracked, the words barely more than a rasp. He swallowed hard, forcing himself to speak. "I didn't use her."

The witch's smile twisted into something darker. "Didn't you? You needed her power, her trust, her belief in your lies. And you took it all, didn't you? You made her think it was destiny, that she was yours. But it wasn't her choice, was it?"

Luka's chest heaved. He wanted to argue, to deny it, but reality was a blade that cut too deep.

The witch pulled back, her expression triumphant. "Oh, Loukas. You've always been such a romantic. But love built on lies is a fragile thing. And when it shatters..." She trailed off, letting the silence speak for her.

She stood, the goblet still in her hand. Luka's eyes followed it, his body betraying him as the hunger clawed at his insides.

"Perhaps next time," she said lightly, turning toward the door. "If you survive that long."

The door slammed shut behind her, and Luka sagged against the wall, the sound of her laughter still echoing in his ears.

He closed his eyes, her words replaying in his mind. He hadn't lied to her for power. He had lied to keep her close, to protect her from a world that would tear her apart. But even he couldn't deny the selfishness buried beneath his noble intentions. The blood ritual had bound them, yes—but hadn't it also given her strength? A purpose?

Yet the truth remained: Ophelia hadn't chosen him. He had taken that choice from her.

Ophelia was fire and fury, a force that couldn't be contained. He'd seen it in her, felt it in her magic. She didn't need him.

But he needed her. Losing her wasn't an option. Not to the witch, not to Gabriel, not to anyone. If he had to tear the world apart to reach her, then so be it.

And if he ever saw her again, he would find a way to make her understand. To make her forgive him.

If she didn't kill him first.

CHAPTER
TEN

Heavy rocking churned Ophelia's stomach, the deep, queasy sensation twisting her insides like a cruel knot. Her head throbbed as if someone were hammering nails into her skull, and the bitter, acidic taste of bile clawed at the back of her throat. Her eyes fluttered open, and the sharp sting of sunlight seared her senses, forcing them closed again.

The rhythmic creak of wood beneath her body and the relentless slap of water against the hull added to the disorientation. It wasn't the bed she remembered from the night before—if it could be called a night. The pounding in her head mirrored the chaotic flashes of memory: Brisa's sharp voice, a crackle of energy, Gabriel's cold grip on her arm. Everything else was a jagged blur, slipping through her grasp like water.

As reality dawned, her stomach heaved. She bolted upright, stumbling toward the edge of the boat. She barely managed to grip the railing before retching over the side. The burning in her throat and the sour taste in her mouth made her stomach lurch again. She felt a cool breeze on her face, salty and biting, as she clung to the railing for dear life.

Below, fish darted to the surface, silvery streaks flashing as they fed on her misery. The sight made her retch again, her body convulsing violently. Tears streamed down her face as she gasped for air, the harsh sunlight doing nothing to ease the pounding in her head.

The boat rocked like a cruel joke, twisting Ophelia's insides with every wave. Her body betrayed her, weak and trembling, the acrid taste of bile still clinging to her tongue. She hated this —being at the mercy of something she couldn't control.

"You're a mess," Gabriel said, voice deep and unruffled, cutting through the haze. There was no trace of ridicule—just a dry amusement that grated on her nerves. He leaned against the mast, the picture of ease, his dark hair still damp from sea spray. The corner of his lips lifted, as though her misery entertained him more than it should.

"Why..." Her voice cracked, raw and broken. She forced herself to swallow and try again. "Why am I on a boat?"

"A sailboat, actually. And because," he said simply, leaning against the mast with maddening ease, "you left us with no choice."

His shirtless form was framed by the backdrop of a perfect blue sky, his skin bronzed and glistening like he'd stepped out of some summer fantasy. His damp, dark hair fell into his eyes. It was exasperating how unaffected he looked while she felt like death would be preferable to being on this boat.

She wiped her mouth with the back of her hand and turned to glare at him. "I didn't ask for this."

"No," he agreed, voice calm as he crouched to her level. His gaze locked on hers, dark and unreadable. "You didn't. But you left us no choice when you decided to turn Trieste into a spectacle."

"I didn't…" she began, but the words faltered. Fragmented memories clawed at the edges of her mind: the taste of whiskey, the burn of magic, her anger spilling over like a broken dam. Her head spun again, and she clutched the railing for support.

"Didn't what? Hurt a witchling and back us into a corner?" His tone was maddeningly patient, as though he had all the time in the world for her denial.

She groaned, closing her eyes as nausea surged once more. "Why didn't you stop me?"

"I tried to," he replied with infuriating calm, his gaze never leaving hers. "You just didn't listen."

She blinked at him, struggling to piece together the events. Flashes of shouting, the heat of a fire, and Brisa's voice rose unbidden in her mind. Her stomach rebelled, churning violently with each wave, though there was nothing left to expel. "Where's Brisa?"

"Below deck," he said. "We used a considerable amount of her air magic to transport us to the Indian Ocean," he said, gesturing at the blue water around them. "She's recovering below deck with some herbs sent by Mo."

"What about Alex?"

"Also below. She's surprisingly good at keeping calm under pressure. And she's been experimenting with her fae healing powers, which you would know if you ever stopped drinking yourself into a stupor and paid attention," Gabriel said, again in an infuriatingly calm voice.

"And where the hell am I supposed to recover?" she snapped, her temper flaring despite her weakened state.

Gabriel's grin returned, a flash of teeth that only deepened her frustration. "You're doing fine where you are."

"Go to hell," she muttered, sinking back onto the deck and letting her head rest against the sun-warmed wood.

"You first," he shot back, his tone light but with an edge that told her he was done coddling her. "But before you do, get yourself together. We're not exactly on vacation here."

She closed her eyes, wishing the world would stop spinning. The boat swayed gently beneath her, the motion almost lulling her to sleep despite the heat of the sun. But Gabriel's voice pulled her back before she could drift off.

"Drink this." A glass of water appeared in her line of sight, held out by his steady hand.

She took it reluctantly, the cool liquid soothing her parched throat. "Where are we going?"

"Toward Nivara Island, hoping that you'll feel some magic call to you," he said, leaning against the mast again. "And before you ask, yes, it's going to take a while. No shortcuts, no magic tricks. Just wind, sails, and patience."

Her head lolled to the side as she squinted up at him. "Why?"

"Because," he said, softening, "Brisa's tapped out. And we don't know how these ancient artifacts can—or even if they will—call to you, Cinis."

"Don't call me that," she muttered, though there was no real bite in her words. She still didn't know what it meant. She refused to ask.

He shrugged, unbothered, and turned his attention back to the sails. The muscles in his shoulders flexed as he adjusted the ropes, his movements fluid and practiced. It was irritating how at home he seemed here, while she felt like a lost and broken thing adrift in the middle of nowhere.

The hatch creaked open, and Brisa emerged, her face pale and drawn. She glanced at Ophelia with a mixture of annoyance and concern, her lips pressed into a thin line.

"You're finally up," Brisa said, arms crossed. "Took you long enough."

Ophelia didn't have the energy to respond. She sipped the water and stared at the horizon, the endless blue stretching in every direction. It should have been calming, but all it did was remind her how far she was from everything she knew.

Alex followed Brisa onto the deck, her movements graceful despite the boat's restless sway. She looked fresh, as if she'd managed to sleep through the turmoil, but her blue eyes carried a weariness that mirrored the charged energy in the air.

"You look unwell," Alex said, though her tone was softer than Brisa's.

"Thanks," Ophelia muttered, her words heavy with sarcasm.

"You should eat something," Alex continued, ignoring the jab. "Even if it's just bread. It'll help."

Ophelia shook her head. The thought of food made her stomach twist. "I'm fine."

"No, you're not," Gabriel said as he stepped between her and the railing. "But you will be. Eventually."

The certainty in his voice made her want to believe him, even if she didn't deserve to. She stared out at the water, the rhythmic rise and fall of the waves mirroring the turmoil inside her.

For now, she didn't have the strength to fight.

The sun hung high, spilling gold over the endless, glittering blue expanse. The boat swayed gently, but to Ophelia, it might as well have been the churning of a violent storm. She slouched against the railing, her eyes fixed on the shimmering waves as she tried to reconcile the fragmented memories of the night before.

Every so often, she caught glimpses of Gabriel moving across the deck with grating ease. His skin glistened under the sunlight, the lines of his muscles shifting with every movement. He didn't say much, but his presence loomed large, a constant reminder of her past failures.

As the afternoon wore on, she forced herself to move. Her hands fumbled with the rigging as Alex demonstrated the knots. "Like this," Alex said patiently, free of judgment. Ophelia nodded, her fingers stiff and awkward but determined. Every knot felt like a small victory against the chaos in her mind.

The sun beat down on her, the sweat dripping from her brow a stark reminder of her weakened state. But as the hours passed, her muscles began to remember, the rhythm of the work grounding her in a way she hadn't felt in weeks. When the sun began to dip toward the horizon, melting the sky to shades of orange and pink, Gabriel called them all to the deck. He stood at the bow, his tall frame silhouetted against the fading light.

"We need to talk about the plan," he said. "Nivara Island isn't close. We've got days ahead of us, maybe more if the wind isn't in our favor. We need to be prepared."

"Prepared for what?" Brisa asked, crossing her arms.

"Anything," Gabriel replied. "The Bell isn't just going to be sitting there, waiting for us to pick it up. If the rumors are true, it's magically guarded—maybe even physically. And we're not the only ones looking for it. We know there is a faction of supernaturals out there working against us, trying to find it first."

A heavy silence fell over the group as his words resonated. The weight of the task ahead pressed down on them, the stakes higher than any of them wanted to admit.

"Then why the hell am I here?" Ophelia asked. "You've made it clear I'm just dead weight."

"You're here," Gabriel said, his gaze locking on to hers,

"because, like it or not, you're part of this. And because we need you."

Ophelia opened her mouth to argue, but the sincerity in his eyes stopped her. She hated it. Hated the way he could make her feel seen, even when she wanted to disappear.

As the sun dipped below the horizon, casting the world in shades of blue and gray, Ophelia found herself alone at the stern of the boat. The gentle lapping of the waves and the hum of the wind filled the silence, giving her a moment of peace.

She leaned against the railing, her fingers trailing over the weathered wood. The cool breeze brushed against her skin, carrying with it the scent of salt and freedom. The vastness of the sea mirrored the hollow ache inside her. How had she let it come to this? How had she become this?

Maybe, she thought, just maybe, she could find a way to fix this.

The sky had deepened into a rich indigo by the time Ophelia made her way below deck. The cramped cabin was dimly lit by a single overhead lamp, its weak glow casting long shadows on the narrow wooden walls. The scent of salt and damp wood lingered in the air, mingling with the remnants of a shared dinner.

Gabriel was already there, shirt back on and leaning back against the corner of the small cabin that served as both a makeshift galley and a communal meeting space. His arms were crossed, his dark eyes following Ophelia as she stepped inside, her posture defensive. Alex sat at the tiny fold-out table, her chin resting on her hand as she scribbled notes in a small journal.

Brisa leaned against the far wall, her gaze flicking between Ophelia and Gabriel, clearly bracing for whatever was about to unfold. "You two are in there," she said, pointing to one of the cabin doors. "Alex and I are in there," she continued, pointing to the other door.

"No way," Ophelia said, crossing her arms to mirror Gabriel's stance. "I'm not sharing a bed with him," she said, pointing at Gabriel.

Brisa shrugged, her indifference only stoking Ophelia's anger.

"And why am I even on this godforsaken boat?" Ophelia asked, frustration spilling over the edges.

Gabriel pushed off the wall, his movements deliberate as he stepped closer. "You're not on this boat for a vacation, Ophelia. You're here because you owe us."

"Owe you?" she snapped, her eyes narrowing. "I refuse to be dragged into this."

"Your choices in Trieste left us with no other option. You nearly started a war, Ophelia," Gabriel said.

Her jaw tightened. "It wasn't that bad."

"Wasn't it?" Brisa cut in. "You hurt a witchling in neutral territory. Do you know how hard it was to cover for you? To convince the Alliance not to hunt you down?"

Ophelia opened her mouth to argue, but their accusations smothered her words. Because she couldn't remember most of it. She clenched her fists at her sides, her nails digging into her palms.

"I didn't ask for any of this," she muttered. "I don't want to be part of this world or your war."

Gabriel stepped closer, filling the small space. "And yet here you are. Like it or not, you're part of this now. You can either keep fighting us, or you can start fighting *for* something."

"For what?" she demanded, her voice rising. "For a world that treats me like an outsider? For a family that only shows up when they need something?"

"For yourself," Gabriel said, voice steady. "Because if you don't start, Ophelia, no one else will."

The room fell silent, the tension so thick it was almost suffocating. Alex glanced up from her journal, her blue eyes filled with quiet concern, but she didn't speak. Brisa crossed her arms and leaned back against the wall, her expression unreadable.

Ophelia's chest heaved as she tried to rein in her emotions. She wanted to scream, to lash out, to run. But there was nowhere to go, no escape from the truth that Gabriel's words had laid bare.

Finally, she turned away, her hands gripping the edge of the table so tightly her knuckles turned white. "Fine," she said, barely above a whisper. "I'll help you find your damn bell. But don't expect me to like it."

Gabriel's lips quirked into a small, almost imperceptible smile. "I don't care if you like it, as long as you do it."

Brisa snorted. "That's about as close to cooperation as we're going to get."

Ophelia glared at her cousin but didn't respond. Instead, she pushed off the table and headed for the narrow doorway leading to her cabin, without saying another word.

The cabin was just as cramped as the rest of the boat, with barely enough room for the small bed that dominated the space. She threw herself onto it, her body sinking into the thin mattress. The gentle rocking of the boat was both soothing and nauseating, a constant reminder of how far she was from solid ground.

She closed her eyes, hoping for sleep to take her, but the sound of the door creaking open shattered the fragile quiet. She didn't need to look to know who it was.

"Go away, Gabriel," she said, muffled against the pillow.

"I need to know you're not going to sabotage this mission," he replied, tone measured.

She rolled onto her side, her eyes narrowing as they met his. "Sabotage? I agreed to help, didn't I?"

"Reluctantly," he said, stepping into the room and closing the door behind him with a click that made her flinch. "That doesn't inspire much confidence."

"Well, I'm sorry if my enthusiasm doesn't meet your expectations," she shot back, sitting up. "Maybe if you hadn't dragged me onto this godforsaken boat without my consent, I'd feel a little more motivated."

Gabriel's eyes darkened, his jaw tightening. He leaned against the wall, his arms crossed. "You think this is easy for me? Babysitting you while we're being hunted by gods know what? When you aren't even yourself? I could have left you in Trieste to deal with the fallout on your own."

"Then why didn't you?" she demanded. "Why didn't you just leave me there?"

His silence was deafening. For a moment, the only sound was the creak of the boat and the distant lapping of waves against the hull. When he finally spoke, his expression had softened, but his jaw remained tight. "Because I couldn't."

His vulnerability caught Ophelia off guard, and she found herself at a loss for words. She looked away, her gaze falling on the small porthole that framed the endless expanse of dark water outside.

"You're impossible," she muttered, lying back down and pulling the thin blanket over her head.

"And you're insufferable," he replied, with maddening ease. "Guess we'll both have to deal."

Ophelia ignored him, closing her eyes and willing sleep to take her as she burrowed into the scratchy blanket. The boat's rocking was incessant, and the creak of wood against water seemed to amplify her frustration. She'd barely begun to relax when she heard the rustle of fabric and the soft thud of boots hitting the floor.

Something about the silence made her uneasy. She peeked over the edge of the blanket, her eyes narrowing when she saw Gabriel shrugging off his shirt. The dim light of the cabin played against his tanned skin, highlighting the defined lines of muscle across his chest and shoulders. Black ink curled along his arms and trailed across his back—intricate tattoos that seemed almost alive in the flickering glow. He turned away from her, reaching for the buckle of his belt, the shifting muscles in his back making the ink stretch and contract like something breathing.

"What the hell are you doing?" she blurted, sitting upright so quickly she nearly knocked her head against the low ceiling.

Gabriel turned slightly, a smirk playing at the corner of his mouth. "Getting ready for bed. What does it look like?"

Her mouth opened and closed as she struggled to form a coherent response. "I—you—don't you have another place to sleep?"

He arched an eyebrow, stepping out of his pants to reveal a pair of fitted black boxer briefs. "Nope. Brisa told you. They claimed the other cabin. That makes us roommates."

She sputtered, her face heating. "You've got to be kidding me."

Gabriel chuckled, the sound low and obnoxiously amused. He tossed his clothes onto a nearby chair before crawling onto the small bed beside her. The narrow mattress barely fit one person, let alone two, and the heat of his body was immediate and overwhelming.

"There's not enough room," she protested, pressing herself against the wall in a futile attempt to create space.

He stretched out beside her, his arm brushing hers as he settled onto his back. "Guess we'll have to make it work."

"This is ridiculous," she muttered, pulling the blanket tighter around herself. "There's no way I'm sharing a bed with you."

"Suit yourself," Gabriel said with a shrug, closing his eyes. "But I'm not sleeping on the floor."

Ophelia glared at him, her hands clenching the edge of the blanket. The cabin was unbearably small, and his proximity was making her skin prickle. She could feel the warmth radiating from him, his steady, slow breathing oddly soothing despite her annoyance.

"Just stay on your side," she grumbled, turning her back to him.

Gabriel didn't respond, and she realized he had already—frustratingly—fallen asleep. She closed her eyes, determined to ignore the fact that she could feel every shift of his body as the boat rocked gently beneath them.

Sleep came slowly, her mind a restless tangle of guilt, anger, and regret. When it finally did, it was light and fleeting. But she woke to the sensation of an arm draped around her waist, pulling her close.

Her eyes flew open, and her breath caught as she realized Gabriel had shifted in his sleep. His chest was pressed against her back, the slow rise and fall of his breath brushing warm air against her neck. His arm was firm but not restrictive, his hand resting just above her hip.

For a moment, she froze, her heart hammering in her chest, unsure of what to do. She could push him away, shove him off the bed entirely. She *should* do that. But as she lay there, feeling the rhythmic slow beat of his heart against her back, something in her stilled. It was grounding in a way she didn't want to admit. "Just this once," she whispered to the dark, the words barely audible over the soft creak of the boat.

CHAPTER

ELEVEN

The boat glided over the waves, its sails taut in the evening breeze. The air smelled of salt and sun-warmed wood, and the soft hiss of the water against the hull blended with the creak of the mast. Ophelia stood at the railing, gripping it tightly as she watched the horizon shift from blue to molten gold. The gentle rocking of the boat, once a source of nausea, was starting to feel soothing—almost meditative.

Gabriel's voice broke the silence, low and calm. "It's beautiful, isn't it?"

She glanced over her shoulder to find him leaning casually against the mast. His faded linen shirt hung open, revealing bronzed skin, and the breeze tousled his dark hair in a way that made him look effortlessly at home here. He wasn't teasing her or hiding behind his usual aloofness. Instead, his expression was open, almost peaceful.

"You look...different," Ophelia said, curious. "Relaxed, even. I didn't think that was possible for you."

He chuckled, the sound as warm as the sunlight glinting off

the waves. "Out here, it's easy to forget the rest of the world exists. No schemes, no grudges, no centuries of baggage. Just the sea and the wind."

Ophelia tilted her head, studying him. "You make it sound like freedom."

"It is," he said, his gaze drifting out to the horizon as his features softened. "Out here, I'm not a vampire or a relic of the past. I'm just me."

Something in his voice caught her off guard. She had always seen him as a creature of control, someone who thrived on being one step ahead. But this version of Gabriel—unburdened, even for a moment—was disarming.

"How long have you been sailing?" she asked, her curiosity piqued.

"Since before I was turned," he said, tone turning wistful. "I was sixteen when I first stepped onto a ship. A navigator's apprentice. It was madness, but it was also exhilarating. The sea is unpredictable, ruthless, but it's honest. You can't outwit the wind or charm the waves. You have to adapt, or you sink."

Ophelia arched a brow. "That's surprisingly poetic coming from you."

He grinned, the corner of his mouth quirking upward. "I won't let that go to my head."

She turned back to the water, her fingers trailing along the railing. "So, what happened? How did you go from an apprentice to this?"

Gabriel was quiet for a moment, the silence heavy with unspoken memories. "I was turned during a voyage," he said finally. "Pirates raided the ship. Most of the crew didn't make it. I would've been one of them if not for...well, let's just say my rescuer had his own reasons for keeping me alive."

Ophelia glanced at him, surprised by the vulnerability in his voice. "Do you miss it? Being human, I mean."

"Sometimes," he admitted. "But the sea doesn't care what you are. Human, vampire, witch—it treats everyone the same. That's why I keep coming back. Out here, I can pretend I'm just another sailor chasing the horizon."

She hesitated, then asked, "Will you teach me?"

Gabriel's eyes lit up, a glimmer of surprise flickering across his face. "You want to learn to sail?"

"Why not?" she said with a shrug. "I'm tired of feeling useless out here. Besides, it beats wallowing in self-pity."

He studied her for a moment, then nodded. "All right, witch. Let's see what you've got."

Gabriel led her to the main mast, where the sails billowed in the breeze like giant ivory wings. The air hummed with tension, the pull of wind against fabric and cord. He handed her a thick rope, its heft providing a sense of stability as she gripped it with both hands.

"This is the mainsheet," he explained. "It controls the angle of the mainsail. Pull it in to tighten; let it out to loosen. Feel the wind on your face, and tell me which way it's coming from."

Ophelia closed her eyes, focusing on the subtle shift of the breeze against her skin. "Right," she said after a moment.

"Good. That's called starboard." Gabriel's praise was quiet but genuine. "Now, pull the mainsheet, just enough to catch the wind."

She tugged on the rope, her muscles straining against the resistance. The sail shifted, and the boat tilted slightly, picking up speed as it caught the full force of the breeze.

"There you go," Gabriel said, voice carrying a note of pride. "You're getting it."

Ophelia grinned, exhilarated by the sudden surge of motion. The boat seemed to come alive under her hands, responding to her movements with a grace that felt almost magical.

"What about that sail?" she asked, nodding toward the smaller, triangular sheet at the front of the boat.

"That's the genoa," Gabriel said. "It works with the mainsail to give us more speed. Watch how Brisa and Alex handle it."

They turned to see Brisa and Alex working in tandem at the bow. Brisa's dark braid swung with each movement as she adjusted the ropes, her hands deft and precise. Alex, her silver hair catching the last rays of sunlight, mirrored her movements with a calm efficiency.

"They make it look easy," Ophelia muttered. She had no idea they even knew how to sail. A pang of envy twisted in her chest. Of course they'd have skills like this, while she felt like she was constantly trying to keep her head above water in every sense.

"They've been at this longer than you," Gabriel said with a wink. "Give it time."

As the sun dipped lower, casting the sky in hues of orange and pink, Gabriel continued to guide her through the basics—tacking and jibing, reading the wind, and keeping an eye on the horizon. His patience surprised her, and for a while, the heaviness in her chest lifted.

By the time they finished, the sky had darkened to a deep indigo, and the first stars were beginning to appear. Ophelia leaned against the mast, her arms aching but her spirits lighter than they'd been in weeks.

"Thank you," she said quietly.

Gabriel tilted his head, his expression softening. "For what?"

"For reminding me that I'm not completely useless," she said with a small, self-deprecating smile.

He reached out, brushing a strand of hair from her face. "You're not useless, Ophelia. You're just lost. But you'll find your way."

The sincerity in his words caught her off guard, and for once, she didn't know how to respond. So she simply nodded, letting the warmth of his words settle over her.

THE NIGHT DEEPENED, and the sea became a vast expanse of black silk punctuated by stars. The gentle creak of the boat mingled with the rhythmic slap of waves against the hull. Below deck, the air was close and thick, carrying the tang of salt and damp wood. Shadows pooled in the corners of the narrow galley, their edges flickering faintly under the weak light of a single lamp.

Ophelia leaned heavily against the narrow table, her breaths shallow and uneven. Her skin itched as if something hot and unbearable pulsed just beneath the surface. The satisfaction of learning to sail earlier had faded, replaced by a dull, gnawing discomfort.

Her body ached in ways she hadn't expected, muscles sore from gripping ropes and shifting sails. But it was the burning just beneath her skin that was harder to ignore. She shifted in her seat, trying to distract herself, but the restlessness refused to abate.

Gabriel entered the galley, his steps light on the wooden floor. He stopped when he saw her, his gaze probing as it swept over her trembling form. "What's wrong?"

"I'm fine," she said, cradling her head in her hands, elbows digging into the table.

"You're clearly not fine, Cinis. What's going on?" he asked.

"It's nothing," she bit out, forcing her head up. But the moment she moved, her vision blurred, and she swayed.

Gabriel was at her side in an instant, his steady grip the only thing keeping her upright. "Dammit, Ophelia," he muttered. "You need to stop pretending you're invincible."

She opened her mouth to retort, but a lancing jolt shot through her chest, stealing her breath. Her vision blurred, and she gripped the edge of the table, her knuckles white. "I just... need a minute," she muttered, barely able to get the words out.

Her muscles spasmed, and she doubled over, clutching her stomach as a wave of nausea washed over her. Her skin burned hot, then cold, and her heart raced as though trying to outrun the pain searing through her body. She clutched her stomach, her breaths coming in short, shallow gasps. The room seemed to tilt, and Gabriel caught her as she slumped forward.

"Ophelia!" His voice was intense now, cutting through the haze. He shook her gently, his hands steadying her shoulders. "Stay with me."

Footsteps echoed on the stairs, and Brisa and Alex appeared in the doorway, their expressions shifting from concern to alarm when they saw her.

"What the hell happened?" Brisa demanded, crouching beside Ophelia, tone clipped with worry.

"She's in withdrawal," Gabriel said grimly. "I should've seen this coming."

Alex knelt on Ophelia's other side, her hands hovering uncertainly before settling on her friend's shoulder. "We need to do something. Now," she said, her usually calm voice shaking.

"It started earlier," Gabriel said, voice tight. "She tried to hide it."

Ophelia groaned, her head lolling to the side. The heat in her body felt unbearable now, as if her blood were boiling. Her skin itched, every nerve screaming for relief. "I just need...a drink," she whispered, raw and desperate.

"No," Alex said firmly, her hand brushing over Ophelia's forehead. "You don't need alcohol. You need help."

Brisa shot Gabriel a glare. "How did you let it get this bad?"

"Don't," he snapped, his patience fraying. "This isn't the time."

Alex closed her eyes, brow furrowing as she focused. Her fingers began to glow, a soft golden light emanating from her touch. Ophelia felt a brief surge of relief, the tension in her chest easing as the magic worked through her.

"She's part vampire and part witch," Alex said, calm but resolute. "We don't know exactly how her body processes alcohol, but withdrawal could do more than just hurt her. It could cause permanent damage. Mixed bloodlines make everything more unpredictable, and the consequences could be severe if we don't act fast."

"How do you know that?" Gabriel asked, his jaw clenched.

"I've been studying my fae ancestry since I learned about my lineage," Alex answered simply, hesitating before continuing. "I don't have enough magic in my veins to heal her. But there's a theory in fae healing magic. Blood can help."

"You mean vampire blood?" Gabriel asked.

Alex nodded. "It's risky, but it could stabilize her. Blood magic can be addictive for witches. She'd have to be careful."

"Luka gave her blood in Trieste, when she was attacked by a vampire," Brisa said.

Gabriel's jaw tightened at Brisa's revelation, his displeasure clear, but he kept his mouth shut, his eyes flicking to Ophelia.

Alex studied her friend, placing a hand on her head. "The more she has it, the riskier it is. But she'll get worse if we do nothing," she said.

Ophelia groaned. "No...I don't want that."

"You don't have a choice," Gabriel said. He rose to his feet, moving to a small, hidden compartment in the wall. He retrieved a dagger, holding it to his wrist.

Brisa grabbed his arm before he could approach. "You understand what this could mean."

Gabriel stared down at Ophelia, his jaw clenched, the dagger in his hand gleaming under the dim light. "This isn't a decision I make lightly," he said. His dark eyes flicked to Brisa and Alex, both watching him with a mix of apprehension and disbelief. "But she doesn't have time for hesitation."

Ophelia's eyes fluttered open, her vision swimming. She saw the knife in Gabriel's hand and shook her head weakly. "Don't...I'll be fine..."

"You're not fine, Cinis," he said, kneeling beside her. "You don't have to fight this alone," he said, his tone carrying quiet urgency. "Let me help you."

He sliced his wrist and pressed it to her lips, tipping it gently. As the first drop of his blood touched her tongue, a rush of warmth spread through her body, soothing the ache in her veins. She swallowed tentatively at first and then greedily, the thick, metallic taste both foreign and comforting.

She felt her strength returning, and the discord within her settled to a whisper. As the blood worked its way through her system, the fever broke, and her breathing steadied. The relief was so profound she could've cried.

Brisa watched Gabriel with a mix of disbelief and something like respect. "You really are an idiot," she muttered, though her tone lacked its usual bite. She leaned back against the wall, her arms crossed. "You're playing a dangerous game," she said.

Gabriel shrugged, his attention focused solely on Ophelia. "She's worth it."

CHAPTER
TWELVE

The glow of dawn filtered through the small cabin window, casting soft golden beams that danced across the narrow bed. Ophelia stirred, the sway of the boat rhythmic and oddly soothing despite the memories of the night before. She blinked, her mind still heavy with sleep, until she became aware of the warmth beside her.

Gabriel lay beside her, sprawled on his back, the sheet low on his hips, exposing the chiseled lines of his torso. His arm was thrown lazily over his head, his hair a tousled mess against the pillow. The sight of him—serene, unguarded—stirred something deep inside her. Her eyes roamed downward, tracing the curve of his collarbone, the shadow of a scar on his ribs, and the slow, steady rise and fall of his chest. Much slower than a human, but she could still mark the rhythm.

She hesitated when her gaze drifted lower, her heart thudding in her chest. The sunlight illuminated every inch of his skin, the golden tones almost otherworldly. He was beautiful in a way that felt unfair, like he belonged to another realm entirely.

"See something you like, Cinis?"

Her breath caught as his voice broke the quiet, low and rough with sleep. Gabriel's dark eyes opened, locking on to hers with lazy amusement. A slow, infuriating smirk curved his lips.

"Need something?" he drawled, the words wrapping around her like a velvet rope.

Ophelia's cheeks flushed, heat rushing up her neck. She tore her gaze away, suddenly finding the woodgrain of the cabin walls fascinating. "You wish," she snapped, sitting up and brushing tangled hair away from her face. She winced at the scent of sweat and salt clinging to her skin. "I was just wondering if vampires even sleep. Guess you do."

Gabriel stretched lazily, his muscles flexing in a way that seemed far too deliberate. "Only when we want to," he said. "Sometimes there are better things to do in bed—"

"You're impossible," she said, cutting him off and swinging her legs over the side of the bed and standing. But the moment she did, the world tilted, and she grabbed onto the edge of the bed to steady herself.

"Careful," Gabriel said, his tone losing its teasing edge. He moved faster than she could track, standing behind her as his hands steadied her by the arms. "You're still recovering."

"I'm fine," she said, shrugging him off. "I just need some fresh air."

"You've been through hell, Ophelia." His voice was softer now, but there was an intensity behind it that made her pause. "You don't have to pretend to be indestructible."

"I've been..." She paused, her hands gripping the edge of the bed as though it might ground her. "I've been a mess. Embarrassing. Broken, even. I haven't just let myself fall apart. I've let all of you down, too. I've ignored everything that matters, everything I should have cared for. And instead of facing it, I've drowned myself in...in all the wrong things. You deserved better from me. I should have been better."

The words spilled out before she could stop them, a confession she hadn't meant to make. Her shoulders tensed as she waited for his inevitable quip, some biting remark that would cut her down. But she felt the bed shift as he stood in front of her, and then his hand was at her throat, firm but gentle, bringing her face toward him. His grip was commanding, his fingers warm against her skin.

"Don't you ever say you're broken," he said with a growl. His dark eyes burned with an intensity that left no room for argument. "What happened to you was cruel. It devastated you. It damaged you. But it didn't break you. Bent, maybe. Scorched? Definitely. But you don't break, not you."

Ophelia swallowed hard, her pulse pounding beneath his touch as he slowly relaxed his hand without moving it.

"You're still the same Ophelia I met in that hallway," he continued, his gaze never leaving hers. "The one who burned my arm without hesitation. The one who stood against the Concilium and the Coven without blinking. You're a warrior, and all warriors carry scars. But don't you dare let those scars define you."

His words hit her like a blow, cracking through the layers of guilt and shame she'd wrapped around herself. "I don't feel like a warrior," she admitted, her eyes welling with tears she refused to let fall. "I feel...lost."

Gabriel's grip tightened slightly, grounding her. "Don't. Don't you dare shy away from who you are," he murmured, softer now. "You're not broken. You're just finding your way back."

His hand shifted, his thumb brushing against the hollow of her throat. "You don't have to prove anything to me, Cinis. I know you can handle yourself, but you don't have to carry it all alone."

Her chest ached, his words pressing against her ribs. She was so sad. And so lonely. But she felt something else stir. Something else deep inside of her. Need. She wrapped her hand around the wrist holding her throat. But instead of breaking free, she squeezed him back, "You don't know me," she said without conviction.

A flicker of amusement crossed his face. "You don't believe that. And I know you, Ophelia. I see into the deepest depths of who you are, and I'm not afraid. I've seen the fire in you, even when you're drowning in your own darkness."

She didn't wait for him to say more. The tension between them was too much, a taut string ready to snap. She started to stand, and he met her halfway, their lips meeting in a crash. It wasn't a tentative kiss—it was a collision, desperate and raw. His mouth was warm, his lips firm and tasting faintly of salt and something sweet.

Gabriel responded immediately, his hand tightening around her throat as he kissed her back with equal fervor. His other hand found her waist, pulling her closer. Ophelia groaned against his mouth, her fingers tangling in his hair as the heat between them grew.

He broke the kiss, his lips brushing against her ear. "I told you that I wouldn't fuck you until you begged. Are you begging now?"

A shiver ran down her spine at his words, her body responding before her mind could catch up. Gabriel's hand slid down her back to her waist, his touch deliberate and unapologetic. He cupped her between her legs, his fingers pressing against her through the thin fabric of her leggings, not even bothering to be gentle.

She gasped, her head falling back. "Never," she said.

"Gabriel..." Her voice was a breathless plea, her body arching into his touch.

"You're not broken," he growled, his lips trailing down her neck as his fingers teased her, igniting sparks of pleasure that made her tremble. "You're stronger than you know. Let me show you. Please."

Her hands found his shoulders, nails digging into his skin as the tension inside her coiled tighter. For the first time in what felt like forever, she wasn't drowning in her grief. She was here, present, alive. "Now look who is begging," she said, breathless.

Gabriel's lips found hers again, softer this time, but no less consuming. His kiss was a promise, a reassurance, and a challenge all at once. He held her together even as he unraveled her, piece by piece, fingers working her through the leggings as she soaked the front of them.

"Ask me," he said in her ear, practically growling. "Tell me what you want me to do to you," he said as he moved his hand to the waistband of her leggings. She resisted the urge to press into his hand, wanting so desperately for him to touch her with nothing between them.

"No," she said, stubborn despite aching for him.

He growled in her ear, nipping at the earlobe. "You don't want me to be gentle, do you?" he asked, his breath hot against her skin. "You need it rough. You need to feel alive again."

In response, Ophelia involuntarily arched her back, pressing her body into his.

"Your body is answering for you, Cinis," he said into her ear. "Your body is begging me to touch it, even if you won't." He ran a massive hand under her leggings, his fingers parting her. Ophelia knew what he'd find there; she felt herself dripping with need. "Fuck, Ophelia..." He rubbed her swollen clit, giving her the friction she so desperately craved. "Your body is telling me exactly what you need."

She moaned, which he covered up with his own mouth as he moved his fingers to her entrance, causing her to gasp with pleasure, her body heating all over.

"When I said I'd only fuck you if you begged, there were some exceptions. Namely, my mouth. Will you come on my face, Cinis? Will you let me suck your clit until you shudder on my tongue?"

Ophelia thought about begging him. She really did. But she couldn't bridge that gap. Not yet. Instead, she nodded. And that was all the consent he needed.

"Thank fuck," he said, pushing her back on the bed and peeling her leggings down without any further teasing. He spread her legs apart and stared down at her, a look of reverence and ownership on his face. "Such a beautiful, perfect pussy, ready for me," he said, kneeling on the small cabin floor, still towering over the bed. "You're about to learn exactly how much this pussy was made for me. Now, you're going to be a good girl and come for me."

She barely had time to make a noise before his tongue found her clit with one long stroke. Her body almost bowed off the bed at the intensity of pleasure that shot through her. But Gabriel pressed her down by stretching his hand up and holding her by the base of her throat. The other hand worked its way through her, finding her entrance and pumping in and out while his mouth sucked on her clit. When she started to moan, he brought that hand to her mouth, silencing her.

She was so needy, so ready, that she felt herself build and explode not long after he started. He kept sucking, bending his fingers inside her to hit that perfect spot as she rode the wave of an orgasm. She finally had to reach down and push his head away when he didn't appear to be stopping.

He leaned back as she stared at him through hooded eyes. His lips glistened with her arousal as he brought his fingers to his mouth, sucking his fingers one by one.

"I've changed my mind," he said.

"About?" Ophelia asked, suddenly self-conscious as she started to lean forward to pull her leggings back up.

Gabriel stopped her, pushing her back down gently. "If it's my time to go, I want *that* to be my last meal," he said as he pulled her leggings up, adjusting them back into place for her.

She blushed, unsure how to act now. She'd spent so long at war with Gabriel. And now, something had shifted. It didn't feel like a truce, more like an understanding between them.

Gabriel backed up and leaned against the door, studying her. "How are you feeling?" he finally asked, breaking the quiet. "I mean, I know you are satiated. I'm referring to the sickness," he said, lips curving.

"So cocky—" Ophelia held up a hand when his smirk deepened. "Don't!"

"You could have found out if you'd only asked, Ophelia," he said, moving his hands deliberately to his pockets and slowly rolling his hips forward.

It took everything in her not to let her eyes trail down to where he so obviously knew she wanted to look. Shaking herself, she answered him honestly. "Better," she admitted, though her voice held a trace of uncertainty. "Whatever was in your blood, it helped. Thank you for that."

Gabriel shrugged, his expression unreadable. "You needed it. And I wasn't going to let you suffer when I could do something about it."

She studied him for a moment, searching his face for any hint of the smugness or teasing she'd grown used to. There was none. He looked...sincere. It was disarming.

"I didn't know…" She trailed off, unsure how to put her thoughts into words. "I didn't realize it could work like that. Blood, I mean."

Gabriel leaned back, his gaze turning distant. "It's complicated. Blood can heal, strengthen, even empower. But it comes with risks, especially for witches. And it's even more complicated because you are part vampire. It's possible that it provides sustenance for you, with none of the side effects. We just don't know."

"Risks?" Ophelia frowned, her stomach knotting at the word. "What kind of risks?"

He hesitated, as if weighing how much to tell her. "Blood magic is addictive. Especially when it's tied to someone powerful. It creates a connection with that vampire. It can enhance your abilities and make you feel invincible. But the more you rely on it, the harder it is to stop."

Her chest tightened. "So you're saying I could become… dependent? Again?" After the last six months with alcohol, she could admit that was the last thing she wanted.

"Not if you're careful," Gabriel said, his tone firm. "You're stronger than you think, Ophelia. This was a lifeline when you needed it most. It doesn't have to define you."

She nodded slowly, her mind racing. The thought of losing control, of becoming reliant on something—or someone— terrified her. She had already spent too much of her life feeling powerless. The idea of trading one addiction for another made her stomach churn.

"Blood magic can bind, Ophelia, but it doesn't have to trap. I don't want to be another chain holding you down. I gave you my blood because I trust you to handle the connection, not abuse it."

"Does it affect you?" she asked quietly.

Gabriel arched an eyebrow. "What do you mean?"

"The bond," she clarified. "You said blood magic creates a connection. Does it change things for you?"

For the first time, Gabriel looked uncertain. He shifted in his seat, his jaw tightening before he spoke. "It's not the same for vampires as it is for witches. For us, the connection is grounding. It strengthens our ties to the people we care about."

A flicker of something unsteady passed through her, but she quickly looked away, focusing on the swirling patterns in the grain of the wooden floor. "So now we're connected?"

Gabriel sat down in the small chair, his elbows resting on his knees. "We were connected before this," he said softly. "You just didn't realize it. Or want to admit it."

Her gaze snapped to his, a mix of confusion and unease flashing in her eyes. "What are you talking about?"

He held her stare, his expression open but unreadable. "You know there's more to this than you've let yourself admit. You felt it the moment we met, whether you wanted to or not."

Ophelia opened her mouth to argue, to deny the truth she felt tugging at the edges of her consciousness, but the words wouldn't come. Because he was right. She had felt it—a pull, a spark, something she couldn't explain but had never been able to ignore.

The silence between them stretched, heavy with unspoken words. Finally, Ophelia broke the tension. "This doesn't mean I trust you," she said.

Gabriel's lips quirked into a knowing smile. "I wouldn't expect you to, Cinis. Not yet."

She narrowed her eyes at him, the familiar frustration bubbling to the surface as she ignored the nickname. "You're unbearable, you know that?"

"It's part of my charm," he replied, leaning back, obnoxiously relaxed.

A small, reluctant smile tugged at Ophelia's lips. For the first time in what felt like weeks, she didn't feel entirely overwhelmed. The turmoil within her had stilled, if only for a moment.

As the day wore on, Ophelia found herself gravitating toward the deck. The open air and the steady rhythm of the waves provided a welcome reprieve from her thoughts. Brisa was at the helm, her focus keen as she adjusted the sails, while Alex sat cross-legged near the bow, a book resting on her lap.

Ophelia hesitated before approaching Brisa, her steps tentative. "Hey."

Brisa glanced at her, her expression unreadable. "You look like you slept."

"I did," Ophelia said, rubbing the back of her neck. "Thanks to Gabriel."

Brisa's lips pressed into a thin line, but she didn't comment, for once holding back. Instead, she focused on the horizon, her hands deftly adjusting the ropes. "We're making good time," she said after a moment. "If the wind holds, we'll be in calmer waters by nightfall."

Ophelia nodded, though her gaze lingered on Brisa's face. "You're mad at me."

Brisa's hands stilled on the ropes, and she turned to face Ophelia fully. "I'm not mad," she said, each word tight. "I'm worried. There's a difference."

Ophelia opened her mouth to respond, but Brisa held up a hand, cutting her off. "I know you're trying, Ophy. I see that. But you're playing with fire. Blood magic is dangerous, and Gabriel's blood...it's not just any blood. It binds him to you in ways you don't fully understand."

"I wasn't given a choice," Ophelia said, crossing her arms over her chest. "Again."

"I know," Brisa said, her expression softening. "But that doesn't make it any less dangerous. You need to be careful."

Ophelia swallowed hard, Brisa's words settling in her chest. "I will be," she said finally.

THIRTEEN

Life on the boat was simple, almost hypnotic in its routine. She woke each morning to the sound of Gabriel's low voice, trading dry remarks with Brisa as they adjusted the sails. The warmth of the sun greeted her, brushing her face with a promise of renewal. Alex's laughter drifted across the deck, a rare sound that revealed a lightness Ophelia hadn't realized her friend possessed.

Ophelia spent her mornings learning the intricacies of sailing from Gabriel. Under his patient guidance, she learned to read the wind and maneuver the ropes with a confidence that had eluded her in recent months. He stood by her side, correcting her form with a touch on her hand or a soft word, steadying her in ways she couldn't explain. They hadn't touched again, but they had a delicate truce.

"You're catching on quickly, Cinis," he said one morning as they worked together to secure the mainsail. The nickname rolled off his tongue like an endearment, stirring something indescribable inside her.

"I had a good teacher," she replied, her lips quirking into a smile.

He laughed, a sound as rich and warm as the sunlight on her skin. "Don't get ahead of yourself. You're still a novice."

The gentle teasing made her feel lighter, as though the burden she'd been carrying was slowly beginning to ease. The sea seemed to mirror her mood, its surface calm and glittering under the sun's rays. For the first time in weeks, the ache of Luka's absence felt less like a jagged wound and more like a distant throb. The memories were still there, but they didn't consume her. Not here.

Brisa and Alex moved about the boat with practiced ease, their unspoken connection clear in the way they worked together. Brisa would call out a command, and Alex would respond without hesitation, her movements fluid and sure. They moved like two parts of a perfectly attuned machine.

"They've got a good rhythm," Gabriel said, following Ophelia's gaze one evening as they stood at the helm.

Ophelia nodded, her arms resting lightly on the wheel. "It's like they've been doing this forever."

Gabriel's lips curved into a small smile. "Some people just fit."

The words lingered in the air, their meaning sinking in as Ophelia watched her friend and cousin. She felt a pang of envy, not for what they had, but for the ease with which they embraced it. She had spent so long running from connections, guarding herself against the vulnerability they demanded. But here, on this boat, she was beginning to see the cracks in her armor.

As the sun dipped below the horizon, casting long shadows across the deck, Ophelia let herself relax into the moment of Gabriel's steady presence beside her, the rhythmic creak of the boat, and the golden light reflecting off the waves. It was enough to make her believe, if only for a moment, that things could get better.

But the sea was never predictable. And as much as it could cradle and soothe, it could also turn wild without notice. Ophelia's gaze drifted toward the horizon, where a line of dark clouds had begun to gather. They were still distant, their edges blurred against the setting sun, but something about them sent a shiver down her spine.

"Do you see that?" she asked, nudging Gabriel's arm.

He followed her gaze, his expression tightening. "Dark clouds."

"Do we need to worry?" A hint of unease crept into her tone.

"Not yet," Gabriel said, though his brow furrowed as he adjusted the wheel. "But it's worth keeping an eye on."

Ophelia nodded, her chest tightening with a flicker of anxiety, a thrum of warning running through her. She shook it off, forcing herself to focus on the present. For now, the boat rocked gently beneath them, its sails catching the soft evening breeze.

"Wind's shifting. Let's adjust the genoa." Brisa called out from the bow. Her voice was crisp but not alarmed.

Gabriel motioned for Ophelia to follow him, and together they worked to trim the sails, their movements quick and efficient. Alex joined them, her silver hair catching the last rays of sunlight as she worked alongside Brisa. The air hummed with energy, a quiet anticipation settling over the boat.

As they finished, Ophelia leaned against the railing, watching the waves ripple in the fading light. The clouds loomed in the distance, a dark smudge on the horizon, but she pushed the thought aside. For now, the sea was calm, and the boat felt like a sanctuary.

She glanced at Gabriel, who stood nearby, his gaze fixed on

the horizon. There was something steady and reassuring about him, a quiet strength that made her feel anchored even when the world threatened to pull her under.

"You're staring again," he said without looking at her, his lips twitching into a smirk.

"Maybe I'm just appreciating the view," she shot back.

He laughed, the sound rolling over her like a wave. "Careful, Cinis. You're starting to sound like you belong here."

She smiled, letting the warmth of the moment settle in her chest. For the first time in a long time, she didn't feel like she was running from something. Instead, she felt like she was moving toward something—something she didn't yet have a name for but was beginning to trust.

THE RHYTHM of life on the boat had grown comfortable but not predictable. The crew moved in sync, like parts of a well-tuned machine. Brisa and Alex had their routines, while Gabriel and Ophelia fell into a steady partnership at the helm. Yet beneath the surface, Ophelia felt a subtle shift in the atmosphere, an undercurrent she couldn't quite name.

One evening, after the sun had dipped below the horizon, Ophelia wandered below deck. The day had been long but satisfying, and her muscles ached in that pleasant way that came from physical effort. As she passed Alex and Brisa's cabin, a sound made her pause.

It was soft at first, a quiet laugh that carried warmth. Then came a low, breathy moan that froze Ophelia in place.

Her hand hovered just inches from the door. She hadn't meant to eavesdrop, but the intimacy in those sounds drew her in, curiosity mingling with guilt. Slowly, almost against her will, she peered through the small crack in the door.

What she saw made her breath catch.

Brisa was perched on the edge of the narrow bed, her dark hair spilling around her face as she leaned down to kiss Alex. Her hands moved with practiced ease, one trailing down Alex's arm while the other slipped beneath her shirt, eliciting a soft gasp. Alex tilted her head back, her hair falling in a curtain around her face, her lips parted in a look of unguarded pleasure.

Ophelia should have turned away. She knew she should have left them to their privacy, but she couldn't look away. There was something raw and beautiful in the way they touched, a vulnerability that took her breath away. It wasn't just the physical intimacy—it was the way Brisa looked at Alex, like she was the only thing in the world that mattered. It was the way Alex's fingers clutched Brisa's shoulders, holding on like she was afraid to let go.

It was love, pure and unfiltered, and it hit Ophelia like a wave.

Her foot nudged the edge of the door, and it creaked loudly. Brisa's head snapped up, her dark eyes meeting Ophelia's through the narrow opening. Alex froze, her expression shifting from bliss to shock as her gaze followed Brisa's.

"I-I didn't mean to," Ophelia stammered, already backing away, her face burning with embarrassment.

She turned and fled up the ladder, her heart pounding in her chest. The cool night air hit her like a slap as she emerged on deck, her cheeks flushed and her mind racing. She gripped the railing, staring out at the dark expanse of water.

"Ophy," Alex's voice called softly from behind her.

She turned to see Alex standing at the top of the ladder, her silver hair mussed and her cheeks still flushed. Though Alex was dressed, her shirt was slightly askew, a small detail that only made Ophelia's embarrassment worse.

"I'm sorry," Ophelia blurted, holding up her hands. "I didn't mean to intrude."

"It's okay," Alex interrupted, steady despite the redness in her cheeks. "I should have locked the door."

Ophelia winced, shaking her head. "I wasn't trying to— I mean, I just— I was looking for— And I heard—" She stopped herself, realizing she was only making it worse.

Alex stepped closer, her expression softening. "It's fine, Ophy. Really."

There was a long pause between them until Alex spoke. Sighing, she ran a hand through her hair. "We weren't hiding it, but we weren't exactly advertising it either. There's been so much going on, and you've been through so much...we didn't want to add to everything."

"You're allowed to be happy, you know," Ophelia said, meeting her gaze. "You don't have to tiptoe around me."

Alex smiled, though it was tinged with sadness. "It's not that simple."

"Why not?" Ophelia asked. "Brisa makes you happy, doesn't she?"

"She does," Alex admitted. "But it's scary. You know me better than anyone. I've never been with another woman before—romantically, I mean. I was raised to believe my life was already mapped out: med school at Yale, marry another doctor—a man—and live this pre-ordained life. Follow the script. And now here I am, on a boat with a bunch of supernaturals, looking for a magical artifact. None of this feels real, and my relationship with Brisa is another part of that," she said.

Ophelia nodded in understanding before Alex continued. "I know I didn't believe you when we were kids, about your episodes or any of it. And I'm very, very sorry for that. But I'm really trying to embrace this part of myself now," she said.

Ophelia wrapped an arm around her best friend as they

stared out at the sea. "This is new to all of us. I know I haven't handled things well the last six months, but I'm ready to do better," she said.

Alex studied her for a moment, before reaching out to squeeze her hand. "Letting someone in fully, trusting them—it's not easy."

They stood in companionable silence for a while, the sound of the waves filling the space between them. Ophelia felt the tension in her chest ease, the embarrassment that had flared earlier forgotten and replaced by the quiet comfort of their shared history. As Ophelia glanced back at the ladder, a small smile tugged at her lips.

"You know, it's a tough position: my cousin and my best friend," Ophelia said, her tone teasing. "If Brisa hurts you, I might have to throw her overboard. But if you hurt Brisa, I might have to throw *you* overboard."

Alex laughed, the sound light and free. "I'll keep that in mind."

Alex's laughter lingered in the air, a fleeting moment of warmth before the first sharp gust of wind silenced it.

FOURTEEN

The wind whispered warnings at first, tugging at the sails and rattling the rigging like a restless ghost. It had been steady and warm all day, filling the air with the comforting scents of salt and sunbaked wood. Now, though, it carried a harshness that prickled Ophelia's skin. She stood at the bow of the boat, her hands gripping the railing as the restless sea stretched endlessly before her. Dark clouds spread like an ink stain across the sky. The ocean's usual rhythm had changed, the waves slapping against the hull with increasing ferocity.

"You feel that?" Gabriel's voice startled her, though it was calm and measured as always. He was standing just behind her, his eyes narrowed as they scanned the horizon.

Ophelia nodded. "The air feels heavier," she murmured. The salty tang of the breeze had a new edge, and her unease was mirrored in Gabriel's stiff posture.

He crossed his arms, his gaze darkening. "Not just heavy. Charged."

The words made her stomach clench. She turned her attention back to the sky, her breath catching as she realized just how much the clouds had grown in the last hour. They were darker now, thickening like a bruise spreading across the horizon.

Behind them, Brisa leaned casually against the railing, the picture of nonchalance. "You two are acting like we've never seen rain before," she said, kicking her boots up onto the lower rung of the railing.

"This isn't rain," Gabriel shot back. "It's a massive storm. And it's coming fast."

Brisa rolled her eyes but straightened her posture, sensing the change in his tone. "Fine. What do you want us to do about it?"

"Alex!" Gabriel barked. "Check the barometer. Now."

The creak of wood signaled Alex's approach as she climbed up from below deck. Her silver hair was tied back, though a few strands clung to her damp forehead. She held the barometer up, her frown deepening.

"Pressure's dropping fast," she said grimly, holding the device out so Gabriel could see.

Ophelia's stomach twisted further. She didn't know much about sailing, but she knew enough to understand what that meant. A pressure drop like this could mean a tropical storm, or even a hurricane, was on its way, unpredictable and merciless.

"Should we change course?" Alex asked, her voice steady but laced with urgency.

Gabriel shook his head. "It's moving too fast. We won't outrun it. We need to prepare."

His tone snapped everyone into motion. Gabriel's orders came swift and firm: "Brisa, Alex, secure the genoa and stow any loose equipment. Ophelia, with me. We need to reef the mainsail before it tears."

The crew scattered, their movements brisk and efficient, adrenaline honing their movements. Ophelia's pulse quickened as she hurried after Gabriel, her hands already reaching for the ropes.

The wind grew stronger with every passing moment, tugging at her hair and clothes. The boat groaned beneath them, the waves slapping harder against the hull. She could feel the tension in the air, a pressure that pressed down on her chest like a weight.

"This weather is moving too fast," Alex called from the other side of the deck, barely audible over the rising wind. "It doesn't make sense!"

"It doesn't have to," Gabriel said grimly. "The ocean doesn't care about our rules. Just focus!"

The wind howled, carrying with it the first drops of rain—light at first, but quickly turning into a driving torrent. Each drop stung like needles against Ophelia's skin as she wrestled with the ropes, her fingers slipping on the soaked lines. The rough fibers bit into her palms as she struggled to secure them. Waves rose higher, slamming against the hull with enough force to make the boat shudder. As the wind shrieked—clawing at her hair and clothes—the boat bucked beneath her like a wild animal.

Above her, the mainsail flapped wildly, fighting against the force of the wind. Gabriel's hands moved quickly, his large frame braced against the violent rocking of the boat. "Pull harder!" he shouted, his hands working in tandem with hers to secure the sail. The force of the wind was staggering, each gust a battle they were losing. "We need to stabilize now!"

"I'm trying!" Ophelia shouted back. "Should we use magic?" she asked.

Gabriel shook his head, his jaw set. "It won't work! The

ocean's power is ancient, natural magic. It's unpredictable. We'd risk making it worse."

Thunder rumbled overhead, a low growl that made the hairs on her arms stand on end. She glanced up just in time to see a jagged streak of lightning split the sky, illuminating the churning waves in harsh white light.

The ocean had grown feral. The waves had grown in size, each one rolling higher than the last, crashing against the hull with ceaseless force. The boat groaned and creaked, its timbers straining under the pressure.

Above them, the mast protested under the stress, its wood bowing dangerously. The tempest seemed vengeful, a wrathful entity intent on devouring them. Thunder cracked overhead, deafening and bone-shaking, followed by a jagged streak of lightning that lit up the sky in blinding relief.

The gale grew with terrifying speed, the waves now towering above the boat like dark, hungry giants. The sky was an angry swirl of black and gray, the occasional flash of lightning illuminating the frenzy. Thunder cracked like the earth was splitting apart, each boom reverberating in Ophelia's chest.

Brisa's voice cut through the din. "The genoa's loose! Alex, I need you!"

Alex was already moving, her hands flying over the ropes as she worked to secure the sail. The wind tore at her silver hair, plastering it against her face.

Ophelia tore her attention back to the mainsail, her heart pounding as she fought to keep her balance. The deck was slick with rain, every step a challenge.

"Gabriel!" she shouted, panic creeping into her voice. "The mast—it's bowing! It's going to break!"

His head snapped up, his eyes narrowing as he assessed the

situation. "Dammit," he muttered under his breath. "Ophelia, get below deck. Now!"

"I'm not leaving you!"

"You'll be safer below!" he barked, his tone leaving no room for argument.

Like hell she would. But before she could respond, a deafening crack split the air as the mast gave way, splintering with explosive force. The top half came crashing down, its jagged edges tearing through the deck and sending splinters flying like shrapnel. Ophelia barely had time to shield her face before a wave crashed over the side, drenching her in icy water.

Brisa and Alex screamed as the impact threw them backward, their bodies tumbling toward the railing.

"Alex! Brisa!" Ophelia yelled, raw with fear. She lunged toward them, but the deck tilted violently, and her footing slipped. A wave crashed over the side, drenching her and carrying debris in its icy grip.

She scrambled to her feet, her eyes scanning the deck for any sign of her friends. She saw Alex first, her hand grasping desperately at the railing. Brisa was further away, clinging to a broken beam as the waves threatened to pull her overboard.

"Hold on!" Ophelia shouted, her words nearly swallowed by the roaring wind.

The next wave was merciless, slamming into the side of the boat with the force of a battering ram and sending her sprawling to the deck.

When she looked up again, her heart stopped. Alex's grip had slipped, her body tumbling into the churning sea. Brisa was right behind her, the force of the wave ripping her from her hold.

"No!" Ophelia's scream tore from her throat as she scrambled to the edge of the deck, her eyes scanning the dark, chaotic waters for any sign of them.

She lunged for the railing, but Gabriel's hand clamped around her arm, pulling her back. "Don't!" he shouted, voice cutting through her panic. "You'll go over, too!"

"They're out there!" Ophelia cried, her eyes wild as she scanned the dark waters.

"They're strong," Gabriel said, his jaw tight. "They'll survive."

The boat pitched violently, another massive wave crashing over the deck and knocking them both off their feet. Ophelia cried out as her shoulder slammed into the splintered wood, pain flaring hot and acute.

Gabriel was at her side in an instant, hauling her to her feet. His grip was iron, anchoring her to the slick, treacherous deck. "We can't help them if we go over, too!" he shouted.

She thought she saw a flash of silver, but it disappeared beneath the waves before she could be sure. "We can't just leave them," Ophelia cried, her eyes wild.

The sea showed no mercy. The waves grew taller, each one a mountain of water that loomed above them before crashing down with relentless force. Lightning illuminated the scene in staccato bursts, the brief flashes revealing the devastation: the shattered mast, the wreckage strewn across the deck, the raw terror etched into Ophelia's face. Another wave knocked Ophelia to her knees.

"Ophelia, get up. Grab the railing!" Gabriel shouted as another wave surged toward them. She obeyed, her hands clinging to the slick wood as the boat was tossed like a toy in the raging ocean.

"What do we do?" she yelled, her words nearly drowned out by the crashing waves.

"We survive!" Gabriel's eyes burned with determination as he scanned the horizon. "No matter what—"

Before he could finish, a towering wall of water rose before them, a monstrous wave that seemed to stretch endlessly upward, blotting out the sky. Ophelia's breath caught in her throat, her chest tightening with terror as she stared at it. The sheer size of the wave dwarfed the boat, its dark, churning mass illuminated by a fleeting flash of lightning. It wasn't just a wave—it was a force of nature, raw and unstoppable, bearing down on them with the fury of the sea itself.

"Hold on!" Gabriel roared, voice tearing through the pandemonium, urgent and commanding.

Ophelia's fingers clamped on to the slick railing, her knuckles whitening as she braced herself. Every muscle in her body tensed, her instincts screaming at her to run, to flee, but there was nowhere to go. The wave crashed down with a deafening roar, its impact a cataclysm that consumed everything.

Water surged over the deck with brutal ferocity. The railing was wrenched from Ophelia's grasp, and she was flung into the maelstrom. Her scream was swallowed by the roar of the water, her body thrown weightlessly into the void of the ocean. The cold hit her like a thousand needles, stabbing and suffocating, stealing the breath from her lungs as the current wrapped around her like a living thing.

For a moment, everything was chaos. Her vision blurred as saltwater burned her eyes, the world a whirlpool of dark, churning green. She kicked and flailed, her arms slicing through the water as she fought against the ruthless pull of the sea. The surface seemed impossibly far, a distant shimmer of light that flickered and danced beyond her reach.

Ophelia's chest burned as her lungs screamed for air. She clawed upward, her body heavy and sluggish against the unyielding current. Panic surged through her veins, jolting and electric, as the realization struck her—she might not make it. The thought was fleeting but chilling, a flash of desperation that fueled her struggle.

Through the mayhem, she caught a fleeting glimpse of Gabriel. His dark figure was clinging to a piece of the wreckage, his silhouette stark against the dim light above the surface. His hand was outstretched, reaching for her, desperation etched into every movement. "Ophelia!" he shouted, voice raw with urgency, though the roar of the sea nearly swallowed it whole.

Her arms reached for him instinctively, her muscles straining with the effort. For one agonizing moment, their fingers brushed, a fleeting connection that sparked a desperate surge of hope. But the sea was merciless. Another wave crashed between them, a wall of water that wrenched them apart as though mocking their efforts.

The force dragged her under, her body tumbling through the depths as the surface receded further and further from her grasp. Her limbs felt leaden, her strength sapped by the crushing cold and the violent currents. The pressure crushed her chest, her lungs straining against the overwhelming need to breathe.

Her mind raced, thoughts scattering like debris caught in a tornado. Flashes of Gabriel's outstretched hand, the desperate determination in his voice, the faces of Brisa and Alex—all of it flickered like a stuttering reel.

The darkness pressed in around her, thick and suffocating, the cold seeping into her bones. Her struggles grew weaker, her body no longer obeying her desperate commands. A sense of eerie stillness crept over her, a quiet acceptance that she couldn't fight anymore.

Her final thought, fragmented and fleeting, was of Gabriel. Then the blackness claimed her, cold and unforgiving, pulling her into its depths.

CHAPTER

FIFTEEN

Ophelia woke with a violent gasp, her body convulsing as saltwater filled her throat and burned her nostrils. Her chest heaved as she choked and coughed, hacking up the seawater that had threatened to drown her. Her limbs felt impossibly heavy, disconnected from her body. Yet, she was floating—buoyant against the gentle, rhythmic push of the waves.

For a moment, disorientation consumed her. She couldn't tell up from down, her mind sluggish and fogged. But then she felt it, a thrumming warmth beneath her skin. Her magic. It was faint and uneven, but it was there. The realization came with a jolt: Her power had worked. Somehow, even while unconscious, it had held her above the water, cradling her like unseen hands. The ocean's embrace, once violent, had shifted to something softer, more deliberate.

But her magic was fading. She could feel the drain in her core, a hollowness that threatened to pull her under as surely as the sea. Every beat of her heart seemed to take more from her, leaving her weaker with each passing second.

The sunlight was blinding. Even with her eyes squeezed shut, it pierced through her eyelids like sharp needles. Blistering and blazing, it stood in cruel contrast to the dark tumult she had been ripped from. With a trembling hand, she wiped her face, but the saltwater stung her skin, intensifying her dazed and disoriented state.

The cold ocean seeped into her muscles, numbing her fingers and toes. Her head lolled to the side as she floated, her energy too depleted to move more than an inch. Waves swelled gently beneath her, lifting and lowering her body in their steady rhythm. The movement was soothing in one way but maddening in another, a reminder of the vastness of the water around her, its indifference to her survival.

She forced her eyes open, squinting against the rays that reflected off the surface of the ocean in a dazzling array of blinding white and shimmering blue. It was too much at first. She groaned softly, shutting her eyes again as her head spun. She didn't want to see, didn't want to confront what awaited her.

But she couldn't avoid it. The realization clawed its way up her chest, lancing and icy: She was alone.

Her eyes snapped open again, this time adjusting to the light. The horizon stretched endlessly in every direction, a vast and unforgiving expanse of glinting water and searing sun. The once-angry clouds had vanished, leaving the sky bright and empty. The air was eerily still, the commotion replaced with an oppressive calm that only heightened her dread.

"Gabriel," she rasped. Her throat ached, and the sound of her own voice startled her. She coughed again, spitting out the lingering taste of saltwater. "Brisa... Alex..."

No response.

She whipped her head from side to side, damp hair sticking

to her face as she scanned the horizon. No one. Only debris and wreckage. No sign of anyone.

The emptiness stretched on forever, vast and endless, and the panic began to bloom in her chest, clawing and suffocating. She spun herself in the water, the effort exhausting, her magic sputtering weakly in her veins. Her limbs felt heavier than before, as though the ocean itself beckoned her to give in.

Her lungs seized, and for a moment, she nearly surrendered to the panic. She let herself drift, her mind racing with a thousand thoughts at once. *Where were they? Could they still be alive? Had they been taken by the sea that had nearly claimed her?*

And then, the realization came with chilling clarity: She was alive because of her magic. If it hadn't worked—if the ocean hadn't somehow answered her desperation—she would be gone, too. She could feel the truth of it lingering in her bones. The power that had surged through her, even as she drifted into unconsciousness, had kept her afloat and breathing. But it wasn't limitless.

She pressed a trembling hand to her chest, where the hum of her magic still stirred. It was weak now, drained to the point of flickering out entirely. The effort it had taken to save her had nearly extinguished her reserves, leaving her dangerously close to being powerless.

The thought terrified her, but there was no time to dwell on it. She had to find them.

Forcing herself to move, Ophelia kicked weakly against the water, her muscles protesting with every motion. The waves, gentle as they were now, seemed impossibly vast and uncaring. Her breaths came in short gasps as she turned her body again, searching for something—anything—that might give her hope.

"Gabriel!" she called again, louder this time, though it left her throat raw. Her voice echoed, swallowed almost instantly by the vastness of the sea. She pressed her lips together, willing herself not to cry. Tears wouldn't help her now, not when every ounce of her strength was needed to survive.

Her gaze swept across the water once more, squinting against the harsh glare of the sun. It was everywhere, reflecting off the waves and making it almost impossible to see. Her heart pounded as the emptiness of the ocean pressed in on her, its vastness a suffocating reminder of just how small she was.

"Come on," she whispered, the words splintering in her throat. "Please...someone...anyone..."

The thought was a lifeline, a fragile thread that kept her moving. She couldn't allow herself to believe it—not yet. Her breaths came in short, panicked gasps as she turned in the water, spinning herself in a slow, desperate circle. Her limbs felt heavier with each motion, the exhaustion creeping closer with every beat of her heart.

And then, through the shimmer of salt and light, she spotted something—a dark shape floating a few yards away. Her heart leapt painfully in her chest, hope and terror surging in equal measure. Was it debris? Wreckage?

Her eyes narrowed against the tyrannical glare of the sun, her vision swimming with spots from the brightness. The shape shifted with the movement of the waves, bobbing gently. A chill coiled through her as she saw it: the unmistakable outline of a man's arm, motionless and trailing in the water.

"Gabriel!" she screamed, the name tearing from her throat with a raw desperation that startled even her. She kicked her legs harder, ignoring the burning ache in her muscles. The salty water stung her eyes, but she didn't care. She had to reach him.

Every stroke felt like an eternity, the distance between them impossibly vast. The waves seemed to conspire against her, pushing her back even as she fought forward. Her hands sliced through the water, her movements frantic and uncoordinated as fear took hold.

"Hold on!" she shouted, though she knew he couldn't hear her.

When she finally reached him, her trembling hands slipped against his cold, wet skin. Her heart plummeted at the touch—it was too cold, unnaturally so. He was floating face down, his dark hair fanned out around his head like a shadow in the water.

"Gabriel," she choked out. Her hands gripped his shoulders, shaking him uselessly as her mind screamed against the possibility of losing him. She used all her strength to flip him over, the motion awkward and clumsy in the water.

His face was pale, far too pale, and his lips were tinged blue. Seawater trickled from the corner of his mouth, and for one gut-wrenching moment, she thought he was dead.

"No," she whispered fiercely, trembling with equal parts panic and determination. "You don't get to leave me. Not like this."

Her hands shook as she pressed them against his chest, her fingers slipping on the wet fabric of his shirt. She leaned closer, her ear hovering above his mouth, but she couldn't hear anything over the sound of the waves and her own pounding heartbeat.

"Come on, Gabriel," she urged. "Breathe."

She positioned her hands again, pressing down on his chest in a desperate attempt to force the water from his lungs. The motion was clumsy, her strength waning with every push, but she refused to stop. Her magic flickered, responding to her desperation, though it was weak and sputtering like a flame about to go out.

"Don't you dare give up," she said through gritted teeth,

her eyes stinging with unshed tears. "Don't you dare." She lowered her mouth to his, preparing to breathe life into him.

Before she could begin, his eyes snapped open, startling her so much she jerked back. Gabriel coughed, spitting out a mouthful of seawater before giving her a lopsided grin, voice hoarse but laced with amusement. "Ophelia," he drawled, "I'm a vampire. The only way for me to face the true death is if my head is chopped off or my heart is shattered. It's uncomfortable not to breathe for that long. I'm happy to pretend that I can't breathe if you want to lower your mouth back where it belongs."

She froze for a moment, staring at him, her mind reeling. Relief crashed into her like a wave, and she let out a laugh that was half sob, punching his shoulder weakly. "You unbelievable bastard," she muttered. "You scared the hell out of me."

His grin widened, even as he grimaced and spat out more water. "It's nice to know you care."

She wanted to scream at him, to let out all the fear and anger that had been building inside her. But there wasn't time for that. They were still adrift, the ocean vast and unforgiving, and Brisa and Alex were still missing.

"Where are they?" Ophelia asked, her voice breaking as she twisted to scan the horizon again. "Did you see them?"

Gabriel's expression turned somber, the teasing light in his eyes dimming. "No," he admitted. "The last thing I remember is the mast breaking and the chaos tearing us apart. After that, nothing."

Her throat tightened painfully. The thought of Brisa and Alex out here, lost or worse, was unbearable. She clenched her fists, her nails biting into her palms as she forced herself to stay calm. "We have to find them," she said firmly. "They're out there. They have to be."

Gabriel's gaze softened, and he reached out to steady her as the waves jostled them. "We will," he said, quiet but resolute. "But first, we need to get out of the water. We're too exposed here."

He was right. The ocean was vast, indifferent, and they were vulnerable. Together, they turned their focus to survival, searching through the debris for anything that could keep them afloat. A large piece of wreckage bobbed a short distance away, a broken section of the deck with jagged edges jutting out like splintered bones.

"Over there," Gabriel said, gesturing with a nod.

They swam toward it, the effort grueling against the relentless pull of the waves. By the time they reached the wreckage, Ophelia's arms and legs felt like lead. Gabriel climbed onto the floating debris first, his movements fluid despite the obvious strain. He reached down, pulling her up against him with ease.

The wooden planks were rough and splintered, digging into her hands and knees as she collapsed onto the makeshift raft. Her chest heaved as she sucked in air, her muscles burning with exhaustion. But at least they were no longer treading water.

"We need to build something sturdier," Ophelia said after a moment, hoarse but determined. "If we can tie more pieces of the wreckage together…"

Gabriel nodded, his expression approving. "Good thinking. Let's get to work."

They scavenged what they could, dragging more pieces of debris to their makeshift raft. It was slow, difficult work; everything was slick with seawater, and her hands were raw and bleeding by the time they finished lashing the pieces together with strips of cloth Gabriel had torn from his shirt. The raft was crude but sturdy enough to keep them afloat.

Once they were settled on the raft, Ophelia let her head fall back, staring up at the endless expanse of sky. The sun was high now, beating down mercilessly, and she could feel her skin prickling under its heat.

"We have no idea where we are," she said quietly, the gravity of their situation settling heavily over her.

Gabriel leaned back beside her, his expression unreadable. "We'll figure it out," he said. "But right now, we need to focus on getting to land. If we can find land, we'll have a better chance of finding Brisa and Alex."

Ophelia nodded, swallowing back the lump in her throat. She couldn't let herself fall apart. Not now. "Okay," she said, steadier. "Let's figure out where to go."

She closed her eyes, reaching out with her water and earth magic. The ocean's energy was vast and overwhelming, but she let herself sink into it, searching for the subtle pull of the currents beneath the waves. Her fingers tingled with power as she focused, her senses extending outward like tendrils.

"There," she said finally, pointing to the left. "The current is stronger that way. I think it's pulling toward land."

Gabriel followed her gaze, shading his eyes as he scanned the horizon. After a moment, he nodded. "Good enough for me. Let's get moving."

As they set off, paddling with broken planks and pushing the raft forward with magic, Ophelia couldn't help but glance back at the empty ocean behind them. Brisa and Alex were out there somewhere. They had to be.

"We'll find them," Gabriel said quietly.

The sun was dipping toward the horizon by the time they spotted it—a dark, uneven smudge breaking the menacing line of sea and sky.

Land.

Ophelia's heart leapt, her exhaustion momentarily forgotten as hope surged through her chest.

"There," Gabriel said pointing, his gaze assessing and intent. "We'll make it."

For the first time in what felt like days, a spark of belief flared in her chest. They weren't lost. They weren't doomed to drift forever. They had a chance now.

Together, they paddled toward salvation, the distant shore drawing closer with every aching stroke.

SIXTEEN

The narrow strip of golden sand came into focus, framed by the dense green of a jungle that loomed like an unbroken wall against the sky.

The waves turned choppier as they neared the shallows, the raft lurching beneath them. Gabriel was the first to move, leaping into the water with powerful strides and gripping the edge of the raft to steady it.

Ophelia followed, her body trembling as she slid into the cool water and waded toward the beach. The moment her feet touched the sand, she collapsed to her knees.

The earth beneath her was firm and real, grounding her in a way the endless sea never could. She dug her fingers into the damp grains, a gasp escaping her lips—a sound halfway between a sob and a laugh.

"We made it," she whispered.

Gabriel knelt beside her, his hand resting gently on her shoulder. "We did," he said quietly, filled with an undeniable strength.

The beach stretched out before them, eerily quiet except for the rhythmic crash of waves behind them. Above, the sky burned with the fading light of the setting sun, casting the jungle in hues of gold and shadow. Ophelia's eyes traced the tree line, the thick foliage looming like a fortress. It was beautiful but unforgiving, a place that promised both sanctuary and danger.

Gabriel helped her to her feet, his touch steadying. "We need to move," he said. "The tide will rise soon, and we don't know what else is out here."

Ophelia brushed the sand from her palms. Her body ached with every step, but she followed Gabriel toward the jungle. The air was thick and humid, clinging to her skin like a second layer. The cries of unseen birds echoed from the canopy, punctuated by the occasional rustling leaves as small creatures darted through the undergrowth.

They pressed into the jungle, the path uneven and treacherous. Gabriel used a sturdy branch to clear the way, slicing through vines and pushing aside low-hanging branches. Ophelia followed close behind, her senses taut. Every shadow seemed to shift, every sound a potential threat.

"Do you think the others made it?" she asked quietly, breaking the silence.

Gabriel didn't answer right away, his gaze focused on the path ahead. When he finally spoke, his voice was measured but tinged with a quiet determination. "If anyone could survive that, it would be Brisa and Alex. They're tough. Resourceful."

Ophelia nodded, clinging to his words. She had to believe they were out there somewhere, fighting to survive, just as she and Gabriel were.

As the light began to fade, they stumbled upon a small clearing nestled against the base of a rocky cliff. The ground was uneven, littered with fallen debris from the jungle, but it offered some semblance of shelter. A shallow cave cut into the rock face, its entrance partially obscured by vines. A small pool of water surrounded the entrance.

"This will do," Gabriel said, wading into the water and then stepping inside the cave. He scanned the interior, his movements cautious and deliberate. "It's dry, and it doesn't look like anything else is living here."

Ophelia followed him inside, sinking to the cool stone floor with a sigh of relief. The cave was small but sufficient, its walls smooth and cool to the touch. The scent of damp earth mingled with the smell of salt clinging to her skin.

Gabriel busied himself gathering wood from the clearing. Once he had built a small hearth, Ophelia used her waning magic to bring fire to the tips of her fingers, lighting the wood. The flames crackled to life, casting flickering shadows on the walls. Ophelia watched him work, her exhaustion warring with an unexpected sense of comfort. Despite everything, he was here.

"You're good at this," she said. The words came out soft, almost reverent.

Gabriel glanced at her, his lips quirking into a small smile. "You pick up a few things when you've been around as long as I have."

Ophelia managed a weak laugh, leaning back against the wall. "How long is that, exactly?"

His smile faded, replaced by something more contemplative. "I was born in the fifteenth century," he said.

Her mouth fell open, but she said nothing. He continued speaking, unprompted.

"My family lived along the shore, and my father was a fisherman. I had seven sisters."

Ophelia smiled at his story.

Gabriel grinned at her. "You learn a thing or two surrounded by so many beautiful women. My sisters were feisty like you." He paused, looking at the fire as if lost in a memory.

"So you were born a human? How did you become a vampire?"

"I was conscripted and learned to sail a trireme, a warship during my time. I wanted to see the world and work my way up in the military. But vampires during that time were looking to increase their ranks. And, as you can see, I'm large," he said, looking down at his body. "I caught the attention of an ancient vampire who was born that way, during the time of empusae. He killed the entire warship just to get to me. Turned me against my will. And I'm still here today."

As he spoke, Ophelia realized how little she truly knew about Luka's past, yet Gabriel offered answers freely.

Luka had at least explained some of the history of the vampires—empusae, as he called them. They were descendants of the goddess Hecate and the spirit Mormo. Zeus was angry with Hecate when he found out she was in love with the female spirit, Mormo. Hecate ignored him, and Empusa was born of the relationship. To punish Hecate, Zeus made Empusa and all her descendants need blood to survive. And that's how the empusae were initially created—born but not made.

She closed her eyes for a moment, letting the sounds of the jungle lull her into a tentative sense of calm.

"I'll tell you more about my family another time," Gabriel said. "But for now, I'd like to get you cleaned up," he said, pointing to the spring next to the cave. "Are you warm enough for that?"

The fire had finally warmed the chill in her bones. "Yes," she said, just as her stomach rumbled.

Gabriel smiled at her, a disarming smile. "I'll get some food if you want to bathe."

She readily agreed. After he'd left through the jungle, she

slipped out of her tattered clothes and left them to dry by the fire. Slipping into the pool, she let the spring water cleanse her wounds and body. She ducked her head under the surface, rinsing the salt from her strands. When she poked her head above again, she found Gabriel standing at the clearing, a makeshift spear in hand with three fish lanced through the middle.

He was staring at her, a wistful look on his face. He waded through the water to the mouth of the cave, placing the fish above the fire, careful to not let them touch the flames as they cooked.

As she watched him, he turned to meet her gaze at last. "Something you need, Cinis?" he asked.

She wasn't sure what made her do it, but she stood up out of the water, her heavy breasts exposed to him. Hesitating only a moment, she answered him, "You."

It was the most he would get from her, and he seemed to know it. He walked through the water to her, grabbing her hair and pulling her head back so that she was facing him. He bent to her lips, crushing his mouth to hers. She wrapped her arms around his neck, pulling him to her as they devoured each other.

Gabriel moved his hands down Ophelia's body, cupping her ass as he lifted her out of the water. She wrapped her legs around him. He never took his mouth from hers as he waded through the water toward the back of the cave. He lowered her to the ground and stepped back, unbuckling his pants and lowering them. When he stood, she sucked in a breath at the sheer size of him. "Fuck," she whispered.

"That's the idea," he said.

She rolled her eyes at him, and he grabbed her by the hair and pulled her head back again so that she could look him in the face. "I promised to give it to you rough, Cinis. I know that's what you need. But you tell me if you need me to slow down, okay?"

She nodded, feeling herself get wetter with anticipation with each word.

"Then don't be a brat and roll your eyes at me when I'm about to fuck the sense out of you."

Ophelia swallowed, her pulse hammering. Gabriel's eyes narrowed to the spot on her neck. He knelt before her, sitting on the ground next to her and touching his fangs to that beating pulse, but not piercing her skin. "Tell me you want me, Cinis. Tell me to fuck you until you forget every bad thing that has happened in your life," Gabriel said. "Be a good girl and tell me what you want."

Ophelia was nearly breathless, her chest heaving up and down, so ready for him. "I-I want you to fuck me, Gabriel," she said, barely able to get the words out.

"Ask me properly, Ophelia. I want to hear you," he said.

"Gabriel...please," she said.

With preternatural speed, he pulled her to him. In seconds, he lay flat on the cave floor with her hovering above his face. "I can't have you uncomfortable on the floor," he said. "So I want you to sit on my face and come until your pussy burns with need for my cock," he said.

"I've never...done this before. Not like this," she said.

Gabriel's grin spread slowly, a dangerous curve that teetered between predatory and teasing, his dark eyes glinting with an intensity that promised trouble. "Cinis, sit that pretty pussy down on my face and ride until you drip with cum."

She hesitated only a moment before lowering herself onto him, her movements tentative. Gabriel's hands shot up, gripping her hips with firm authority, pulling her down with deliberate strength. His tongue met her with devastating precision, and any hesitation melted as waves of pleasure overtook her.

She cried out his name, her body shuddering uncontrollably as he consumed her completely.

When her trembling subsided, Gabriel eased her off him with a surprising tenderness. He stood effortlessly, lifting her as though she weighed nothing, and carried her to the smooth, cool floor of the cave. Lowering her gently, his dark eyes locked onto hers, brimming with unspoken promises.

"Normally, Cinis," he said, voice low and rough, "I'd want to see your eyes when I take you." His hand drifted down to stroke the length of his thick cock, swollen with need. "But I know what you need right now. Turn around. Hands on the wall."

An electric thrill coursed through her as she obeyed, her body responding before her mind could catch up. She bent forward, her palms pressing against the cool stone, her back arching slightly as her hips instinctively met his.

Gabriel slid himself along her, letting her slickness coat him until he was poised at her entrance. His breath was hot against her ear, his words sending shivers down her spine. "Better hang on, Ophelia."

With a single powerful thrust, he filled her completely, stealing the air from her lungs. She gasped, her fingers curling against the wall as her body adjusted to the intensity of him. Gabriel's pace was relentless, each stroke deep and commanding, sending shockwaves through her with every movement.

His hand gripped her hip, steadying her as his other slid around to find her clit. His touch was unyielding, stroking her with a deliberate rhythm that matched his thrusts. Her world narrowed to the heat of his body against hers, the overwhelming pleasure building inside her until it was unbearable.

"Gabriel," she gasped, the sound raw as her body tightened around him. His name became a desperate cry as they reached the peak together, shuddering in unison, the cave filled with their ragged breaths.

As her knees threatened to give out, Gabriel caught her, his strength unwavering as he held her close. He pressed a kiss to the curve of her shoulder, his lips soft against her overheated skin. Gabriel scooped her up effortlessly, carrying her back to the spring. The cool water lapped at her skin as he cleaned her with a quiet, deliberate care, washing away every trace of their shared intensity. The intimacy of the moment almost made her blush, but his calm, matter-of-fact demeanor stripping the act of awkwardness. When he was satisfied, he lifted her once more and carried her to the fire, settling her gently onto a pile of dry clothes he had prepared.

Turning to the fish, he tested them and took them away from the smoke. He brought the fish to her, taking a chunk of the meat and putting it in her mouth. She chewed slowly, her gaze flickering to Gabriel. She hated how much his calm steadied her—and how much she wanted to cling to it. They finished the meal in near silence, the fire crackling softly beside them.

"Do you think we'll find them?" she asked after a while, barely above a whisper.

Gabriel settled beside her, solid and reassuring. "We will," he said firmly. "But for now, we need to rest. We'll need all our strength for whatever comes next."

Ophelia nodded, lying back on the ground. The firelight danced across the walls of the cave, casting shadows that flickered and shifted like restless spirits. The warmth of the flames was a welcome contrast to the damp night air, and Ophelia found herself leaning closer to Gabriel, enjoying the warmth of his body. Though her clothes had dried, the ocean's chill still clung to her skin. It was a stark reminder of how close she'd come to being lost to the sea.

She broke the silence. "Do you ever get tired of it?"

Gabriel glanced up, his brow furrowing slightly. "Tired of what?"

"Surviving. Fighting. Losing people," she said, watching the shadows dance across his face.

His expression softened, the hint of a smile tugging at his lips. "All the time," he admitted. "But giving up isn't an option. Not for me, and not for you."

Ophelia looked away, her fingers curling into a fist. "Maybe I'm not this unbreakable force you seem to see. I feel like I'm holding on by a thread."

Gabriel leaned closer. "You've survived things that would've crushed anyone else, yet here you are. You're not done fighting."

She wanted to believe him, but doubt lingered in the back of her mind, like a shadow she couldn't shake. "What if I can't?"

He moved even closer, filling the small space between them. "If you falter, I'll be there. I'd set the world ablaze if it meant keeping you safe," he said simply. "But I don't think I'll need to."

Her chest tightened at the quiet certainty in his tone. She forced herself to meet his gaze. His dark, steady eyes held a depth that both comforted and unnerved her. "Why do you keep fighting for me, Gabriel? After everything?" she asked, voice cracking.

Gabriel's lips quirked into a small smile, but there was no amusement in his expression. "Because you're worth fighting for," he said softly.

For a moment, she couldn't speak. The fire crackled between them, filling the silence with its gentle warmth.

As the night deepened, the sounds of the jungle grew

louder. The air pulsed with an energy that was both foreign and familiar.

Gabriel shifted beside her, his movements drawing her attention. He was closer now, his shoulder brushing against hers. "We'll find them," he said quietly, as if reading her thoughts. "Brisa and Alex are survivors, just like you. We don't leave anyone behind."

Ophelia nodded, her throat tight. "I just...I can't lose them, too."

"You won't," he said, each word steady and unflinching. "Not as long as I'm here."

She turned to look at him, her eyes searching his face for any sign of doubt. But all she saw was resolve, steady and unshakable. For the first time in a long while, she felt like she could breathe.

CHAPTER

SEVENTEEN

Ophelia pushed through the dense foliage, her legs aching from the steep climb and the sweltering heat. They'd been searching for hours, scouring the unfamiliar terrain for any clue about where they were or how to get help. Her heart pounded—not from exertion, but from a mix of hope and fear. Gabriel followed close behind her, silent but watchful, steadying her in a way she couldn't quite explain.

Her mind buzzed with questions she hadn't dared to ask before. For months, she had tried to ignore her supernatural lineage, to live as if she could escape it. But now, curiosity and necessity had taken over. She'd been pestering Gabriel, desperate for answers.

"You can be out in the sun," she began, brushing a thick vine out of her way. "And you won't burn up into ash. And you don't sparkle. So why aren't you pale with no melanin?"

Gabriel, ever patient, answered as he always did—without hesitation. "Vampires retain the appearance they had when they turned. My skin was this golden tan color when I died, and that's how I remain as a reborn vampire. Our appearance is only enhanced, to make us more beautiful. Predatory, really. It's a tool for hunting. But our core traits, like skin color, remain unchanged. We are still our essence, just elevated."

Ophelia frowned, processing his words. "So no supernatural makeover? You don't go all pale and creepy just because you're a vampire?"

Gabriel chuckled, brushing a low-hanging branch out of her way. "No, Cinis. We're predators, not ghosts."

"And I thought vampires could go days without sleeping," she pressed, glancing over her shoulder at him. "But you sleep all the time."

His grin was wolfish. "Was I really sleeping? Or was I just trying to share a small bed with you?"

"You're *such* a bastard," she muttered, rolling her eyes. "And why are you warm? I thought vampires were cold."

"Another myth. If our blood didn't circulate, how would everything else work?" Gabriel's grin widened, the mischievous glint in his eyes unmistakable. "You need blood circulation for certain...functions. For instance, you need blood to go to your—"

Gabriel smirked at her when she held up her hand, cutting him off.

"That's enough! I get the idea," she said, blushing slightly at the memory of the night before. And rubbing her thighs together at the thought. She could sense Gabriel's satisfaction without even looking at him.

"What about breathing and your heartbeat?" she asked, trying to regain her composure. "In your sleep, you breathe slower than humans. And I still hear your heartbeat—faint, but there."

"Watching me sleep, Cinis?" His teasing tone softened as he continued. "You're right. Vampires still breathe, and our hearts still beat, but much slower. Our bodies are optimized, efficient. We conserve energy for speed, strength, and lethality. Everything we do is designed to make us better hunters."

Ophelia fell quiet, mulling over his answers as they trudged forward. The jungle around them was alive: the rustle of leaves, the distant cries of unseen birds, and the persistent hum of insects. The air was heavy with the scent of damp earth and greenery, the heat pressing down on her like a physical weight.

Just as she was beginning to feel the strain of the climb, something cut through the background noise. A faint voice, carried on the wind.

Ophelia froze, holding up a hand to signal Gabriel to stop. Her eyes narrowed as she strained to hear it again, her pulse quickening. The sound was muted, barely distinguishable from the symphony of the jungle, but it was there.

"Did you hear that?" she whispered.

Gabriel tilted his head, listening intently. His focused eyes scanned the shadows ahead. "Yes," he said, voice low but sure. "Someone's there."

Ophelia could feel magic near her, another witch. And another supernatural signature she couldn't quite place. It had to be them.

Without waiting, Ophelia broke into a run, branches whipping at her arms as she pushed forward. The sound grew louder—a voice, then two. Laughter. Her chest tightened, hope surging like a tidal wave.

"Ophelia!" a voice called, clear and unmistakable.

Ophelia stumbled into a clearing, her breath catching in her throat as she saw them. Alex stood there, her silver hair matted with dirt, her face streaked with grime, but her blue eyes were bright with relief. Brisa was next to her, looking just as battered. The sight of them made Ophelia's knees weak.

"You're alive," Ophelia breathed, barely able to find her voice.

Alex was the first to close the distance, pulling Ophelia into a tight embrace. "We thought we'd lost you," she said, trembling with relief. "We've been searching everywhere."

Brisa joined them, wrapping her arms around both women. "Took you long enough," she said, her tone light but eyes shining with unshed tears. "I was starting to think Gabriel finally did you in."

"Not yet," Gabriel said, stepping into the clearing with a wry grin. "Though she's doing her best to keep things interesting."

Ophelia laughed, a sound that felt strange and wonderful in her throat. The grip of fear and exhaustion began to lift, replaced by the overwhelming relief of knowing they were all together again. She clung to Alex and Brisa as if letting go might make them disappear.

When the hugs loosened, Brisa took a step back, her gaze turning thoughtful. "You know," she began, glancing between Ophelia and Gabriel, "we wouldn't be completely lost here if Celeste and my dad were trying to find us."

Ophelia stiffened at the mention of her mother. "What do you mean?"

Brisa shrugged, brushing a leaf off her shoulder. "Witches are tied to their family by more than just blood. Magic leaves a signature, a thread connecting those who share it. The stronger the bond, the easier it is to follow."

Gabriel added, "The magic is instinctive, like a homing signal. And because witch magic is matriarchal, it's especially strong between mothers and daughters, or sisters."

Brisa nodded. "If Celeste is out there, she'll find you when you need her. She already did once."

Ophelia's jaw tightened. "If she wanted to, she would've found us by now."

"She will," Brisa said firmly, her eyes steady on Ophelia's. "You're her daughter, whether you like it or not."

The group settled near the clearing's edge, exhaustion pulling them down. The late afternoon sun filtered through the jungle canopy, casting dappled shadows on the ground. Despite their reunion, the silence hung heavy, each of them lost in their own thoughts.

Ophelia sat with her knees pulled to her chest, her fingers absently tracing patterns in the dirt. The relief of finding Alex and Brisa had already started to wane, replaced by the gnawing uncertainty of their situation. Brisa's words echoed in her mind: *If Celeste is out there, she'll find you when you need her.*

The idea of Celeste finding her way to them should have comforted her, but it didn't. If anything, it left her feeling exposed, vulnerable. "Why hasn't she come already?" she muttered, more to herself than anyone else.

Gabriel, sitting a few feet away whittling a piece of driftwood into a makeshift spear, glanced up. "Magic like that isn't instant," he said, his tone calm but firm. "It takes time. Focus."

Brisa, crouched nearby and brushing dirt from her boots, added, "She probably had to figure out where you even were. Lineage magic isn't perfect; it's like following the feeble hum of a thread through mayhem. It takes precision and intent."

Ophelia scoffed, shaking her head. "She hasn't exactly been big on intent when it comes to me. What if she's not looking at all?"

Alex frowned. "Ophelia, she's your mom. Whatever's happened between you two, she wouldn't leave you here to die."

"That's easy for you to say," Ophelia shot back, her tone harsher than she intended. "She didn't disappear on you when you were a child, leaving you to grow up not understanding supernatural power."

Gabriel shifted closer, his expression unreadable. "She'll come," he said simply.

Ophelia stared at him, her chest tightening. How could he be so sure? How could any of them? She wasn't even sure she wanted Celeste to come. The tangled mess of their relationship threatened to choke her, and she clenched her fists to keep from spiraling.

The minutes dragged on, each one stretching into eternity. The jungle around them buzzed with life. But to Ophelia, even the air seemed to be holding its breath.

Gabriel's presence was usually a balm, but even he seemed restless now. His hawk-like gaze flicked constantly to the trees, scanning for movement. Brisa paced, muttering under her breath, while Alex sat cross-legged, her hands pressed together as if in prayer.

The tension wrapped around Ophelia's chest, a crushing grip that refused to relent. Every shadow seemed too long, every rustle of leaves too loud. She closed her eyes, trying to steady her breathing, but her mind refused to quiet. What if Celeste couldn't find her? What if she didn't want to?

Then, just as Ophelia felt the stirrings of despair, something shifted.

It was subtle at first—a slight pulsing in her chest, like a string being plucked deep inside her. She froze, her eyes snapping open. The jungle around them seemed to still, life fading into an eerie silence.

"Do you feel that?" she asked.

Gabriel nodded, his eyes narrowing. "Magic."

Brisa's head shot up, her expression tensing. "It's her," she said, voice tight with certainty.

The pull grew stronger, a gentle but insistent tug in Ophelia's chest. It was as if an invisible thread had latched on to her, guiding her toward something—or someone. The air around them grew heavy, charged with energy. A shimmer rippled through the clearing, barely visible.

Ophelia's heart pounded, her hands trembling as she gripped the ground beneath her. "Is this what it feels like?" she asked, barely more than a whisper.

"Like being reeled in," Brisa murmured. "Lineage magic is primal. Instinctive. You can't ignore it when it's this strong."

The vibration in Ophelia's chest intensified, almost overwhelming, as if her very blood recognized the being drawing nearer. Her breath hitched, her emotions warring within her: relief, dread, anger.

The jungle seemed to exhale all at once, the silence breaking with the distant sound of footsteps.

"They're here," Gabriel said, rising to his feet, his hand instinctively moving to the hilt of his blade.

Ophelia's pulse thundered in her ears as she stood, her gaze fixed on the edge of the clearing. For a moment, everything stilled again, the air thick with anticipation.

The air seemed to pulse with energy, a rhythmic vibration that thrummed in Ophelia's chest. It was unlike anything she'd felt before, unfamiliar yet oddly resonant, as though her own magic were responding to something ancient and unyielding. She glanced around the clearing, her heart hammering.

"What's happening?" Ophelia asked, voice edged with panic.

Gabriel moved closer to her, his hand resting on the hilt of his blade. "Stay sharp. This feels...powerful."

Brisa's eyes darted toward the jungle, her brow furrowing. "It's them," she murmured, half in awe. "It has to be."

Before Ophelia could ask who *they* were, the world around her shifted. The air bent, shimmering like heat waves rising from the pavement. A crackling sound filled the clearing, like distant thunder rolling through the jungle.

Then, it happened.

The space just beyond the clearing warped and twisted, as though an invisible hand were folding the air itself. A gust of wind rushed outward, carrying with it the scent of ozone and something earthy—burnt sage, perhaps. The shimmering intensified, forming a swirling vortex of light and shadow, its edges traced with glowing runes that seemed to pulse in time with the vibration in Ophelia's chest.

A shiver of apprehension pulsed through her as two figures stepped through.

Celeste emerged first, her movements calm and assured. She looked as if she'd walked straight out of a whirlwind, her dark hair billowing around her, steely eyes scanning the clearing with practiced precision. There was an unshakable confidence in the way she carried herself, as though she'd done this a thousand times before.

Behind her came Mo, his husky frame steady and imposing. His usually casual demeanor was replaced with a quiet intensity, his gaze flicking over each of them as if assessing for injuries.

The vortex vanished as quickly as it had appeared, the shimmering air settling back into its natural state. The jungle felt startlingly still in its wake, as though it were holding its breath.

Ophelia stumbled back a step, her mind racing. "What...the hell was that?" she demanded.

Celeste's dark eyes met hers, and for a moment, there was silence. Then she spoke, her tone as composed as ever. "It's called threading."

"Threading?" Ophelia repeated, the word foreign on her tongue.

"It's the act of folding space," Celeste explained. "By weaving magic into the threads of reality, witches can collapse the distance between two points, creating a passage. Well, some witches can. I can."

Ophelia stared at her, the explanation doing little to settle her confusion. "You can just...move through time and space like that?"

Celeste's lips twitched into a smile. "Not exactly. Threading doesn't break the rules of time. It's more like finding a shortcut, a quicker path to where we need to be. But it's not without limits. It requires a powerful connection, a clear anchor, and an incredible amount of magic."

"And you never thought to tell me about this?" Ophelia snapped, voice rising.

Celeste sighed, brushing a curly strand of hair from her face. "You weren't ready."

Ophelia's jaw tightened, her anger bubbling to the surface. "Not ready? We've been stranded on this island, and you didn't think *this* was the time to mention you could pull me out of thin air?"

"I had to find you first," Celeste said firmly. "Threading isn't as simple as snapping your fingers. It requires focus and preparation. Your magic signature was scattered. Finding you through all that chaos wasn't easy."

Brisa stepped forward, her words softening the tension. "She's telling the truth, Ophelia. Lineage magic is strong, but threading isn't something you just *do*. It takes time, and it drains you."

Ophelia's gaze shifted to Celeste, and for the first time, she noticed the strain in her mother's posture—the slight tremble in her hands, the pallor of her skin. It was subtle, but it was there.

"Threading takes a toll," Celeste admitted, quieter now.

"But I wasn't going to leave you here. When Brisa didn't check in with Mo, we knew something was wrong. You may not believe me, but I've been tracking you since the moment we realized you'd disappeared."

Ophelia's chest tightened, her emotions warring within her. Relief, anger, confusion—they all fought for dominance. She wanted to believe her mom, but trust didn't come easily.

Gabriel crossed his arms, his intense eyes narrowing. "And now? What's the plan?"

Celeste straightened, her exhaustion replaced by determination. "Now we get you off this island. All of you."

The clearing fell into an uneasy silence after Celeste's declaration. Ophelia's eyes remained fixed on her mother, trying to reconcile the woman before her with the countless unanswered questions that had haunted her for years. Relief mingled with resentment, creating a tangled knot in her chest.

Celeste moved closer, her expression unreadable but her movements deliberate. "You don't look too worse for wear," she said, her tone calm but edged with something softer—concern, perhaps.

Ophelia stiffened, crossing her arms over her chest. "You don't get to act like you care now."

Celeste stopped mid-step, gaze locking onto Ophelia. "I never stopped caring."

"Really? Because disappearing for most my life and then reappearing without any explanation says otherwise," Ophelia shot back, voice rising. The anger she'd tried to suppress surged to the surface, raw and unfiltered. "You left. No explanation. Just gone. And now you show up, expecting me to act like it never happened?"

Gabriel shifted uncomfortably behind her, his eyes darting between mother and daughter. Brisa and Mo exchanged a glance, but neither intervened.

"I never wanted to leave," Celeste said, steady, though a flicker of vulnerability crept into her words. "I thought I was protecting you."

Ophelia let out a bitter laugh. "By abandoning me? Leaving me to figure out all of this"—she gestured wildly around her—"on my own?"

Celeste's shoulders sagged, the exhaustion in her posture suddenly more pronounced. "You don't understand what it cost me to stay away. But if I'd stayed, you would've been dragged into things you weren't ready for. I thought I was giving you a chance at a normal life."

Ophelia's chest tightened. "Do you even know what my life has been like? Elijah raised me, not you. He and Sebastian are the ones who—" She shook her head, tears stinging her eyes.

Celeste stepped forward, her hand reaching out hesitantly. "I know I failed you, Ophelia. I'm not asking for forgiveness. I just want to keep you safe now."

Ophelia's anger faltered, replaced by a pang of guilt she wasn't ready to admit. She glanced at Gabriel, who gave her a small nod, his expression unreadable.

Brisa, who had been uncharacteristically silent until now, grinned. "Family reunions, huh? Never simple."

The tension in the clearing eased slightly at her remark. Ophelia let out a weak laugh, the sound breaking through the heaviness in her chest. She glanced at Celeste, emotions still swirling, but her words came quieter. "You've got a lot to answer for."

Celeste nodded solemnly. "And I will. But first, we need to get off this island."

Celeste moved toward the center of the clearing, her movements purposeful despite the visible strain on her body. She reached into the folds of her jacket and pulled out a small crystal sphere, its surface shimmering in the fading light.

Ophelia's brow furrowed as she watched her mother kneel and place the crystal carefully on the ground. "What are you doing?" she asked, her tone wary.

"Preparing to thread us off this island," Celeste replied, her focus entirely on the sphere as she traced intricate patterns in the dirt around it with her finger. The lines glowed, like embers catching fire.

Ophelia hesitated, glancing at Gabriel, who gave her a reassuring nod. "I thought you said threading took a lot of magic," she said. "Are you sure you're up for this?"

Celeste didn't look up. "It does. But we don't have the luxury of waiting. The longer we stay here, the harder it will be to get to safety."

Mo crouched beside her. "She knows what she's doing. Just stay close, and don't let go of anyone, no matter what," he said.

Brisa stepped closer, her expression serious.

"Threading a group is different than just moving one person," Celeste explained. "The spell will need to pull all of us along the same thread. If you let go, you'll break the connection."

Ophelia swallowed hard, her heart pounding. The thought of being left behind, lost between threads of magic, sent a shiver down her spine.

Celeste glanced up briefly, her gaze steady. "Everyone needs to be touching. I can't guarantee your safety if the connection isn't strong."

Gabriel moved to stand beside Ophelia, his hand brushing hers before gripping it firmly. His strength was a silent reassurance. Brisa linked arms with Mo, who stood protectively at Celeste's side.

The air grew heavier as Celeste muttered an incantation under her breath, low and melodic. The crystal began to glow brighter, its light spreading outward in shimmering waves.

The runes etched into the dirt flared to life, casting an eerie blue glow across the clearing.

"What does it feel like?" Ophelia asked, barely above a whisper.

Celeste's lips curved into a smile. "It feels like stepping through a thread of magic, pulling yourself and others along the weave. It's disorienting, but it's over quickly. Just hold on, and whatever you do, don't fight it."

Mo grinned. "You get used to it. Sort of," he said.

The wind picked up suddenly, swirling around them in a tight vortex. Ophelia's hair whipped across her face as the magic intensified, the shimmering light growing brighter until it was almost blinding. The air hummed with power, the vibration resonating deep in her bones.

The ground beneath her feet seemed to dissolve, replaced by a sensation of weightlessness. It was as though the world had fallen away, leaving only the threads of magic to guide them. Ophelia's breath stuttered as a rushing wind pressed against her skin, pulling her forward with an unstoppable force.

She clung tightly to Gabriel's hand, her heart racing as light and shadow blurred into a dizzying swirl. The sensation was both exhilarating and terrifying, like being swept up in a current she couldn't control.

And then, as suddenly as it had started, it was over.

The wind died down, the light faded, and solid ground returned beneath her feet. Ophelia stumbled, her legs shaking as she struggled to find her balance. Gabriel's steady grip kept her upright, his dark eyes scanning their surroundings.

They were no longer on the island.

EIGHTEEN

They had landed in a sanctuary, a haven carved into the side of a jungle mountain. Long-tailed monkeys darted through the trees, their high-pitched calls filling the humid air. A series of elegant, open-air structures nestled among the dense trees, their design a harmonious blend of nature and architecture.

"Where are we?" Ophelia asked as she turned in a slow circle, taking in the lush surroundings.

"Nivara Island," Mo answered, his tone carrying a note of reverence.

Before Ophelia could process the name, a familiar figure emerged from one of the buildings, moving with fluid grace.

The air seemed to still as the woman approached, her aura magnetic.

"Mira?" Ophelia whispered, the name escaping her lips like a breath of air after surfacing from deep water. Recognition swept over her, accompanied by a flood of emotions: surprise, relief, and a quiet, aching sense of familiarity.

The woman smiled, her dark eyes warm and knowing.

"Ophelia," she said, her voice a soothing balm that seemed to ease the tension in the air. "Welcome to my home."

Everything about Mira exuded peace and warmth. Her long, dark hair flowed freely, streaked with strands of white that caught the dappled sunlight filtering through the jungle canopy. She was dressed in a deep green tunic that shifted, her bare feet making no sound on the earth.

For a moment, Ophelia was transported back to her teenage years, when Mira had been a stabilizing force in her chaotic life. Sebastian had steered an angry and unruly Ophelia to Mira's yoga studio. But she'd been more than a yoga instructor; she had been a guide, helping Ophelia channel her power into something manageable.

Back then, Ophelia hadn't understood the depth of Mira's influence. Now, standing before her again, she realized just how much she owed to the woman who had taken such a risk to help her. As a moira—a supernatural known for an ability to share visions of a person's destiny—Mira didn't want to be used for her gifts. But she'd still helped Ophelia.

Ophelia felt a wave of emotion wash over her as Mira opened her arms, the gesture both welcoming and grounding. "You look tired," Mira said softly, pulling her into a warm embrace. "But you're here, and that's what matters."

Ophelia melted into the hug, the tension she'd been holding in her shoulders easing for the first time in days.

"You run this place?" Ophelia asked as they broke apart.

Mira nodded, her expression serene. "I do," Mira replied with a soft smile. "It's a refuge for those like us—supernaturals who've lost their way or need time to heal. Everyone here is in some form of recovery, whether from magic, addiction, or life itself. You'll find no judgment here, only space to breathe and be."

Gabriel, who had been standing a few steps behind,

inclined his head respectfully. "This is a remarkable place," he said, his dark eyes scanning the elegant structures around them.

Mira's gaze shifted to him, narrowing slightly in quiet observation. "You carry a weight," she said, gentle but firm. "A heaviness that does not belong to you alone."

Gabriel's jaw tightened, but he didn't respond. After a moment, a smile tugged at his lips. "I'll keep that in mind."

Mira's attention shifted back to the group, her warmth extending to all of them. "You're all welcome here. We'll get you settled in the guest quarters. But first, let me show you the heart of Nivara."

As they followed Mira through the retreat, Ophelia marveled at the place. The path wound through the jungle, connecting open-air buildings crafted from bamboo, stone, and thick vines. Every structure seemed to belong, blending seamlessly with the lush surroundings. Large, open spaces allowed the jungle breeze to flow freely, carrying the scent of blooming flowers and damp earth. Everything about Nivara exuded intentionality: the arrangement of seating areas, the cascading greenery that framed every view, the way the sunlight filtered through the canopy.

"This is where the healing begins," Mira said as they entered a wide, circular pavilion at the retreat's center. A ring of low cushions surrounded a fire pit, the embers glowing even in the daylight. "You'll find that the energy here is different, softer. It encourages reflection and renewal."

Brisa lingered near the edge of the group, her arms crossed tightly over her chest. "How long do we stay here?" she asked.

"As long as you need," Mira replied without hesitation. "There's no rush, no expectation. You'll leave when you're ready."

Celeste observed Mira, an unreadable expression on her face.

As the group began to disperse, exploring the pavilion and the surrounding spaces, Mira touched Ophelia's arm lightly. "Walk with me."

Ophelia followed her mentor down a narrow path that wound through the trees, the sounds of the others fading into the background. The jungle seemed to embrace them, the leaves whispering secrets on the breeze.

"You've changed," Mira said after a while, her expression contemplative.

"I've been through a lot," Ophelia admitted, her gaze fixed on the path ahead. "More than I know how to handle."

Mira stopped, turning to face her. "And yet you're still standing."

Ophelia let out a hollow laugh. "Barely. I feel like I'm falling apart most days."

Mira's expression softened, and she reached out, brushing a strand of hair from Ophelia's face. "Falling apart is a part of healing, Ophelia. It's how we let go of what no longer serves us. You're not broken. You're transforming."

Ophelia's throat tightened, the words striking something deep within her. "I don't know if I can keep going," she whispered. "Not like this."

"You don't have to," Mira said. "You don't have to do it alone, and you don't have to have all the answers. Just take the next step. That's all."

For a moment, they stood in silence, the weight of the conversation settling between them. The sounds of the jungle —chirping insects, distant bird calls, and the soft rustle of trees—faded into the background, leaving only the steady rhythm of Ophelia's breathing and Mira's calm presence.

Mira smiled, a warm, reassuring expression that seemed to dissolve some of the tension in the air. "You're stronger than you think, Ophelia. You always have been."

Ophelia nodded. The words seeped into her, touching the raw places she tried to keep hidden. She nodded, unable to find the words to respond. Instead, she let Mira anchor her, grounding her in a way she hadn't felt in what seemed like forever.

"Come," Mira said, her hand resting lightly on Ophelia's shoulder. "There's still much to see."

The evening sun cast dappled patterns of light and shadow on the forest floor. Ophelia followed Mira down a winding path, her bare feet brushing against the smooth stones that lined the walkway. The air was cooler in the shade, carrying the earthy scent of moss and blooming flowers.

Mira led her to a small meditation pavilion, tucked away in a secluded corner of the sanctuary. The structure was simple yet elegant, open on all sides with a thatched roof and soft cushions scattered across the smooth wooden floor. The pavilion seemed to belong to the jungle, as though the trees themselves had parted to cradle it.

Mira moved with practiced grace, settling into the center of the pavilion with her legs crossed. Her posture was impossibly straight, her hands resting lightly on her knees. She closed her eyes, exuding an effortless serenity. "Come, sit with me," she said, a melody of calm that seemed to resonate with the very air around them.

Ophelia hesitated, her movements awkward and uncertain as she stepped into the pavilion. She lowered herself onto a cushion across from Mira, her shoulders stiff, her breathing uneven. Compared to Mira's effortless grace, Ophelia felt clumsy and out of place. "I don't even know where to start," she admitted.

Mira opened her eyes, her gaze steady and kind. "Start with where you are now," she said gently. "The rest will follow."

Ophelia took a shaky breath, letting her gaze drift to the jungle beyond the pavilion. The trees seemed to sway in time with the rhythm of her thoughts, their leaves whispering secrets she couldn't quite grasp. "I feel lost," she said finally. "Like I've been carrying all this pain and anger for so long, and now I don't know how to let go."

Mira reached out, her hand resting lightly on Ophelia's. Her touch was warm, steady, and grounding. "You've endured more than most," she said softly. "But carrying that pain doesn't make you stronger. It only weighs you down."

Ophelia's throat tightened, her gaze dropping to the worn cushion beneath her. "I don't know who I am without it," she admitted. "If I let go of the pain...what's left of me?" she whispered.

"You are more than your pain," Mira said firmly. "More than your losses, your fears, or the mistakes you've made. You are the fire that rises from the ashes, the spark of life that refuses to be extinguished."

The words hit Ophelia with unexpected force, breaking through the walls she'd built around herself. Her chest tightened, her vision blurring as she blinked back tears. "How do I find that part of me again?"

"By forgiving yourself," Mira said simply. Her tone was neither harsh nor pitying. It was a steady truth, offered without judgment. "Forgiveness isn't about excusing what happened. It's about freeing yourself from the chains of guilt and shame. It's about choosing to move forward, even when it feels impossible."

Ophelia shook her head, voice cracking. "I don't think I can."

"You can," Mira said, her unwavering tone wrapping

around Ophelia. "But it will take time. And you don't have to do it alone."

The tears spilled over then, hot and unstoppable. Ophelia pressed her hands to her face, her shoulders shaking as the weight she'd been carrying finally began to crack under the strain. She wept, the sobs raw and unfiltered, spilling out of her like a flood.

Mira didn't say anything. She didn't try to soothe her with empty words or tell her everything would be fine. She simply sat there, steady and unwavering, a quiet reminder that Ophelia didn't have to carry it all by herself anymore.

When the sobs finally subsided, Ophelia lowered her hands, lungs shuddering as she tried to steady herself. Mira offered her a soft cloth, and she took it gratefully, dabbing at her damp cheeks.

"Thank you," Ophelia said, the words rough but earnest.

Mira smiled, her dark eyes filled with quiet compassion. "You've already taken the first step, Ophelia. Trust that you'll find your way."

Mira reached into the folds of her tunic, pulling out a small, vibrant stone that shimmered in hues of blue and white. She held it out to Ophelia, who took it with tentative fingers.

"Moonstone?" Ophelia asked, a smile tugging at her lips as she recognized the stone from her past.

Mira nodded. "Remember what I taught you? The moonstone symbolizes wisdom and new beginnings. Meditate with it as your focal point, and it will guide you. Let it help you find forgiveness—not just for others, but for yourself."

Ophelia clutched the stone tightly, its cool surface a comforting weight in her palm. As she stepped out of the pavilion and back onto the winding path, the jungle seemed a little brighter, the air a little lighter.

She wasn't healed—not yet, and not even close—but for the first time, she understood that healing wasn't a destination. It was a journey she'd been afraid to take. But she was finally ready to try.

NINETEEN

LUKA

The cell was suffocating, cloaked in a darkness broken only by the sickly glow of runes etched into the damp stone walls. Their light pulsed weakly, like the dying embers of a fire, casting jagged shadows that tormented him.

Luka sat slumped against the wall, his arms shackled high above his head, the iron biting into his wrists. The cold seeped into his bones, though the dull ache of his injuries had long since numbed him to discomfort. The silence was oppressive, broken only by the rhythmic drip of water from somewhere above, each splash echoing like a taunt.

His body bore the evidence of endless torture—days or weeks, he could no longer tell. Time blurred in the void, marked only by fresh wounds layered over barely healed scars. Deep gashes lined his torso, sluggishly healing only to be reopened. Bruises painted his now-pale skin in shades of blue and yellow, stark against the darkened chamber. His once-pristine hair was matted, sticking to his forehead with dried blood and sweat. Though sunken, his eyes still held a spark of defiance.

He shifted, the movement scraping his already raw wrists against the iron cuffs. He bit back a groan, unwilling to give his captor the satisfaction of hearing his pain. A familiar sense of foreboding settled over him as he thought of her—the witch who seemed to derive endless pleasure from his suffering. Luka's jaw clenched as he stared at the floor, refusing to let his mind wander to the one person she seemed fixated on. The one who looked eerily like her.

Ophelia.

Her name lingered, unbidden and unwelcome, a thread of light in the dark corners of his mind. Shame raged.

The sound of approaching footsteps broke through the stillness, pulling him from his thoughts. His body tensed instinctively, every muscle coiled as though he could somehow defend himself in his weakened state. The air grew heavier, tinged with the metallic scent of blood magic. He didn't need to see her to know who it was.

The witch.

She swept into the chamber, her silhouette framed by the crimson glow of the runes in the corridor, moving like a shadow given form. Her presence curled through the room like inescapable smoke. And though Luka kept his head down, he felt her gaze settle on him.

A stabbing, sudden pain jolted through his body, emanating from the runes carved into the wall behind him. They flared to life, bathing the chamber in crimson light as they siphoned his strength, leaving him gasping. The witch stepped closer, her lips curving into a small, cruel smile.

"Nothing, Luka? No barbed retorts, no grand declarations of vengeance? I expected more from you." She tilted her head, her yellow-green eyes gleaming with amusement. "How disappointing."

Still, Luka didn't respond. He felt his body weaken further

as the runes drained him, but his pride refused to let her see his pain. She sighed dramatically, crouching down to meet his gaze.

"You're stubborn," she said. "It's admirable, really. But ultimately futile. Everyone breaks, Luka. Even you."

He finally looked up, his eyes burning with a flicker of defiance. "Then you've underestimated me," Luka said, voice a raw whisper, but no less resolute.

Her smile widened, serrated and predatory. Reaching out, she traced a line of dried blood on his cheek. "I know you better than you think. I know your weaknesses, your regrets. I know why you tied that poor witch to you, even when you knew she wasn't yours."

Luka's jaw tightened, a deliberate show of composure. He met her gaze, allowing just enough defiance to flicker in his eyes to provoke her without revealing the true depth of his resolve.

"Ah, yes," she purred, circling him slowly. "You thought binding her to you would save you both. Did you honestly believe that trickery would go unnoticed? That it wouldn't catch up to you eventually?"

"She doesn't belong to you," Luka growled, voice hoarse but steady. "She never will."

The witch's laughter echoed off the stone walls, a sound both chilling and musical. "Oh, Luka," she said, dripping with condescension. The witch's smile never wavered as she leaned closer, her breath cold against his ear. "You still don't see, do you? I don't want to claim her. I don't need to." She crouched in front of him again, her face inches from his. "Because, whether you like it or not, she's already mine."

She pulled back, studying him with clinical detachment, as though he were a puzzle she was eager to solve. "Tell me about Ophelia."

Luka's chest heaved as he fought the urge to lash out, his muscles trembling with rage and exhaustion.

The witch straightened, sighing theatrically. "Fine. If you won't talk about her, let's talk about you." She tapped the dagger lightly against her chin as though deep in thought. "Why did you bind her to you, Luka? Why risk everything for a woman who was never truly yours?"

His silence stretched on, and the witch's patience frayed. She grabbed his chin with one hand, forcing him to meet her gaze. "Answer me," she hissed, the words sharp enough to draw blood.

Luka's eyes burned with defiance, even as her grip tightened. "Because I wanted to protect her," he said finally, barely masking his regret. "I thought binding her to me would shield her from what's coming. I thought I could save her from herself."

The witch's laughter was stinging and maniacal. "Save her from herself? Or from you?"

Luka didn't flinch, his stare unwavering. "From all of this," he said, voice steady despite the pain. "From people like you."

The witch released him with a derisive snort, stepping back. "Oh, Luka," she said, shaking her head. "You still cling to the illusion of being a savior," she said, full of disdain. "But you're nothing more than a placeholder, a shadow in a story that was never yours. And she? She's the catalyst."

"Do you know what she is, Luka? Do you know why she was born? Why she survived?"

Luka's throat tightened, but he didn't answer. The witch's smile widened, sensing his unease.

"She isn't merely a witch," the witch said, her voice a blend of awe and malice. "She's a force waiting to be unleashed, a keystone in a power structure you can't begin to fathom. And soon, she'll understand what you never could."

Dread curled in his gut, though he didn't let the fear show. "Then tell me. What is it you want?"

The witch straightened, brushing imaginary dust from her cloak as she turned her back on him. "Ophelia's blood carries answers you will never understand," she said, almost wistful. "But I will."

Her words hung in the air like a curse, as Luka's mind raced with questions. What could she mean? What answers could Ophelia's blood possibly hold? He clenched his fists tighter. "You're wrong," Luka growled, rough but fierce. "She's more than that. She's—"

"More than you'll ever deserve," the witch interrupted, her tone mocking. She stood, turning the dagger over in her hands. "But don't worry. You'll see soon enough. When she realizes what she truly is, she won't need you. She won't need anyone."

She paused by the door, her gaze flickering back to him. "But I'm curious, Luka. Do you think she knows? Do you think she'll forgive you when she learns what you've done? That you bound her out of selfishness, not love?"

Luka's chest labored with the effort of holding his anger in check. "I'll find a way," Luka said, unyielding. His gaze burned through the darkness, a flicker of light refusing to be snuffed out. "I always do."

TWENTY

The air in Mira's sanctuary was thick with the heady aroma of blooming frangipani, and the distant murmur of waves crashing against the island's shore reverberated around the space. The room was open to the warm evening breeze, its edges framed by flowing white curtains that danced like specters in the dim light. The polished stone floor felt cool against Ophelia's bare feet as she settled onto a circular mat.

Closing her eyes, she exhaled slowly, letting the world around her fade into the periphery. Mira had said this place held a unique energy, one capable of bridging the gap between the physical and the spiritual. Whether that was true, Ophelia couldn't say. But she needed answers, and she was willing to try anything.

The moonstone Mira had gifted her rested on the mat before her, its pale surface gleaming. She extended her hands, palms facing the sky. Her voice remained steady as she recited the incantation Mira had taught her, though her heart thudded nervously in her chest.

The first stirring of energy prickled against her skin, like the light touch of static electricity. Her lungs constricted as the sensation deepened, wrapping around her like invisible vines. And then, she felt the familiar pull—a magnetic force that seemed to tug at her very core.

When she opened her eyes, Galla Placidia stood before her, clad in flowing white robes that caught an ethereal light of their own. Her eyes sparkled with mischief as a knowing smile played at her lips.

"Nipotina," Galla said, tilting her head in feigned exasperation. "You're disturbing me again. Must you always?"

Ophelia let out a shaky breath, her relief overshadowed by frustration. "You always say that, yet here you are. Maybe your peace isn't as sacred as you claim."

Galla chuckled. "Audacious as ever. What do you want this time, little one?"

Ophelia straightened, meeting Galla's gaze head-on. "The Kala Ghanta. I need to find it."

For a moment, Galla said nothing, her expression unreadable. Then she began to pace, her bare feet gliding over the floor as if she weren't entirely bound by gravity. "Ah, the Bell. A relic of immense power, yet the supernaturals bicker over its location like children squabbling over a lost toy." She stopped, eyeing Ophelia. "Why should I help you find it?"

"Because if it falls into the wrong hands, it could end everything," Ophelia said, steady despite the knot tightening in her chest. "You've seen what's happening, haven't you? The Alliance is fracturing. The balance is breaking."

Galla sighed theatrically. "Always so dramatic, Ophelia. Fine, I'll help you. But only because watching you flail about, trying to decipher riddles, is getting tiresome." She leaned in, her voice dropping to a conspiratorial whisper. "The Bell is tied to ancient trade routes. Look to the Caribbean, to the paths carved by sailors and conquerors. The Bell rests where the old meets the new, though its keepers have long forgotten their charge."

Ophelia frowned, her mind racing to piece together the clue. "That's not much to go on."

"It's enough," Galla said. "You have magic, do you not? Use it."

Ophelia clenched her fists, but before she could respond, another thought surged to the forefront of her mind. This one was heavier and harder to ignore. "Why did you tell me Luka was my twin flame? At the Eye of the Earth, you said he would help me."

Galla's eyes narrowed on Ophelia. "Careful, nipotina. Words are powerful things. I told you that your twin flame would stand with you at the Eye of the Earth, and he did, did he not?"

A hollow ache opened in Ophelia's chest as the memory of Luka's final moments—his sacrifice, his unwavering devotion—flashed in her mind.

Galla stepped closer, her gaze unrelenting. "I said your twin flame would be there, yes. I did not say that *Luka* was your twin flame. You would do well to listen to what is said, not what you want to hear."

Doubt flickered through Ophelia, gnawing at the edges of her resolve. Was everything she believed about Luka—about herself—wrong? "Then who—"

"No more questions on that," Galla interrupted curtly. "Answers will become clear in time. For now, focus on the task at hand."

Ophelia's jaw tightened, but she nodded. "What else should I know?"

Galla's expression grew grave, her tone replaced with something far heavier. "Someone close to you will deceive you, nipotina. You must be vigilant. But remember, deception doesn't always mean malice. It is often the tool of desperation."

The warning sent a chill down Ophelia's spine, but she forced herself to stand taller. "And my mother? She's hiding something. What is it?"

Galla's bemused smile returned, though it was tinged with melancholy. "Your mother's secrets are hers to keep—for now. But trust me when I say this: One day, you may thank her for them."

Galla's words settled heavily on Ophelia, but before she could ask more, the air around her ancestor began to shimmer. Galla lifted her chin, a hint of mischief returning to her expression. "I've given you enough for now, nipotina. Use it wisely. And for heaven's sake, let me rest for a century before calling me again."

With a flourish of her hand, Galla vanished, the energy in the room dissipating like mist in the morning sun.

Ophelia remained seated, her mind churning with the enigmatic clues and warnings. Frustration warred with determination, but as she took a steadying breath, she resolved to trust her instincts and move forward.

The Bell of Time, deception, her mother's secrets—everything was connected. She just needed to find the threads that tied it all together.

THE SUN WAS SETTING, painting the ocean in streaks of molten gold and crimson. Waves lapped gently against the shore, their rhythmic whispers blending with the distant calls of seabirds. Ophelia followed the footprints in the sand, her heart heavy with the questions swirling in her mind. She had spent too long burying her feelings about her mother's absence, letting them fester into a quiet rage. But Galla's cryptic words had stirred something in her—a need for answers, no matter how painful.

She found Celeste sitting on a large driftwood log near the water's edge, her shoulders slouched as she stared out at the horizon. Her hair, a cascade of brown curls streaked with hints of gray, moved gently in the ocean breeze. For the first time, Celeste looked fragile, less like the powerful witch Ophelia had built up in her mind and more like a mother weighed down by years of secrets.

Ophelia approached cautiously, her bare feet sinking into the cool sand. She paused a few steps away, unsure of how to start. "You always seem so far away," she finally said, cutting through the quiet.

Celeste turned, her expression soft but wary. "Ophelia," she murmured, her tone a mix of surprise and relief. "I didn't hear you coming."

"That's because you're always lost in thought," Ophelia said, folding her arms. Her words carried more edge than she'd intended, but she didn't back down. "What are you thinking about this time? Or should I say, who?"

Celeste's lips pressed into a thin line, and she turned her gaze back to the ocean. "It's not that simple," she said after a moment.

Ophelia stepped closer, her frustration bubbling to the surface. "Nothing with you is simple, is it? I don't understand why you left. Why you abandoned me."

Celeste flinched at the word, but she didn't turn away. "Abandoned?" she repeated softly, the word sounding bitter in her mouth. "I never abandoned you, Ophelia. I left to protect you."

"From what?" Ophelia demanded. "You've had years to

explain, but you've never told me the truth. You just left me to figure it all out on my own."

Celeste sighed, her shoulders slumping further. "If I had stayed, you wouldn't be standing here today. Powerful forces were hurting our family, and I was the only thing standing in their way. Staying would have painted a target on your back."

"Maybe I would've preferred that!" Ophelia's voice cracked with emotion. "At least then I wouldn't have spent my whole life wondering why I wasn't enough for you to stay."

Celeste's head snapped up, her eyes shimmering. "You were more than enough," she said fiercely. "There are very few things in this world that could keep me from my first-born daughter. But keeping you alive was one of them."

Ophelia froze, something inside her cracking at the raw emotion in Celeste's voice. It wasn't enough to erase the years of pain, but it was a crack in the armor she had built around her heart. "If you were trying to protect me, why didn't you tell me anything when you came back? Why are you still keeping secrets from me?"

Celeste hesitated, her gaze falling to the sand. "Because some truths are more dangerous than the lies that replace them," she said quietly. "I've made mistakes, Ophelia. I've been reckless with my own life, but I couldn't afford to be reckless with yours."

"And my father?" Ophelia pressed. "Who was he? Why can't you tell me anything about him?"

Celeste's jaw tightened, and she shook her head. "I can't answer that," she said firmly. "To do so would risk everything. Your safety. Your future."

Ophelia felt the familiar sting of frustration, but before she could lash out, Celeste continued. "I can tell you this much: Your father is not an ordinary man. He is extraordinary in ways that terrify me. I left for you, Ophelia, but also because of him.

Because he would have destroyed us both, even if he didn't mean to." Celeste's lips parted slightly, brushing a stray hair from Ophelia's face. "There's so much I want to tell you, but I can't—not yet."

"That's convenient," Ophelia muttered, stepping back. "You say you're protecting me, but it feels like you're punishing me instead. Punishing me for something I didn't even do." Ophelia knew she was being stubborn, but she couldn't let go of the part of her that hurt so deeply. *Where had her mother been all these years?*

Celeste's expression softened as her hand fell to her side. "I don't expect you to understand, and I don't expect you to forgive me. But I never stopped loving you, Ophelia. Not for a single moment." The words carried years of regret. "I only hope we can find our way back to each other."

Ophelia stared at her mother, her heart a tumult of emotions—anger, sadness, hope. "I don't know if I can forgive you," she admitted. "Not yet."

Celeste nodded, her eyes glistening with unshed tears. "When you're ready, I'll be here."

They stood in silence for a moment, the sound of the ocean filling the space between them. The tension hadn't disappeared, but it felt lighter, as if a thread of understanding had begun to weave itself through the rift between them.

As Ophelia turned to leave, she glanced back at her mother, still seated on the driftwood. The sunset bathed Celeste in hues of gold and orange. For a brief moment, Ophelia saw not the enigmatic witch, but a woman burdened by impossible choices.

TWENTY-ONE

As the sun rose, brushing the waves with soft hues of pink and gold, Ophelia sprinted along the shoreline. Her labored breaths blended with the ocean's constant song. Gabriel ran ahead of her, his pace effortless, his steps barely leaving imprints in the wet sand. He turned his head just enough to smirk at her, a glint of challenge in his dark eyes.

"Come on, Cinis," he called, voice carrying over the sound of the waves. "Is that all you've got?"

Ophelia gritted her teeth, refusing to let him see how much her legs ached or her lungs burned. "I'm letting you win," she shot back, pushing herself harder.

Gabriel's laughter rolled through the air, warm and infuriating. "Is that so? Because it looks like you're struggling to keep up."

The shifting sand made her movements clumsy, a stark contrast to Gabriel's smooth strides. Her magic buzzed, tempting her to cheat, but she resisted. This was about proving something to him and to herself.

The gap between them closed as the beach curved sharply. Gabriel slowed just enough for her to catch up, though his grin made it clear he wasn't taking her seriously. Ophelia shoved past him, her shoulder brushing against his, and for a brief, triumphant moment, she was ahead.

"Not bad," Gabriel admitted, his tone more approving now. "But let's see how you handle this."

Without warning, he veered off the shoreline toward a rocky outcrop. Ophelia hesitated for half a second before following, her focus narrowing to the challenge ahead. The rocks were slick with sea spray, the footing treacherous, but Gabriel scaled them with the ease of someone who had been doing this for centuries.

"Showoff," she muttered under her breath as she hauled herself up after him.

"Less talking, more climbing," he teased, offering her a hand as she struggled to find purchase on a particularly slippery ledge. She ignored it, shooting him a glare before pulling herself up on her own. His laughter echoed above her.

When they finally reached the top, the view stole her breath more effectively than the run had. The ocean stretched out endlessly, the rising sun igniting the waves in a dance of gold and silver hues. Gabriel stood at the edge of the cliff, the wind ruffling his dark hair as he turned to look at her.

"Beautiful, isn't it?" he said softly, his usual teasing replaced by something quieter, more reflective.

Ophelia nodded, unable to find the words to describe the way the sight made her feel—small, yet connected to something vast and infinite.

But the moment didn't last.

"All right," Gabriel said, turning back to her with a glint in his eye. "Now we train."

"Train?" she echoed, barely catching her breath. "After that?"

"You're warmed up," he said with a shrug, as if it were the most obvious thing in the world. "Perfect time for combat training."

Ophelia groaned but followed him to a flat stretch of ground farther inland. Gabriel turned to face her, his stance relaxed but predatory. "Show me what you've got."

"I'm not in the mood for your games," she said, crossing her arms over her chest.

"This isn't a game, Ophelia," he said, his tone hardening. "You have power, but you need control. And you need to be able to defend yourself without relying on magic. If you can't do that, you'll be vulnerable."

The words hit their mark. Luka had taught her the same thing. She dropped into a fighting stance, her feet braced against the uneven ground. Gabriel nodded approvingly, then darted forward with a speed that took her by surprise. She barely managed to sidestep his attack, her heart racing as she turned to face him again.

"Too slow," he said, circling her like a predator stalking its prey. "Anticipate my movements. Don't just react."

She focused on his body, the subtle shifts in his weight, the way his eyes flicked toward her shoulder before he struck. This time, she blocked his blow, her arm absorbing the force of his attack. A spark of satisfaction flared in her chest.

"Better," he said, his lips curving into a grin. "But you're still thinking too much. Trust your instincts."

The sparring intensified, their movements faster and more fluid. Gabriel pushed her to her limits, his attacks relentless but controlled. Ophelia felt the strain in her muscles, the sting of sweat in her eyes, but she didn't back down. Each time she blocked or dodged an attack, a little more confidence settled into her bones.

Finally, Gabriel stepped back, holding up a hand. "Enough."

Ophelia straightened, her chest heaving as she wiped her brow. "Was that satisfactory, Your Majesty?" she panted, a smile tugging at her lips.

Gabriel chuckled, tossing her a water bottle he'd brought from the villa. "You're getting there," he said, voice humming with approval. "But don't let it go to your head. You've still got a long way to go."

Ophelia took a long drink, the cool water soothing her parched throat. She felt a flicker of pride at his words, even if she wouldn't admit it out loud.

As they made their way back down the rocks, the sun climbing higher in the sky, she realized that the tension coiled in her chest had loosened, if only a little.

They wound their way to the library, a quiet refuge tucked away in one of the secluded wings of the villa. Sunlight poured in through tall arched windows, illuminating the rows of ancient books and casting golden patterns on the polished wooden floor. The scent of aged paper mingled with the salty tang of the ocean breeze that drifted through the open windows.

The library was filled with ancient texts in languages only Mo could decipher. Yet, they were all assigned the task of searching for clues about the Bell's location in the Caribbean, assuming Galla's vague answer could even be trusted. Ophelia ran her fingers along the spines of the books, reading their titles aloud. "*The Mysteries of Chronomancy, Navigating Temporal Magic, The Secrets of the Kala Ghanta...*"

She pulled one off the shelf, its leather cover cracked with age. As she opened it, the scent of old parchment filled the air.

Gabriel, lounging at a nearby table with his feet up, watched her with a lazy grin.

"Find anything useful, Cinis?" he asked, voice a mix of amusement and curiosity.

"Maybe," she said, flipping through the pages. The text was in an ancient script she could barely decipher. "Though it'd help if I could actually read this."

Gabriel stood, crossing the room with his characteristic grace. "Let me see."

He leaned over her shoulder, his breath warm against her neck as he scanned the text. Ophelia's pulse quickened, though she told herself it was from the exertion of the morning. His proximity was distracting in a way she wasn't ready to admit.

"It's Old Latin," he said after a moment. "Something about the Bell being a key to balancing time. But the rest is metaphorical, as usual."

Ophelia groaned, closing the book with a thud. "Why can't anyone in this world just say what they mean?"

Gabriel chuckled, the sound low and warm. "Where's the fun in that?"

She turned to face him, her frustration evident. "This isn't funny, Gabriel. We need answers. This Bell could be the key to stopping whatever's coming, and all we have are riddles and half-truths. As usual."

Gabriel's expression softened, his teasing fading as he met her gaze. "We'll figure it out, Ophelia. We always do."

The sincerity in his voice caught her off guard, and for a moment, she forgot about the books, the Bell, and everything else. It was just them, standing in the quiet of the library, the sunlight casting a golden halo around them.

"I don't know how you do it," she said, quieter now. "How you stay so calm when everything feels like it's falling apart."

Gabriel's lips curved into a small, almost wistful smile. "I've had centuries to practice."

Ophelia's laugh was soft, almost reluctant. "That doesn't make me feel any better."

"Then let me try something else," he said, his tone shifting. There was a hint of mischief in his eyes now, but also something deeper, something that made her breath catch.

Before she could respond, he leaned in, his hand brushing against hers on the edge of the table. The touch was light, almost hesitant, but it sent a jolt through her. She looked up at him, her pulse hammering in her ears.

"Gabriel..." she began, but words failed her.

He didn't say anything, but he didn't need to. The way he looked at her, like she was the only thing that mattered, said enough. Slowly, he reached down, his fingers brushing a strand of hair from her face. The gesture was so tender, so unlike the Gabriel she knew, that it left her feeling unmoored.

"I know you're scared," he said softly. "But you're not alone in this. You never have to be alone."

Her throat tightened, and for a moment, she thought she might cry. Instead, she leaned into his touch, letting herself believe his words, if only for a moment.

The library seemed to fade around them, the world narrowing to just the two of them. Gabriel tilted his head, his gaze dropping to her lips. Her heart raced, her body caught between anticipation and fear.

But before either of them could move, the sound of a book falling shattered the moment. They broke apart, both turning toward the noise. A stray gust from the open window had knocked over a stack of books and papers on a nearby table.

Ophelia cleared her throat, stepping back and smoothing her hands over her clothes. "We should get back to work," she said, a little too brisk.

Gabriel hesitated, then nodded, his usual smirk returning, though it didn't quite reach his eyes. "Of course, Cinis. Back to saving the world."

THE AFTERNOON SUNLIGHT HAD SHIFTED, casting long shadows across the library floor. The room had grown quieter, save for the occasional rustle of turning pages or the creak of Gabriel's chair as he leaned back, his boots propped on the edge of the table. They'd been combing through texts for hours, finding little more than frustrating fragments of knowledge about the Kala Ghanta.

Ophelia sat cross-legged on the floor amidst a growing pile of discarded books. She flipped through another ancient tome, muttering under her breath about obscure authors and their obsession with riddles. Gabriel, now watching her with an amused expression, finally broke the silence.

"You know," he began, "I don't think the Bell's mysteries will unfold through sheer force of will."

Ophelia shot him a glare but couldn't help the small smile tugging at her lips. "And I suppose you have a better method?"

He leaned forward, elbows on his knees, his dark eyes glinting. "Patience."

"Patience," she repeated, rolling her eyes. "From the man who can barely sit still."

Gabriel's laugh was soft, genuine. "Fair point, Cinis."

She looked at him, her smile fading as she took in the relaxed curve of his lips and the way the sunlight played across his sculpted features. It struck her, not for the first time, how easily he could disarm her with just a look, a laugh, or a single word. He wasn't supposed to feel safe, yet somehow, he did.

"You never told me," she said, interrupting the quiet,

finally breaking down and asking. "Why do you call me that? Cinis."

Gabriel's expression shifted, softening as he met her gaze. "Ashes," he said simply. "Because that's what you rose from, Ophelia. You've been burned, broken, and beaten down, but you keep rising. Stronger. Fiercer. Like a phoenix rising from the ashes."

Her breath hitched, her chest tightening as his words sank in. She looked down, unable to hold his gaze, her fingers twisting in her lap. "Sometimes I don't feel like I'm rising. Most days, it feels like I'm still burning."

Gabriel stood, crossing the room to crouch in front of her. He tilted her chin up with a single finger, forcing her to meet his eyes. "That's because the fire isn't finished with you yet," he said, voice low and steady. "But it won't consume you, Ophelia. It'll forge you."

His words struck something deep within her, something raw and vulnerable. She swallowed hard, blinking against the sudden sting of tears. "You make it sound so simple."

"It's not," he admitted. "But you don't have to face it alone."

The air between them was electric, charged with an unspoken tension neither of them could ignore any longer. Gabriel's hand lingered on her chin, his thumb brushing her jawline in a touch so gentle it made her ache. She wanted to say something, to break the moment, but words failed her.

"Ophelia," he murmured, her name a reverent whisper.

Her name on his lips sent a shiver down her spine. The way he said it, like a prayer and a plea, sent a tremor through her. She searched his face, her defenses faltering under the sincerity in his eyes. For once, there were no masks, no smirks or barriers, just raw vulnerability.

Instead of speaking, she let herself act. Closing the distance between them, she leaned in and brushed her lips to his in a tentative kiss. It was hesitant at first, testing the boundaries of what they were both willing to give.

Gabriel responded immediately, his hand sliding to the back of her neck, pulling her closer as the kiss deepened. His lips moved against hers, firm yet gentle, as though he was memorizing her. The world around them disappeared.

Her hands found the hem of his shirt, gripping it tightly as she pushed him back into the chair. Gabriel arched an eyebrow in amusement, but he didn't resist. His gaze smoldered as she leaned over him, her body tantalizingly close. The low cut of her shirt made her breasts spill forward, and his hands moved instinctively, reaching for her.

But she swatted his hands away. "Not yet," she teased, sinking to her knees between his legs.

His breath caught as she reached for his belt, unfastening it with deliberate slowness. Her eyes never left his, a silent challenge flickering in her gaze. When she freed him from his pants, his cock stood thick and ready, and she leaned forward, letting her tongue run along the length of him.

"Ophelia..." Gabriel growled, rough and barely contained.

She took him in her hand, her fingers wrapping firmly around the base as her tongue circled the sensitive head. Gabriel let out a shuddering breath, his hand coming to her hair, tangling in it as she began to bob her head. Her movements were slow at first, teasing, her lips gliding over him as she stroked the rest of his length with her hand.

"Good girl," he rasped, his grip tightening in her hair as she quickened her pace. "Taking my cock so perfectly...fuck, Ophelia."

She could feel him tense beneath her touch, the salty taste of his pre-cum proof of how close he was. But just as he began to tremble, his release imminent, Gabriel pulled her head back with a firm tug on her hair.

She let out a frustrated whimper, her lips parted in protest, but he hushed her with a devilish grin.

"Not yet," he said, thick with restraint. "I've had centuries to learn control. And right now, I need to feel you ride me."

Her cheeks flushed, heat pooling low in her stomach as his words settled over her. She turned away from him, slowly lowering her workout shorts and bending at the waist, exposing herself to his hungry gaze. Gabriel leaned forward, his breath warm against her as he parted her with his tongue, tasting her.

"Perfect," he muttered, reverent.

When she turned back to face him, she found his eyes dark with desire, fixed on her. "Lose the rest," he commanded, his tone leaving no room for argument. "I want you bare. I want you riding me with nothing between us."

She swallowed hard, her body clenching with anticipation as she peeled off her top and bra, standing before him completely exposed. The risk of their location—a public library, the possibility of being caught—only heightened her arousal.

She climbed onto his lap, positioning herself over him as he held her steady. Slowly, she lowered herself onto his cock, her body stretching to accommodate him as she sank to the base. Gabriel groaned, his hands gripping her hips tightly as he pulled her closer.

"Fuck, Ophelia," he murmured against her neck, his teeth grazing her skin.

Her movements were slow at first, rolling her hips against him as his hands roamed her body. One hand found her breast, his fingers pinching one nipple while his mouth claimed the other, his tongue and teeth sending sparks of pleasure coursing through her.

Her pace quickened, the friction of her clit against him driving her higher and higher. When she finally came, her release tore through her like a wave, and she cried out his name, her nails digging into his shoulders.

But Gabriel wasn't done. He grabbed her hips, adjusting her angle as he thrust up into her, hitting a spot that made her vision blur. Another orgasm built quickly, crashing over her as he followed, his release spilling inside her as his teeth scraped her neck, claiming her in a way that felt primal and possessive.

She slumped against him, her body trembling from the lingering echoes of her release. Gabriel's arms wrapped around her, holding her close as their breathing slowed.

"You're unbelievable," she murmured against his chest.

He chuckled, the sound low and satisfied. "And you're everything, Cinis."

TWENTY-TWO

The library was dimly lit, the soft glow of a nearby lamp casting warm light over the ancient tomes scattered on the table. The air was thick with unspoken tension, but for once, it wasn't the kind that gnawed at Ophelia's nerves. Gabriel stood close behind where Ophelia sat, his fingers tracing the edge of a book, the warmth of his presence both distracting and grounding.

"Ophelia," he murmured, low enough that only she could hear, "you're thinking too much."

She turned to meet his gaze, ready to retort, when the heavy doors of the library burst open, slamming against the stone walls with a resounding thud.

"Seriously?" Ophelia muttered, snapping her head toward the noise.

Brisa stormed in, arms laden with books, followed closely by Mo, who balanced a precarious stack of maps and scrolls. Celeste entered last, her movements graceful but purposeful.

"You have to see this," Brisa said, a mix of excitement and urgency. "My dad found something."

Celeste crossed the room, her movements controlled, though her eyes were alight with excitement. "The Kala Ghanta's origins," she added, her tone measured.

The air in the library was thick with anticipation as Mo unfolded the delicate parchment he'd brought with him. The pages bore intricate Sanskrit characters that shimmered, as though imbued with ancient magic. He cleared his throat, drawing everyone's attention.

"This text," Mo began, tracing the characters with a steady finger, "is a chronicle written by a faction of witches during the creation of the Bell of Time. It's more than a historical account. It's a map and a warning."

Ophelia leaned forward, her irritation at the interruption now replaced by curiosity. Gabriel stood beside her, arms crossed, watching Mo with a calm intensity.

Mo continued, his tone grave. "The text confirms that the Bell cannot be near the Indian Ocean. It was never designed to function in regions dominated by fire and earth elements. The Bell's magic is tied to water and air; its essence thrives in balance. The Indian Ocean, with its volcanic energy, would destabilize the artifact. Instead, the text speaks of ancient currents that lead to the Caribbean Sea."

"Exactly where Galla said it would be," Ophelia said quietly.

Celeste furrowed her brow, gesturing to the map they'd spread across the table. "The Caribbean? Do we have any more specifics?"

Mo nodded, his expression tightening. "The text references an island that matches the description of a place on this map." He pointed to a small dot labeled *Isla del Aquelarre*. "It's isolated, rich in supernatural history, and was a hub for trade and exploration centuries ago. If the Bell is anywhere, I think it's here. Isla del Aquelarre."

The name sent a ripple of unease through the room.

Gabriel stepped forward, his brow pulled together. "Coven Island," he said, heavy with suspicion.

Mo nodded. "Roughly translated, yes. The name itself suggests a gathering place for witches, but the supernatural energy there is said to be incredibly potent. The island was used as a sanctuary during ancient conflicts, and it's rumored that several powerful artifacts were hidden there."

Brisa plopped down in a chair next to Ophelia, her eyes lit with interest. "It makes sense. The Caribbean trade routes were pivotal for supernatural factions. If they wanted to keep the Bell away from prying eyes, they'd hide it somewhere like this."

Ophelia's fingers grazed the edge of the map as her eyes roamed over the delicate ink work. The small, unassuming island sat surrounded by vast blue waters, a world apart. "How certain are you about this?"

Mo adjusted his glasses, lips twitching. "Quite certain," he said.

"Then what's the plan?" she asked.

Celeste placed a hand on the map, commanding the room. "We find a way to get there. Quietly. If the Bell is on Isla del Aquelarre, it's only a matter of time before someone else realizes it, too."

"And when they do," Brisa added, devoid of emotion, "they won't be as interested in destroying it as we are."

Gabriel's expression darkened. "If they're not already on their way."

Mo cleared his throat again, breaking the silence. "There's more," he said, his tone heavier now. "This text doesn't just point us to the Bell's location. It also describes the cost of destroying it."

Ophelia's stomach twisted. "Cost?"

Mo hesitated, his fingers brushing the edges of the page as though reluctant to share. "The Kala Ghanta can't simply be destroyed. It demands a sacrifice. A supernatural must go back to the moment of its creation and tether themselves to it. Once they do, they can never return. The sacrifice would effectively trap the Bell in a temporal loop, preventing it from ever being used again."

The room went still, the implications sinking in.

Brisa leaned back in her chair, twirling a strand of hair between her fingers. "So what happens to the Bell then? Does it just implode?"

Mo glanced at her, his expression weary but resolute. "Once the Bell accepts the sacrifice, its magic is drained completely. It becomes inert. Silent, lifeless. It will never work again. And no one—not even the one who made the sacrifice—can undo what's been done."

Brisa frowned, her fingers tapping her arm in frustration. "So it just sits there? All that power, locked away forever?"

"Yes," Mo said quietly. "But that's the point. It's the only way to ensure it can never be used again, by anyone."

"You're saying whoever destroys the Bell," Ophelia began, "will be trapped in the past. Forever."

Mo nodded solemnly. "Yes."

Brisa's face darkened. "So we're looking for someone with a death wish?"

"No," Mo replied firmly. "We're looking for someone with courage. The sacrifice wouldn't just destroy the Bell. It would undoubtedly save countless lives."

The room fell silent again. The enormity of the decision loomed over them, unspoken but understood.

Ophelia clenched her fists, her nails biting crescent moons into her palms. She could feel the tension in the room shift, her own thoughts spiraling. The idea of sacrifice wasn't new to her, but the thought of volunteering herself—or worse, asking someone she cared about—made her stomach churn.

Brisa broke the silence. "We need to focus on getting to Isla del Aquelarre first. We can't do anything until we locate the Bell."

Celeste nodded, her expression resolute. "Agreed. We'll need to prepare for whatever we find there."

Ophelia glanced at Gabriel, his jaw tight and eyes unreadable. She wondered if he was thinking the same thing she was—that the cost of this mission might be higher than any of them could bear.

His jaw clenched, his hands curling into fists at his sides. "Who created this thing?" he asked.

Mo glanced at Celeste, then back at the text. "A coven of witches created it. It was meant to manipulate time, reverse catastrophic events, or stop wars before they began. But, as with all power, it became a weapon. When the witches realized what they'd created, they tried to undo it. But the Bell wouldn't allow itself to be unmade."

"Why not destroy it outright?" Brisa asked, her tone skeptical.

"Because of the tethering spell," Mo explained. "It binds itself to its creator, or anyone who attempts to wield it. The sacrifice ensures that the Bell's power is neutralized without releasing its energy into the world. It's the only way to stop it permanently."

Ophelia stared at the map, the island's jagged outline seemed more menacing now, more dangerous. The thought of someone she cared about—someone like Gabriel—being sacrificed to destroy the Bell made her chest tighten painfully.

"And if we don't destroy it?" she asked, already fearing the answer.

Mo's gaze was steady, unflinching. "Then whoever finds it

first could use it to rewrite history. Entire civilizations could be undone. Wars could be started—or erased. The balance of the world would be shattered."

The revelation cast a heavy shadow over them.

Finally, Gabriel spoke, cutting through the stillness. "Then we'd better make sure we get there first."

The determination in his tone ignited a sense of resolve in Ophelia. She straightened her spine, her jaw tightening as she nodded.

Brisa was already gathering the scattered books, her movements quick and efficient. "We'll need supplies. A way to reach the island without drawing attention."

"I'll handle that," Celeste said. "I know people who can help."

"And the rest of us?" Ophelia asked.

Mo gave her a small, encouraging smile. "We prepare. This isn't just a search anymore. It's a race."

As the group began to disperse, the air in the room remained charged with unspoken fears and unvoiced doubts. Ophelia lingered by the map, her fingers brushing the faded ink as she tried to imagine what awaited them on Isla del Aquelarre.

Gabriel's voice broke her reverie. "We'll figure it out," he said softly.

Ophelia nodded, her resolve hardening. "We have no choice."

For now, the only path forward was clear: They had to find the Bell. And they had to destroy it—no matter the cost.

TWENTY-THREE

The low hum of the private jet quieted as the wheels hit the tarmac, jolting Ophelia from her restless thoughts. Through the small window, the lush landscape of Isla del Aquelarre unfolded before her as if conjured from myth. Vivid greens of dense jungle framed the narrow runway, while beyond, the turquoise waters of the Caribbean sparkled under a sun that seemed too bright, too perfect.

Between the edges of the jungle and the ocean, she caught glimpses of crumbling buildings, their once-majestic facades now weathered and overtaken by vines, standing as silent reminders of the island's faded grandeur. The island was now inhabited by both supernaturals and mortals who had forged a fragile coexistence amid the ruins. Its beauty was almost disarming, but to Ophelia, it felt like a mask, hiding something she couldn't yet name.

Her fingers brushed the edge of her sunglasses as she adjusted them, shielding her eyes from more than just the sun. The tension that had coiled in her chest since they left Nivara Island refused to loosen. She tried to brush it off as travel fatigue or the oppressive humidity that she could already feel creeping through the plane's sealed cabin, but she wasn't so sure.

Outside, the others disembarked and moved with practiced efficiency. Celeste and Mo were already organizing the unloading of supplies, their movements decisive and purposeful. Brisa stood a few paces away, her posture casual, but her eyes roved over the surroundings like a predator assessing its territory. Alex lingered near her, looking uneasy, glancing from the jungle to the sky as if expecting something to go wrong at any moment.

Ophelia stayed in her seat, gaze fixed on the jungle's edge. The island thrummed with an energy that seemed to press against her skin, almost humming beneath it. It wasn't unpleasant, but it was unsettling, like a barely distinguishable whisper she couldn't quite make out.

"You all right?" Gabriel's voice broke through her reverie.

Ophelia turned to see him standing at the top of the stairs, his dark eyes fixed on her with a familiar intensity. His broad frame cast a shadow into the cabin, and she suddenly felt very small in her seat.

She nodded, forcing a smile. "Yeah. Just the heat, I guess."

Gabriel raised an eyebrow, his skepticism clear, but he didn't press her. Instead, he extended a hand toward her. For a moment, she hesitated, staring at the hand as if it might somehow make her feelings too visible. Then, with a quiet sigh, she slipped her fingers into his and let him pull her to her feet.

The moment she stepped outside, the air wrapped around her like a wet blanket—thick with humidity and the scent of salt and vegetation. It was almost suffocating, yet it buzzed with life.

Her boots hit the cracked runway, and the peculiar hum

beneath her skin intensified. It was subtle but impossible to ignore, as though the island itself was greeting her.

"Feel that?" Brisa's voice came from her side, soft but tinged with awe.

Ophelia glanced at her cousin, who had appeared seemingly out of nowhere, her angular features highlighted by the sunlight. "It's like the whole place is breathing," Ophelia murmured, her words half question, half realization.

Brisa tilted her head toward the jungle. "It's pulsing with magic," she said, her usually sarcastic tone momentarily absent.

The words sent a chill down Ophelia's spine despite the heat. That was exactly it. She scanned the jungle for any sign of movement, but there was nothing, just the restless stir of the jungle and the distant call of birds.

The group gathered near the edge of the tarmac, the plane behind them a lifeless silhouette against the vibrant backdrop of Isla del Aquelarre. The sun blazed overhead, its rays unrelenting as sweat beaded on everyone's brows. Mo stood at the center of their huddle, a map unfurled in his hands, its edges curling slightly in the humid air.

Ophelia shifted as her unease settled deeper. Her gaze flickered to Celeste, who stood a few paces away with her arms crossed, her face as unreadable as ever. Brisa leaned against a stack of crates, her sparkling pink nails catching the light as she examined them with exaggerated nonchalance.

Mo's voice broke the uneasy quiet. "If the Kala Ghanta is here, we'll feel its power the closer we get. A magical artifact of that magnitude can't exist without leaving some sort of signature."

Ophelia barely registered his words. The buzz coursing through her had grown more pronounced, like an itch she couldn't scratch. The island's magic seemed to weave through the air, brushing against her senses, drawing her focus to the jungle as though it were trying to tell her something.

"So basically," Brisa said, dryly, "we're just wandering around the jungle, hoping we trip over it?"

"Pretty much," Mo replied, not looking up from the map.

Brisa sighed dramatically, her fingers drumming against the crate. "Excellent plan. Truly inspiring."

Alex, who had been standing quietly nearby, finally spoke up. "Where do we start?"

Mo's finger traced a line on the map, stopping at a marked point. "There's an old post on the northern tip of the island. It's been abandoned for decades, but it used to belong to a powerful coven. If they were involved with hiding the Bell, it's the most likely place to start."

"Why would they hide it there?" Ophelia asked, forcing herself to focus on the conversation.

"Seclusion," Celeste said, calm and measured. "This island is isolated, and its natural magic would make it difficult for anyone to find the Bell unless they knew exactly what they were looking for."

"And how long will it take to get there?" Gabriel asked.

Mo straightened, folding the map carefully. "A half day's trek, maybe more. The terrain's rough, and the jungle's thicker the farther north we go."

"Perfect," Brisa muttered, pushing off the crate and adjusting her ponytail. "I just love hiking through sweltering jungles with nothing but mosquitoes for company."

"We need to move," Celeste cut in, her tone brooking no argument. "The longer we wait, the greater the risk that someone else finds it first."

Ophelia adjusted her stance, gaze drifting back to the jungle. The pull she'd been feeling all morning was stronger now, almost insistent. She wondered if anyone else felt it or if it was just her, a thread connecting her to something she couldn't yet name.

As the group began to move, Gabriel fell into step beside her, eyes scanning the surroundings with quiet precision. "You okay?" he asked for the second time that day.

Ophelia nodded, though the tension in her chest hadn't eased. "I'm fine," she said, though even she didn't believe it.

The jungle swallowed them whole, its dense foliage closing in like the walls of an ancient cathedral. Every step forward felt like breaking into a sacred, untamed world, one where the rules of civilization held no sway. The air was thick with the scent of damp earth and blooming flowers, each breath heavy with humidity that clung to their skin. The sun filtered through the canopy in fragmented beams, creating shifting patterns of light and shadow on the ground beneath their feet.

Ophelia fell into step behind Celeste, her senses on high alert. Each whisper of shifting foliage or snap of a twig set her heart racing. Insects buzzed, tormenting her and a constant reminder of the jungle's vitality. But what unnerved her most was the pull of magic beneath it all, a constant thrumming that seemed to emanate from the very soil, seeping into her with every step.

"Watch your footing," Mo muttered, glancing over his shoulder as he navigated the uneven terrain with the map clutched in one hand. "The path gets rough from here."

"What path?" Brisa shot back. She swatted at a mosquito with an annoyed flick of her hand, her usual acerbic wit dulled by the crushing heat. "This is less of a path and more of a suggestion."

Despite her cousin's grumbling, Ophelia couldn't ignore the beauty around her. The jungle's vibrant greenery pulsed with unseen energy. Vines twisted like serpents around towering trees, their leaves glistening with moisture. Flowers bloomed in bursts of red and orange, their colors so vivid they seemed almost unnatural. Birds called out from the canopy above, their cries echoing through the dense underbrush.

Gabriel was a steadying force beside her. He moved with the ease of someone who had faced worse terrain, dark eyes scanning their surroundings with quiet vigilance. His hand rested casually on the hilt of his blade, but Ophelia could see the tension in his posture. He was on edge, and that only heightened her own unease.

As they pressed deeper into the jungle, the pull Ophelia had been feeling grew stronger. It was like a thread wrapped around her chest, tugging her forward with increasing urgency. Her magic responded instinctively, a hum beneath her skin that she couldn't ignore.

She stopped abruptly, eyes narrowing as she scanned the trees around them.

"What is it?" Gabriel asked, voice low.

"I don't know," Ophelia murmured, her gaze darting from shadow to shadow. "It's like someone's here. Watching us."

Gabriel stiffened. "Do you see anything?" he asked.

"No," she admitted, frustration creeping into her tone. "But I can feel it. It's...familiar, somehow."

Celeste, who had been leading the group, paused and turned back to them. Her expression was calm, but her steely eyes betrayed her wariness. "Stay focused," she said. "This part of the island isn't as uninhabited as it looks."

Her words sent a chill down Ophelia's spine, despite the smothering heat. She exchanged a glance with Gabriel, whose jaw was set in a grim line.

The group continued on, their movements slower now, more deliberate. The jungle seemed to grow denser with each step, the undergrowth pressing closer as if it were trying to keep them out.

Ophelia's mind raced as she walked, her senses tuned to every sound, every shift in the air. The pull of the island's magic was almost overwhelming now, tugging at her like an invisible hand. It felt deeply personal, as if the island itself recognized her.

But that was impossible.

Wasn't it?

The jungle's density seemed to reach a crescendo as they moved further into its depths, the air growing heavier with each passing moment. The sunlight that had once dappled the forest floor was now almost completely swallowed by the canopy, leaving their path shrouded in a dim, green-tinted haze. Every step was a struggle against the thick underbrush, vines clinging to their legs as if trying to pull them back.

Ophelia's magic was restless now, thrumming with an intensity she couldn't ignore. It wasn't just the island anymore —it was something else, something specific. A presence, distant but unmistakable, brushing against the edges of her awareness.

And then, as if the jungle itself had taken a breath, the ceaseless noise of birds and insects fell silent.

Ophelia froze, her body going rigid as her ears strained to catch a sound—any sound—but there was nothing. Just the muffled rustle of leaves in the breeze and the sound of her own heartbeat pounding in her ears.

"Do you hear that?" she whispered to Gabriel, who had stopped a step behind her.

"Hear what?" he asked, voice low but edged with concern.

"That's just it," Ophelia said. "There's nothing."

Gabriel's dark eyes narrowed, his hand tightening on the hilt of his blade. "Stay close," he said, his tone leaving no room for argument.

The rest of the group continued ahead, oblivious to the

eerie stillness. But Ophelia's attention was elsewhere. Her gaze was drawn to the left, to a cluster of trees where something shimmered in the distance. It was like light reflecting off water, a flicker of movement at the edge of her vision.

"I'll catch up," she murmured, already stepping off the path before Gabriel could stop her.

"Ophelia, wait—" he started, but she was already moving, her magic pulling her forward like an invisible thread.

The jungle seemed to close in around her as she veered off the trail, the air growing thicker and more suffocating with each step. The shimmering light ahead grew brighter, almost beckoning her, and she quickened her pace, her heartbeat thundering in her chest.

And then she saw it.

The clearing was small, almost impossibly so, as though the jungle had reluctantly made space for what stood at its center. A figure cloaked in dark fabric loomed there, their silhouette malignant against the shadows. The cloak rippled unnaturally, like smoke caught in a breeze that didn't exist.

But it wasn't the cloak that froze Ophelia in her tracks.

It was the face.

Her face.

Not an exact replica, but close enough to make her stomach twist. The woman's features were more severe, her scorching yellow-green eyes glowing faintly in the dim light. Her midnight-black hair was cut shorter and pulled back, her tanned skin shimmering with an almost otherworldly sheen. Confidence and danger radiated from her, the unnatural twist of her lips both familiar and alien.

"Who are you?" Ophelia demanded, voice steady despite the racing of her heart.

The woman tilted her head slightly, studying her with

unsettling intensity. "Who are *you*?" she mimicked, smooth and unnervingly similar to Ophelia's.

Ophelia's fingers curled into fists, her magic flaring beneath her skin. "I asked you first."

The woman's grin widened, her glowing eyes cold and calculating. "You've felt it since you landed, haven't you? The pull. The connection."

"What are you talking about?" Ophelia snapped, her lithe body tensed, ready for anything.

The woman stepped closer, her movements impossibly fluid. "We share the same blood. The same power."

A cold realization settled over Ophelia, her chest tightening. "What are you saying?"

The woman's words dripped with disdain. "Think about it. Why else would you feel drawn to this island? To me?" she asked.

Ophelia's magic surged, her instincts screaming at her to act, to protect herself.

The woman laughed, a low, chilling sound that sent a shiver down Ophelia's spine. "You really have no idea, do you? How quaint."

Before Ophelia could respond, the woman moved with inhuman speed, gliding across the clearing as though she were weightless. One moment she was several feet away, and the next she was standing directly in front of Ophelia, her hand raised as though to touch her face.

Ophelia reacted instinctively. Her magic burst forth in a wave of golden and red light, slamming into the woman and sending her staggering back. The force of it rippled through the clearing, rattling the treetops and sending a few small branches crashing to the ground.

The woman regained her balance effortlessly, brushing herself off as though she were more amused than hurt. "You've got fire," she admitted, her lips curling with something unreadable. "But it won't be enough."

Ophelia clenched her fists tighter, her jaw set. "Who are you?" she demanded again.

The woman's expression grew darker. "You'll find out soon enough," she said, tone laced with menace. "But not today."

Before Ophelia could react, the woman raised her hand, and shadows swirled around her like a living storm. In the blink of an eye, she was gone, leaving the clearing eerily empty.

"Ophelia!" Gabriel's voice called from behind her, his footsteps crashing through the undergrowth.

She turned to see him emerge from the trees, his blade drawn and his face filled with concern. His dark gaze swept over her, taking in the still-glowing aura of her magic.

"What happened? Are you hurt?"

"I'm fine," she said quickly. Her mind was still spinning from the encounter. "But I think I just found something—or someone—we weren't looking for."

Gabriel's eyes narrowed, his grip tightening on his blade. "We need to get back to the others. Now."

Ophelia nodded, but as they made their way back to the group, her thoughts were consumed by the woman's words and the undeniable connection she had felt. Whoever that woman was, she wasn't done with Ophelia.

Not yet.

Ophelia's heart still pounded as she and Gabriel retraced their steps through the jungle. The merciless heat pressed down on her, but it was nothing compared to the weight of her thoughts. The encounter replayed over and over, the woman's haunting familiarity and those chilling words echoing like a refrain. *We share the same blood.*

Beside her, Gabriel was silent, his tension palpable. His dark eyes scanned their surroundings, and his hand never strayed far from the hilt of his blade. He didn't press her for details, not yet, but Ophelia could feel the unspoken questions radiating from him.

"Ophelia, are you going to tell me what just happened?" he finally asked.

She shot him a hard look. "I don't even know what just happened."

"You were gone for too long," he said, his tone edged with frustration. "I was looking for you when I heard the commotion. What did you see?"

Ophelia sighed, brushing a damp strand of hair from her face, glancing around her. She half-expected the woman to reappear, her laughter echoing in the jungle. "There was someone," she admitted. "A witch. But she looked like me. Almost exactly like me."

Gabriel's brows furrowed. "What do you mean, like you?"

"Same height, same build, same eyes. Even the same hair," Ophelia said in disbelief. "But she wasn't just a reflection. She was real. And she knew things about me, about my magic."

Gabriel's jaw tightened, his hand gripping the hilt of his blade. "What did she want?"

Ophelia hesitated, the memory of the woman's cryptic words swirling in her mind. "She didn't say. Not directly. But she was powerful, Gabriel. I could feel it."

"Did she hurt you?"

"No," Ophelia replied quickly. "Not exactly."

Gabriel stopped walking and turned to face her fully, his dark gaze intense. "What do you mean, not exactly?"

"I hit her with my magic," Ophelia admitted, her tone defensive. "It didn't do much. And then she just...left."

Gabriel's expression darkened, his grip tightening on his blade. "No one just leaves. Not without a reason. Did she say anything else? Anything we can use?"

Ophelia exhaled slowly, her mind racing to piece together the encounter. "She mentioned blood. That we share the same blood. But I don't know what she meant, and she didn't stick around to explain."

Gabriel's dark eyes searched hers, his intensity unwavering. "We'll figure it out," he said finally. "But right now, we need to get back to the others. Whatever this is, it's not something you should face alone."

They continued down the path in tense silence, the jungle gradually thinning as they approached the clearing, where the rest of their group had stopped to regroup. The scene that greeted them was deceptively serene.

Brisa and Mo were bent over a large map spread across a flat rock, their heads close together as they argued quietly. Celeste leaned against a tree as she scanned the surroundings with penetrating, watchful eyes. Alex sat near the edge of the clearing, sharpening her dagger with slow, deliberate strokes.

Brisa glanced up as they approached, her terse voice breaking the quiet. "Where the hell have you been?" Her eyes narrowed in irritation.

Ophelia ignored her cousin's tone, brushing past her to stand beside Mo and the map. "What did you find?" she asked, steady despite the turmoil still churning inside her.

"Nothing, unfortunately," Mo said, barely glancing up. Frustration was evident in the way he traced the map with his finger, muttering under his breath. "The outpost was empty. Not even a hint of magic."

"That's not the only thing," Celeste said abruptly, pushing off the tree she leaned against. Her sharp gaze settled on Ophelia. "You used magic. Why?"

Ophelia stiffened at her mother's words, her jaw tightening. "How do you know about that?"

Mo finally looked up, a small, knowing smile tugging at the

corner of his lips. "Your magic leaves a ripple in the air when you use it. Experienced witches can sense it."

Gabriel shot Ophelia a pointed look, but she ignored him.

"I was approached by another witch," Ophelia said reluctantly. "She taunted me and claimed we'd meet again. Then she just disappeared. It was strange, to say the least." Ophelia knew she was being vague, but something about the encounter felt off. She couldn't quite pinpoint what it was, but she couldn't shake the feeling.

A murmur rippled through the group, their voices overlapping as they speculated about the encounter.

Celeste stepped closer, her expression grave. "We need to be prepared for whatever we find here. The coven that created and hid the Bell was powerful. If their magic still lingers, it could be as much a trap as a safeguard."

"And what about this witch Ophelia saw?" Alex asked, her wide blue eyes filled with apprehension. "Could she be tied to the Bell?"

"It's possible," Mo said, stroking his chin thoughtfully. "She could have a connection to the Bell or to the magic that created it. Either way, we need to tread carefully."

Gabriel's gaze lingered on Ophelia for a moment before he addressed the group. "We'll deal with it. But first, we need rest. If we're going to search again tomorrow, we can't do it half-dead from exhaustion."

The group nodded in agreement, the tension easing slightly as they shifted their focus to the immediate task of setting up camp.

Ophelia stepped away from the others, her thoughts churning. The encounter with the witch had rattled her more than she wanted to admit. She couldn't shake the feeling that this was only the beginning, that whoever that woman was, she wasn't done with Ophelia yet.

CHAPTER

TWENTY-FOUR

The hotel perched precariously on the edge of the cliffs, its weathered stone walls seeming to rise out of the rock itself, as though it had always been part of the rugged landscape. Below, the turquoise waters crashed in rhythmic bursts, their foam catching the fading light of the setting sun. The building's rustic charm offered little in the way of luxury, but it exuded a sense of resilience, as if it had weathered countless storms and still stood defiant.

Inside, the wooden floors creaked beneath Brisa's boots as she dropped her bag with a loud thud that jarred Ophelia from her restless thoughts. "This will do for now," Brisa said, her tone clipped, her movements haggard with exhaustion. She moved toward the window, her gaze dragging over the darkening ocean as though expecting danger to rise from its depths.

Mo, ever methodical, placed a stack of maps and leather-bound notes on the small, rickety table at the room's center. He adjusted his glasses, his fingers already flipping through yellowed pages as he muttered, "I'll need a few hours to cross-reference these texts. If the Bell is near here, as Galla described, there should be something in the local records to confirm it."

Celeste leaned against the doorframe, her arms crossed, eyes watchful. "We may not have that kind of time," she said, her words slicing through the room. Her gaze darted to Ophelia, then to the open window, as if she expected an ambush at any moment. "The witch Ophelia encountered isn't working alone. Others will come. They always do."

Ophelia remained silent, her body unmoving as tension coiled tightly in her chest. The room felt too small, its walls pressing in on her like an unseen force. Somewhere beyond those cliffs, the Bell waited. She couldn't see it, couldn't hear it, but she could feel its pull, a constant, unrelenting weight that pressed against her ribs and tugged at her very core.

"You're quiet," Gabriel said from his place near the doorway. He studied her, his arms crossed loosely, calm but watchful.

Ophelia turned to him, the corner of her mouth twitching upward in an attempt at a smile. "Just thinking," she said. "It's been a long day."

Gabriel's dark eyes softened, though his expression remained guarded. "Take a breath," he said, as though it were the easiest thing in the world.

"I need air," Ophelia said abruptly, pushing back her chair and standing before anyone could respond. The room was suffocating, the gravity of the Bell's pull and the razor-edged tension between her companions unbearable. "I'll be back."

"Ophelia—" Brisa began, sharp and terse. But Gabriel silenced her with a slight shake of his head. His gaze never left Ophelia's face as he said, "Let her go. She knows where we are."

Without another word, Ophelia slipped out the door, the sound of her boots fading down the narrow hallway.

The air outside was a stark contrast to the stifling tension in the hotel room. Heavy with the scent of salt and citrus, the humid breeze clung to Ophelia's skin like a second layer, the wind tangling her midnight-black hair as she descended the narrow stone path leading to the beach. Above her, the cliffs loomed dark against a sky painted in fiery hues of orange and violet, the sun dipping low on the horizon.

When her boots touched the sand, she kicked them off without hesitation. The cool, grainy surface squished between her toes. She stared out at the vast expanse of turquoise water, the rolling waves glowing amber under the dying light. The scene was breathtaking, the kind of beauty that belonged on postcards and travel brochures. But Ophelia felt no peace.

The pull of the Bell thrummed, insistent and inescapable. It wasn't a sound or a voice, but an almost magnetic force, an invisible thread pulling her toward the waves. She wrapped her arms tightly around herself, pacing along the shore as her mind raced.

Her thoughts churned, turbulent as the sea. Questions she couldn't answer crowded her mind: *Why was the Bell calling to her? Why now? What did it want?* She paused, eyes narrowing on the horizon, searching for something she couldn't see but could feel as surely as the tide against her ankles.

The steady roar of the waves filled the silence, inexorable in their pull and retreat. A part of her wanted to follow the pull, no matter the cost. But another part of her, the part that had spent a lifetime not understanding who she was, screamed for her to turn back.

Her pacing slowed, and she stopped at the water's edge. The foam licked at her bare feet, cool and fleeting. She closed her eyes, inhaling deeply, letting the salty air fill her lungs. The pull of the Bell was strongest here, where the land met the sea. It called to her, a silent command she couldn't ignore.

"I need answers," she whispered, the words almost lost to the wind.

The declaration felt like an invocation, a plea to the forces that had entangled her in this web of magic and destiny. Deep down, she knew where to turn. There was one being who could guide her, one who had walked this path long before her and carried their bloodline's history.

Ophelia sank to her knees in the damp sand, pulling the moonstone from her pocket. The smooth, luminous surface glinted in the fading light. She rolled it between her fingers, its coolness steadying her nerves as she focused on its energy. Mira had given her the stone for this very purpose: to call upon her ancestors when the path ahead seemed impossible to navigate.

She inhaled deeply, centering herself. Her breaths grew slow and measured, each one pulling her further into a meditative calm. The world around her began to fade, the cloying edges of the present softening until she felt suspended in a quiet, timeless void.

"I call upon the bloodline that runs through me," she murmured, her heart pounding. "I call upon Galla Placidia."

The air shifted. A vibration rippled through the sand, subtle at first, then growing stronger. The salty breeze carried a new scent—smoky and ancient, like burning cedar and forgotten ruins. Ophelia kept her eyes closed, her focus unbroken, as the energy around her built to a crescendo.

And then, she felt it: a presence. Powerful, familiar, and undeniably real.

She opened her eyes slowly, a golden shimmer dancing in the air before her.

And then the woman appeared.

Galla Placidia stepped from the shimmering haze as if emerging from a dream, her figure both ethereal and commanding. Her robes flowed like molten gold, catching the light of the setting sun and refracting it into a spectrum of brilliance. Her hair, dark and streaked with silver, cascaded over her shoulders in soft waves, framing a face both regal and severe. Her piercing yellow-green eyes glinted with the wisdom of centuries—and a touch of exasperation.

"Nipotina," Galla said, dry but tinged with amusement. "You disturb my rest yet again. You are nothing if not persistent."

Ophelia rose to her feet, brushing the damp sand from her knees. "You don't exactly make yourself easy to reach," she shot back. Despite her frustration, there was something undeniably reassuring about Galla, like stepping into the embrace of an ancient, thorny tree whose roots ran deep into the earth.

Galla's lips quirked as she approached, her steps slow and deliberate. "Perhaps because I value my peace. But you, little one, seem determined to shatter it at every opportunity." She stopped a few paces away, her gaze sweeping over Ophelia with an intensity that felt like a physical weight. "You're stronger now," she observed, voice softening slightly. "The last time we spoke, you were trembling like a leaf."

"I don't have time for riddles or small talk," Ophelia said, folding her arms across her chest. "I need answers."

Galla's grin widened, her amusement evident. "Ah, the eternal impatience of youth. Do you think the world owes you its truths, nipotina?"

"No," Ophelia shot back, her frustration rising. "But I think you do. You dragged me into this mess."

Galla laughed, the sound melodic and clashing, like the chime of bells over a battlefield. "Dragged you? Oh, dear child, you were born into this 'mess.' Your blood carries a legacy that predates even my time. I merely nudged you toward the truth."

Ophelia clenched her fists, forcing herself to take a

steadying breath. "Fine. If you're so wise, then answer me this: the Kala Ghanta. It's here, isn't it?"

Galla tilted her head, her expression unreadable. "You already know the answer to that," she said, maddeningly calm. "You feel it."

"I need confirmation," Ophelia insisted. "Where is it? How do I find it?"

Galla's gaze shifted to the horizon, her eyes distant as if peering into a world beyond this one. "The Bell rests beneath the waves, hidden in a city long forgotten by mortals. A place of immense power, abandoned when its magic became too dangerous to contain."

Ophelia's pulse quickened. "A city? Underwater?"

"Marisante," Galla said, reverent. "It was a sanctuary for supernaturals, a haven where magic flourished. But ambition and greed corrupted it. The city fell, consumed by the very power it sought to harness. Now it lies beneath the sea, a graveyard of secrets."

"And the Bell?" Ophelia pressed, her awe barely contained beneath the urgency.

"It lies at the heart of Marisante," Galla said simply. "Waiting. Watching. It calls to you, as it has called to every descendant of its creators. You are its blood, nipotina. It recognizes you. It knows you carry the power to wield it. Or to destroy it."

A chill ran down Ophelia's spine. "Why me? Why us?"

Galla's expression softened, a rare flicker of tenderness crossing her face. "Because the Bell is bound to our bloodline. It was forged by your ancestors, infused with their magic, their will, and their sacrifice. It is as much a part of you as your heartbeat."

Ophelia's jaw tightened. "I don't want to wield it. I want to end this."

"Then you must heed its call," Galla said, firm. "Let it guide you to where it lies. But be warned, nipotina: the closer you get, the stronger its influence will become. The Bell does not surrender its power willingly. It will test you, tempt you, and twist you if you are not vigilant."

Ophelia's hands clenched tightly into fists. "I don't care about its power. I just want this to be over."

Galla studied her in silence for a long moment, her piercing gaze seeming to strip away every layer of doubt and fear. "You are brave, little one," she said finally. "Foolish, but brave. Remember: The Bell cannot be destroyed without sacrifice. When the time comes, you must be ready to make that choice."

"I will," Ophelia said, as the promise settled heavily on her chest.

Galla nodded, a hint of pride in her eyes. "Then go. Follow the magic. It will lead you to Marisante, and to your destiny."

The golden shimmer around Galla began to fade, her figure dissolving into the evening air like smoke carried away on the wind. But her voice lingered, clear and crisp: "And Ophelia, beware of those who walk beside you. Not all who smile are your allies."

And then she was gone.

The beach was quiet once more, the only sound the rhythmic crash of the waves. The sun had dipped below the horizon, leaving the sky painted in deep blues and purples. Ophelia exhaled slowly, her hands unclenching as she tried to ground herself in the present.

The Bell's pull was stronger now, a relentless hum beneath her skin. Whatever lay ahead, she knew one thing with absolute certainty: There was no turning back.

The ocean echoed around her as Ophelia stood on the beach, staring at the darkening horizon. The pull of the Bell was constant and maddening, but it wasn't the only weight pressing on her chest. Gabriel's voice broke the silence, low and steady, like the tide.

"Ophelia."

She turned to see him standing a few feet away, his figure a dark silhouette against the twilight sky. The sight of him—calm, composed, and undeniably steadfast—made her heart ache. He had been her anchor through the turmoil of these last few months, but tonight, she wasn't sure if she was ready to face him.

Gabriel stepped closer, his expression unreadable. "You've been quiet since we landed."

Ophelia hesitated, her arms crossing over her chest in a defensive gesture. "I needed time to think."

"About the Bell?" he guessed, his gaze searching hers.

"About everything," she admitted.

The space between them felt charged, the tension growing with each passing second. Gabriel didn't move, but his presence seemed to fill the air around her, grounding her even as her thoughts threatened to spiral.

"I've known for a while," she said finally, forcing herself to meet his eyes. "I've felt it in every touch, every look, every moment we've shared. I just didn't want to admit it."

Gabriel's expression softened, a rare, unguarded smile breaking through his usual stoicism. "And what is it you've known?"

"That you're my twin flame. My life mate," she said, the words heavy but certain. Her chest tightened, her vulnerability laid bare.

"Took you long enough to say it," he teased, though his voice carried an unmistakable depth of emotion.

Ophelia huffed a soft laugh, shaking her head. "Of course, you already knew."

"I've known from the moment I met you," Gabriel said, quiet but resolute. "But hearing you say it changes everything."

Ophelia hesitated, a flicker of uncertainty crossing her face. She took a deep breath and asked the question that had been clawing at her chest. "What about Luka?"

Gabriel's smile faded, his jaw tightening. His dark eyes grew stormy, the calm surface giving way to something far more volatile. "What about him?"

Ophelia swallowed hard, the confusion and guilt swirling inside her. "He believed I was his life mate. I don't understand. Was he wrong?"

Gabriel's voice was cutting, almost acidic. "He wasn't wrong. He was a liar."

The bluntness of his words made her flinch. "What do you mean?"

Gabriel's jaw worked for a moment, as though he were trying to temper his frustration. When he spoke, his tone was steady but laced with quiet anger. "Luka knew you weren't his life mate. But he performed the blood ritual on you anyway—without your understanding of what it meant."

A hollow pang clenched in her chest, his words sinking in. "He knew?"

"He knew," Gabriel confirmed, his gaze unwavering. "He bound you to him. Not out of love, but out of desperation. He wanted to keep you tethered to him in a way you couldn't escape."

Ophelia's knees felt weak, and she stumbled back a step, her hand rising to cover her mouth. "But why would he do that?"

"Because Luka couldn't stand to lose," Gabriel said, voice dark and full of disdain. "He thought if he could claim you, he'd win. But it was never his choice to make."

The revelation hit her like a tidal wave, the betrayal cutting deeper than she'd expected. With everything she had learned, she'd tried to reconcile the man she loved with the reality of who he'd been. And now, this truth felt like a final, crushing blow.

"His death released you from that bond," Gabriel said, stepping closer. His tone softened, his gaze steady. "You're free now, Ophelia. Truly free."

She swallowed hard, trembling as she asked, "And if he were still alive?"

A shadow crossed Gabriel's face, his expression darkening with something primal and unyielding. "If Luka were still alive," he said quietly, his words edged with steel, "we'd have a problem. Because I would make sure he never came near you again."

The intensity of his tone stole her breath. For a moment, they stood in silence, Gabriel's words hanging between them.

"You deserve better," he said finally, softening. "Better than manipulation and lies. You deserve something real."

Ophelia's throat tightened, a mix of anger, grief, and gratitude swirling inside her. "I don't even know what's real anymore," she admitted, barely audible.

"You will," Gabriel promised, his hand reaching out to gently clasp hers. "We'll figure it out. Together."

A flicker of fear crossed her face, a reminder of the risk they both knew but rarely spoke of. "You know what this means, don't you? I'm only part vampire. What if—"

Gabriel stepped closer, his dark eyes steady and unwavering as they held hers. "I know the risks, Cinis," he began, his tone soft but resolute. "But I also know I've spent centuries waiting for this—for you. I'm not afraid."

He paused as though searching for the right words, his expression uncharacteristically open. "Do you know what it's like to exist for centuries without purpose? To watch the world change, to see everything and everyone you care for slip through your fingers while you remain? I told myself I didn't need anything more than survival. That attachments were dangerous, fleeting, and never worth the pain."

His jaw tightened, his gaze flickering with a vulnerability he rarely allowed anyone to see. "But then you came along. Stubborn, infuriating, reckless—you shattered everything I thought I understood about myself. And I hated it at first. I hated that you made me feel alive again. That you made me want something I thought I could never have."

The raw honesty in his words cut through the barriers Ophelia had built around her heart. He reached out, his hand brushing against her cheek, his touch warm and grounding. "But the truth is, I don't just want you, Ophelia. I need you. You've reminded me what it is to fight for something real, something worth risking everything for. And now that I've found you, I can't—I won't—go back to that empty existence."

His voice dropped even lower, his eyes locking on to hers with an intensity that left no room for doubt. "I'll face every danger, every challenge, every impossible choice, because the one thing I can't do is live without you. I refuse to."

A lump formed in Ophelia's throat as she stared at him, her chest tightening at the conviction in his words. Gabriel's hands moved to cradle her face, his thumbs brushing gently over her cheeks. "You've brought me back from the brink, Cinis. You've shown me what it means to hope again, to feel again. And I'll fight for us—for you—with everything I have."

His confession lingered between them, heavy and unbreakable. Gabriel's lips curved into the faintest smile, his gaze softening. "So, no, I'm not afraid. Not of the risks, not of what we'll face, not of what this bond means. The only thing I fear is losing you."

His words wrapped around her like a protective shield,

steadying the chaos that had been tearing at her from the inside out. For the first time, she allowed herself to lean into him, not just physically, but emotionally. She let go of the doubt, the fear, and the walls she'd carefully built around her heart. She let herself trust the bond that had been undeniable from the very beginning.

"I love you, too," she said finally, steady and sure despite the storm of emotions threatening to overwhelm her. The words hung in the air between them, soft but charged, like the first rays of sunlight breaking through the dawn.

Gabriel's smile returned, softer this time, his dark eyes glimmering with something she hadn't seen before. It was as if her words had lifted a burden he'd carried for centuries, one he hadn't fully realized was there. "Then we face whatever comes next," he said as steady as a vow. "Together."

Ophelia didn't wait. She closed the distance between them, her hands reaching up to grasp the collar of his shirt as she pulled him to her. Their lips met in a rush of heat and longing, the kiss fierce and consuming. It wasn't soft or tentative; it was raw, a culmination of everything unsaid between them, everything they'd fought against and finally surrendered to.

Gabriel responded instantly, his arms wrapping around her as though he could hold her there forever. One hand slid up her back, tangling in her hair, while the other pressed against the small of her back, anchoring her to him. The world around them seemed to fade, leaving only the warmth of his touch and the intoxicating taste of his lips.

Ophelia felt herself melt into him, her body fitting against his as though they were two pieces of a puzzle finally clicking into place. His kiss was unyielding, demanding in its intensity, but it was also laced with tenderness—a promise in every brush of his lips, every gentle tilt of his head.

Her hands clutched his shirt, magic sparking into a golden

glow that glimmered between them. She didn't care if he felt it; in this moment, there was no room for hiding, no space for holding back. She poured everything she felt into the kiss: her fear, her hope, her love. And she felt his own emotions crash against hers like waves against the shore.

When they finally broke apart, both of them were breathless. For a moment, they stood there, tangled in each other's arms as the ocean whispered against the shore behind them. The Bell's silent call still lingered in the background. But in Gabriel's arms, Ophelia felt something she hadn't allowed herself to feel in far too long: peace.

CHAPTER

TWENTY-FIVE

The early morning sun filtered through gauzy curtains, casting soft, golden rays over the rustic hotel suite. Dust motes floated lazily in the light, a quiet contrast to the tension reverberating in the air. Ophelia stood at the edge of the worn wooden table, its surface cluttered with maps, notes, and Mo's leather-bound journal. Her fingers absently traced the edges of a faded map of the Seven Color Seas, her gaze anchored on the spot Galla had marked as Marisante's hidden resting place beneath the waves.

"This is it," she said. An edge of tension rippled beneath her words. "We need to reach Marisante before anyone else. It's the only way to ensure the Bell doesn't fall into the wrong hands."

The group had gathered in the largest suite the hotel could offer, its modest furnishings no match for the enormity of their task. Brisa perched on the arm of a chair, her short legs crossed as she twirled a strand of her dark hair between her fingers. Alex leaned against the back of the sofa, her silver hair glinting like spun moonlight in the morning glow.

At the table, Mo and Celeste studied the maps with identical expressions of focused intensity. By the window, Gabriel stood silhouetted against the sunlight, his shoulders blocking part of the view. His arms were crossed, but his eyes remained fixed on Ophelia, unreadable but unwavering.

"Mo and I will stay here," Celeste said, cutting through the tension. "We'll monitor the situation and keep an eye on the island. If anything goes wrong, I'll thread to you."

"And if you can't?" Gabriel asked, his tone calm but edged with a challenge.

Celeste's piercing gaze met his, unflinching. "Then you'll have to handle it. But I won't let it come to that."

Brisa broke the moment with a chuckle, tossing her braid over her shoulder. "At least we're not taking another sailboat. A jet boat is much more my speed."

Gabriel raised an eyebrow, a characteristic smirk tugging at his lips. "You'd be surprised what you can learn on a sailboat, Brisa. Patience, for one."

Brisa rolled her eyes dramatically. "Patience is overrated."

Despite her playful tone, the tension in the room was far from broken. "If Marisante is anything like Galla described, we'll need to be prepared. There's no telling what kind of magic is still active down there," Alex said.

"And no telling who might already be there," Gabriel added as his expression darkened. "We can't afford to make mistakes."

"Agreed," Ophelia said, meeting his eyes with quiet determination. "We stay together. We move quickly. And above all, we trust each other." Still, a nagging doubt tugged at the edges of her mind. Galla had warned that someone would betray her. She could feel it coming. But as Ophelia looked around at the faces of her family and friends, her gut insisted that it couldn't be any of them. *Could it?*

Her words settled over the room like a solemn vow. For a moment, no one spoke, the gravity of their mission tightening around them. Then, one by one, the group moved to make their final preparations.

Brisa examined the magical seals on their gear with surprising precision, muttering under her breath as she reinforced each one. Alex carefully folded a waterproof map into her pack, her movements deliberate. Gabriel remained by the window, his silhouette steady against the vibrant backdrop of the sea.

Ophelia adjusted the zipper of her jacket, her mind already miles ahead. When Brisa sidled up to her with a grin, Ophelia forced herself to focus. "Ready to dive for buried treasure?" Brisa asked, though her eyes betrayed her nerves.

"Always," Ophelia replied, her smile small but sincere.

Celeste, watching from the table, spoke up one last time. "Be careful. All of you." Her voice held the faintest waver, a crack in her usual composure.

Ophelia nodded, her mother's concern looming over her. "We will."

Turning to Gabriel, Brisa, and Alex, she gestured toward the door. "Let's go."

The group filed out, stepping into the blinding sunlight. The ocean's roar greeted them, a constant reminder of the power that lay beneath its shimmering surface. The sleek jet boat waited at the dock, ready to carry them toward the unknown.

Ophelia took a deep breath, the salty air filling her lungs. The pull of Marisante vibrated against her senses, a magnetic force drawing her closer to destiny. She met Gabriel's gaze, his expression calm but resolute.

"This is it," she said. She kept her tone even, her nerves locked beneath the surface.

Gabriel's hand found her shoulder, his grip warm and grounding. "We'll find it," he said, voice sure. "Together."

She nodded, drawing strength from his resolve. As they boarded, the boat's engine roared to life under Gabriel's command, cutting through the water with practiced precision. The sea glinted like liquid jewels under the late-morning sun, shifting effortlessly between hues of emerald, sapphire, and turquoise, a breathtaking contrast to the foreboding pull that guided their path.

Ophelia leaned against the railing, her fingers curling tightly around the edge as her eyes fixed on the horizon. The pull in her chest deepened, its urgency both exhilarating and unsettling. It was as though Marisante itself was calling her, whispering promises she couldn't yet understand.

"Beautiful, isn't it?" Brisa's voice interrupted, light and casual.

Ophelia turned to see her cousin leaning against the opposite railing, her hair whipping in the wind. Brisa's expression was calm, but her probing eyes betrayed a simmering tension beneath the surface.

"It is," Ophelia admitted, her tone quieter than she intended. Then, after a beat, she added, "But it feels wrong. Like it's waiting for us."

Brisa tilted her head, a genuine smile tugging at her lips. "Probably is," she said lightly, though her eyes were serious. "But hey, when has that ever stopped us?"

A small, fleeting smile crossed Ophelia's face. "Fair point."

The boat surged forward, its speed slicing through the gentle swell of the waves. Gabriel stood steady at the helm, his silhouette framed by the vast expanse of water and sky. Alex sat at the bow, her silver hair catching the sunlight as she studied the waterproof map spread across her lap. The scene was peaceful, but an undercurrent of anticipation threaded through the air, a tension that pressed against Ophelia's senses.

"We're getting close," Alex called over the hum of the engine, her finger tracing a faded route on the map. "The coordinates are just ahead."

Gabriel slowed the jet boat to a gentle crawl, the engine humming softly as the group peered over the edge of the vessel into the crystalline waters below. The ocean here was an impossible blue, so clear that the coral reefs beneath them seemed close enough to touch. Shafts of sunlight pierced through the surface, illuminating the underwater world with an almost ethereal glow.

"We'll stop here," Gabriel announced, his tone steady as he cut the engine. The silence that followed was filled only with the gentle lapping of the waves against the boat's hull.

Ophelia leaned over the side, her eyes scanning the depths. The pull of Marisante was almost overwhelming now, a steady drumbeat coursing through her. The water shimmered as if alive, the outline of a vast structure just barely visible far below. That familiar vibration returned, stronger this time, rippling through her, urging her to stay alert.

"This is the spot," she said, resolute. "I can feel it."

Brisa joined her, leaning over the railing with an arched brow. "You're sure? Because all I see is a bunch of fish."

"It's there," Ophelia said, unyielding now. "I know it is."

"Then we don't waste time," Gabriel said, biting through the tension. He turned to Alex, who was already rolling up the map and securing it in her bag. "Gear up. We go in together."

The group moved with practiced efficiency, each of them slipping into diving suits and checking their equipment. Brisa muttered something under her breath as she secured her oxygen tank, her usual sarcasm subdued by the gravity of the moment.

"Ready to play underwater archaeologist?" she quipped, though her tone lacked its usual bite.

"Just stick together," Ophelia said firmly as she adjusted the straps on her gear. "No splitting up. Not for any reason."

Gabriel stepped forward and placed a hand on Ophelia's shoulder, his dark eyes locking with hers. "I'll take point. You stay in the center. Brisa and Alex will cover the sides."

Ophelia nodded, her chest tightening with a mix of anxiety and determination. "Let's do this."

One by one, they slipped into the water, the cool embrace of the ocean enveloping them. Ophelia paused for a moment, adjusting to the weightlessness as the pull of Marisante seemed to intensify. The world around them was a kaleidoscope of color, teeming with life as schools of fish darted through coral formations that gleamed like submerged jewels.

Brisa activated her magic, weaving an air spell that ensured a steady flow of oxygen for the group. Ophelia mirrored the spell, her power blending seamlessly with Brisa's, the dual magic forming a protective barrier that shielded them from the crushing depths.

As they descended, the light from the surface began to fade, replaced by an eerie glow that seemed to emanate from the ocean itself. The pull in Ophelia's chest guided her like a compass, drawing her deeper into the unknown. The shadowy outline of an ancient structure began to take shape below them, its jagged edges and intricate carvings coming into focus.

Alex signaled with her hand, pointing toward the silhouette of what appeared to be a massive archway. The structure was enormous, its stonework covered in glowing symbols that pulsed, as though alive with dormant magic.

"This is it," Brisa said through the communication spell woven into their gear. "This is Marisante."

Ophelia's heart pounded as they swam closer. The archway's carvings reacted to their presence, glowing brighter until the surrounding water vibrated with energy. It was as if the city itself was waking up, aware of their intrusion.

"Everyone stay sharp," Gabriel said. "Whatever's down here has been waiting a long time."

Ophelia reached out, her fingers brushing the edge of the archway. Magic surged, the connection so powerful that it took her breath away.

As the current pulled them through the gate, the world blurred into an overwhelming rush of light and shadow, as if the ocean itself had fractured into shimmering threads of magic. Ophelia felt the pressure build in her chest, a momentary panic as the water closed around her completely—until, just as quickly, it dissipated. The sensation was strange, as though she had passed through a thin, invisible membrane.

When the motion finally stopped, Ophelia stumbled forward, her boots landing not on the slick ocean floor but on smooth, dry stone. The air here was warm and tasted of salt, though her lungs expanded with ease. She instinctively reached for her throat, expecting the telltale weight of water, but found nothing but air.

The sudden shift left her breathless, and as her eyes adjusted, she took in their new surroundings. The chamber was massive, its size almost incomprehensible. Towering columns reached up to a ceiling shrouded in darkness, their surfaces carved with intricate symbols that pulsed with an otherworldly light. The air was warm and dry, but it was weighed down by an ancient energy that seemed to press against their skin. The scent of salt lingered, a reminder of the ocean that still surrounded them.

Brisa let out a low whistle that echoed in the cavernous space. "Well, this isn't creepy at all."

Ophelia ignored her, her gaze sweeping over the room. The walls were adorned with carvings that seemed to shift and shimmer. Figures locked in battle, creatures she couldn't name, and symbols she didn't recognize danced along the stone, illuminated by the glow of the carvings. She couldn't shake the feeling that the city itself was studying them.

"This is impossible," Alex murmured, stepping closer to one of the walls. Her silver hair glinted in the dim light as she traced her fingers over a glowing symbol. "It's like we're on dry land—breathing, moving—and we don't even need air or magic to do it." She glanced over her shoulder, eyes wide with awe as she found Brisa. "This place...it's been untouched for centuries, but it feels like it's waiting for us," she said.

"It probably is," Brisa muttered, gripping the hilt of her blade tightly. Her usual smirk was gone, replaced by a wary tension. "And I don't like how quiet it is."

They peeled off their diving suits, the heavy material clinging to their skin, and exchanged them for the lightweight clothes they'd packed. To Ophelia's surprise, the fabric was already dry, as if the magic of Marisante had willed it so. The sensation was strange, almost as though the city itself was taking care of them, but it did little to ease the unease prickling at the back of her neck.

Gabriel moved to stand beside Ophelia, his presence solid and reassuring despite the unease that prickled at the edges of her senses. His dark eyes scanned the chamber, his hand resting on the hilt of his weapon. "Stay close," he said, voice low. "We're not alone."

Ophelia nodded, though her chest tightened at his words. She could feel it, too—the subtle shift of the air, the vibration beneath her boots, the almost imperceptible movement in the shadows. It wasn't just the carvings that seemed alive. Something—or someone—was watching them.

They moved as a group, their footsteps muffled against the stone floor. Every sound seemed amplified in the heavy silence: the rustle of their clothing, the clink of gear, the steady drip of water from somewhere unseen. Ophelia's senses were on high alert, magic pulsing through her veins as though resonating with the city's power.

"This place is a death trap," Brisa said, light on the surface, but her grip on her blade betrayed her nerves. "I hope we don't have to stick around long enough to see how it ends."

Alex crouched near a crumbled statue, her fingers brushing against a jagged edge. "These carvings tell a story," she said, her words tinged with awe. "I just wish I knew what it was."

Ophelia's focus remained ahead, drawn inexorably toward the light spilling through another archway. The pull in her chest grew stronger, a magnetic force that seemed to guide her steps. The city wasn't just ancient; it teemed with magic older and darker than anything she'd encountered before.

"Ophelia," Gabriel said softly, breaking through her thoughts. She turned to find him watching her, his expression unreadable but his dark eyes filled with concern. "What do you feel?"

She hesitated, the words sticking in her throat. "The city is calling to me," she admitted. "Like it knows I'm here."

Gabriel nodded, his hand brushing against hers briefly. "Then we follow it. But carefully."

The malevolent magic grew heavier, pressing down on them with every step. Shadows danced along the walls, their movements too deliberate to be tricks of the light. A whispering sound, like the murmur of distant voices, drifted through the chamber, sending a chill down Ophelia's spine.

"This feels wrong," Brisa muttered. "We shouldn't be here."

"Probably not," Gabriel replied, his tone grim. "But we don't have a choice."

They stepped through the archway, and the chamber that unfolded before them stole Ophelia's breath. It was vast, almost cathedral-like, with columns that stretched endlessly upward, their surfaces covered in intricate carvings that pulsed with magic. The air shimmered with energy, dense and electric, as though the chamber itself watched their every move. Light spilled from the glowing symbols, casting long shadows that danced across the stone walls like restless spirits.

At the heart of the chamber stood a raised platform, its surface etched with the same glowing markings, though they radiated a fiercer light. Two figures occupied the platform, their stances rigid and charged with hostility. The tension between them was palpable, the kind that pressed against the skin and made the air seem heavier.

"Celeste?" Ophelia's voice was barely above a whisper, but the word seemed to echo through the chamber, bouncing off the walls like a haunting refrain. Her chest tightened painfully, every ounce of breath stolen by the sight before her. Her mother's unmistakable silhouette came into focus, and with it, a crushing realization. Celeste's back was to them, her posture coiled with barely restrained energy, one palm held out toward the other figure, as though she were commanding or protecting them.

For years, Ophelia had clung to the memory of her mother as a protector, a guide she longed to find again. But now, standing here, all she could see was the shadow of betrayal. The mother she had spent her life yearning for was not here to save them; she was here to deceive them.

The second woman turned slowly, her movements deliberate, and Ophelia's stomach twisted as the light revealed her face. Her features were almost too perfect, as if carved from marble. Dark hair was pulled back into a severe braid, emphasizing the unforgiving angles of her cheekbones. And then there were her eyes—Ophelia's own piercing yellow-green stare, but with a glint of malice that set her teeth on edge.

Recognition swept through her, unbidden and unwanted.

"Eris, no!" Celeste's voice cracked, raw with desperation. She stepped forward, her hand outstretched, but Eris held her ground, a sickly grin curling her lips.

"Just in time," Eris said, dripping with mockery. "I've been waiting to meet my prodigal sister."

CHAPTER
TWENTY-SIX

sister. The word struck Ophelia like a physical blow, forcing the air from her lungs. She'd felt the truth stirring in the jungle—unspoken, undeniable—but hearing it aloud from Eris's lips sealed the realization with a crushing finality.

The resemblance was uncanny, as though they were reflections fractured by opposing forces. Eris's face mirrored Ophelia's. Yet, the similarities only served to amplify the differences. Eris's stance brimmed with chaotic energy, every movement exuding wild, unrestrained power.

Ophelia's fists tightened at her sides, her magic sparking at her fingertips. "I don't know what you want," she said. "But I'm not interested."

Eris tilted her head, her expression warping into something that wasn't quite a smile but held the same unsettling satisfaction. "Oh, dear sister," she said, patronizing. "So cold. So quick to dismiss me. All I've done is guide you to the truth. Isn't that what you've been searching for all along?"

"The truth?" Ophelia's voice cracked, her fury breaking

through her carefully maintained control. "You've been stalking me since the moment I stepped onto this island. What kind of twisted family reunion is this?"

Celeste, standing just to the side, dropped her gaze to the floor, her body tense but silent.

Eris laughed, sharp and bitter, the sound echoing against the carved stone walls. "Oh, Ophelia, you're so naïve. You think I wanted this? To be the forgotten one? The outcast?" Her eyes burned with a mix of fury and pain. "Do you know what it's like to be hidden away, to be treated like a secret too shameful to reveal? While you"—she jabbed a finger at Ophelia, her eyes narrowing into slits—"grew up protected, chosen, and adored?"

"Protected?" Ophelia spat, her laugh brittle and hollow. The sound echoed in the cavernous space, harsher than the cold air. "You think my life has been easy? Do you think I've had everything handed to me? I've lost more than you could possibly imagine."

Eris stepped forward, the glow of the runes on the walls intensifying with her movement. "*You've* lost?" she demanded, trembling with years of suppressed rage. "Do you know what I lost? Everything. I was the child she didn't want. The one she left behind. I struggled with powers she feared, powers she refused to nurture. And you—" Voice cracking, her fingers curled into fists. "You were the reason she walked away. You were her perfect, precious firstborn. And I was nothing."

The accusation struck Ophelia hard, but she held her ground, the heat rising in her chest. Her words came out like steel, hard and unyielding. "You don't know anything about me. You think my life was perfect? You think I was spared the pain, the loss, the isolation? You're wrong."

Eris's lips twisted into a bitter smile, her eyes gleaming with a dark triumph. "I know enough," she said coldly. "I know she chose you. I know she built her legacy around you. And I know that the Kala Ghanta is the key to everything I've ever been denied."

Ophelia's stomach twisted violently. "What do you mean?" she demanded, stepping closer. She ignored the warning glance Gabriel shot her, her focus locked on Eris.

"The Bell was forged by our bloodline. Only we can wield its power. Only we can control it. And only we can unlock its secrets," Eris said.

The chamber darkened, the glow of the runes flickering like dying embers. A cold weight pressed against her ribs at the implications of Eris's words. "You want to use the Kala Ghanta," she said, trembling with disbelief and fury.

Eris's smile widened, unhinged and maniacal. "Why destroy something that could give me everything I've ever wanted? The Bell isn't just a weapon—it's freedom. It's control. It's power. And it's mine."

Eris's words hung in the air, reverberating in the charged silence. Her predatory smile widened, radiating a volatile energy that made the air feel heavier as she took another step closer to Ophelia.

"You'd risk the world for that?" Ophelia demanded. "Do you even understand what the Kala Ghanta is capable of?"

Eris tilted her head, her expression one of calculated amusement. "I understand it perfectly," she replied, her tone smooth and cutting. "It's a masterpiece. A weapon forged by those who understood what true power is meant to do. In the right hands, it could reshape everything. The weak would finally kneel, and I..." A sinister edge tainting her words. "I would never be powerless again."

The arrogance in Eris's voice set Ophelia's teeth on edge. Her fists clenched at her sides, magic simmering beneath her skin. "You don't care who you hurt, do you?" Ophelia asked, stepping closer. Her yellow-green eyes burned with anger. "You don't care about the cost."

Eris's eyes gleamed with cold amusement, a spark of something dangerous flickering in their depths. "Why should I?" she countered, like a dagger slipping between ribs. "Power always comes with a price, dear sister. Those who understand that price are the ones who deserve to wield it."

"Power for the sake of power is meaningless," Ophelia shot back. "You'd tear the world apart just to make yourself feel whole. That's not strength, Eris. That's desperation."

For a brief moment, a flicker of something raw and unguarded crossed Eris's features. But it was gone as quickly as it appeared, replaced by a cold, detached mask. "Call it what you want," she said. "But when I'm holding the Kala Ghanta, none of that will matter."

The tension in the chamber was electric, the air thick with unspoken challenges. Eris's confidence was a palpable force that pressed against everyone in the room. Ophelia's mind raced, searching for a way to break through to her sister—or at least buy time.

"This isn't over," Eris said suddenly. "But I have preparations to make."

Before anyone could react, she raised her hand, and a surge of dark magic erupted around her. Shadows twisted and writhed around her form like living tendrils. In a heartbeat, she was gone, leaving the chamber in a foreboding silence.

Ophelia stood frozen, her chest heaving as she tried to process what just happened. The lingering traces of Eris's magic buzzed in the air, a grim reminder of her sister's growing power.

"She's gone," Alex said, breaking the quiet. "For now."

Ophelia's gaze shifted to Celeste, who lingered near the chamber's edge. Her mother's face was pale, her tense posture betraying unspoken truths. The silence between them was suffocating, strained by the heaviness of too many lies and too much time.

"You have some explaining to do," Ophelia said. The trembling in her hands belied the control she tried to maintain. "No more secrets, no more half-truths. I need the whole story, and I need it now."

Celeste straightened, her poise returning as she met Ophelia's fiery gaze. But there was no mistaking the flicker of unease in her eyes. "Ophelia," she began, almost pleading. "I was trying to protect you—"

"Save it," Ophelia snapped, cutting her off. Her anger surged, fueled by years of unanswered questions and the sting of betrayal. "You've been trying to 'protect' me my entire life, and look where it's gotten us. Eris is out there, wielding magic that could destroy everything, and you never thought to warn me? To prepare me?"

Celeste's lips pressed into a thin line. "I didn't know she would find you," she said quietly, her tone laced with regret. "I thought I had hidden her away, far from anyone who could manipulate her or use her against you."

"Hidden her?" Ophelia echoed with disbelief. "You abandoned her. You left her to fend for herself while you kept me in the dark about everything!"

"I didn't abandon her," Celeste said, her composure cracking. "I tried to help her. I did everything I could to teach her control, to guide her magic. But Eris...she was different. Her power was wild, unstable. She nearly destroyed an entire coven when she was just a child. I had no choice but to keep her away, for her sake and for yours."

Ophelia shook her head, a bitter laugh escaping her lips. "You call that protecting her? You made her into the monster she is now."

Celeste flinched, the accusation hitting its mark. "You don't understand," she said softly. "Eris's magic is tied to the darkest parts of our bloodline. No matter what I did, it consumed her. It made her dangerous."

"And you thought hiding her—and lying to me—was the solution?" Ophelia shot back. "You didn't trust me to handle the truth. You didn't trust me to make my own decisions."

"I thought I was protecting you," Celeste said again, her tone almost desperate. "I thought I was doing what was best for both of you."

Ophelia's anger burned brighter, but beneath it was a deep well of hurt, raw and unyielding. "You don't get to decide what's best for me," she said, voice cracking. "Not anymore."

Celeste hesitated, her gaze flickering to the others in the room. Brisa and Alex stood silently, their expressions a mixture of shock and anger. Before she could speak again, Ophelia broke the silence.

"And Leander?" she asked. Her question hung in the air like a thunderclap.

Celeste's eyes widened, surprise flashing across her face. "How did you know?" she asked.

Ophelia's jaw tightened. "It wasn't hard to figure out. The way he looked at you, the way his magic felt familiar. And now Eris—her power, her abilities. It all makes sense."

Celeste's shoulders sagged, her secrets visibly bearing down on her. "Leander is your father," she admitted, voice trembling. "Both of yours."

The room seemed to close in around Ophelia, the revelation caving in on her like a physical weight, even though she'd already suspected. She swallowed hard, her mind racing. "So, what?" she said bitterly. "You thought I'd be safer if I didn't know the truth? You thought ignorance would protect me?"

"I thought knowledge would put you in danger," Celeste

said. "Leander is one of the oldest vampires alive. His enemies are countless, and his power is unmatched. If anyone knew you were his daughters…"

"They'd come for us," Ophelia finished, the realization sending a chill down her spine. "Just like Eris has."

"Yes," Celeste whispered, her words catching as they broke apart.

Ophelia closed her eyes, exhaling slowly as she tried to process the tangled web of truths and lies. Her anger hadn't abated, but beneath it was a growing resolve. "Eris is after the Kala Ghanta," she said finally. "And we're going to stop her. But when this is over, we're having a long talk."

Celeste nodded, her expression a mix of guilt and determination. "I'll tell you everything," she promised. "But right now, we need to focus on the Bell."

Ophelia squared her shoulders, pushing her emotions to the back of her mind. "Brisa," she said, turning to her cousin. "What's the plan?"

Brisa stepped forward, her air magic rippling around her. "We track her down. And we stop her. No matter what it takes."

Ophelia met Celeste's gaze one last time, eyes hard and unyielding. "Whatever it takes," she said, echoing the words with a grim finality.

TWENTY-SEVEN

They ventured deeper into Marisante, a once-glorious city now crumbling under the weight of time and abandonment. The Kala Ghanta's pull was unrelenting, an invisible thread drawing Ophelia forward. It throbbed in her chest, matching the rhythm of her heartbeat, as though the artifact itself was guiding her path.

The cobblestone streets beneath their feet glistened in the dim light, slick with the lingering humidity of the subterranean air. The remnants of a forgotten world loomed around them—arches that once stood tall now fractured and jagged, spires tilted as if bowing to the inevitable decay. Statues of long-dead rulers stared down with empty eyes, their features worn smooth by time, yet their presence still carried a sense of gravitas.

The silence was broken only by the muffled shuffle of boots against stone and the occasional clink of gear. Even the air seemed reluctant to stir, thick with an unnatural weight that pressed against Ophelia's chest. Every breath felt heavier than the last. Somewhere in the distance, a whisper carried through the ruins, the sound almost too delicate to hear but enough to set her nerves on edge.

Ophelia scanned the area, her fingers brushing the hilt of the dagger at her waist. It felt heavier than usual, though she knew it was only her imagination. Her gaze flicked toward Gabriel, who moved with the quiet assurance of someone who had seen too many battles to let unease show. His broad shoulders were taut, his hand resting near the blade strapped to his side, ready for the slightest hint of danger.

Brisa trailed behind, her eyes vigilant and watchful, though her usual smirk was absent. Instead, her hands flexed at her sides, traces of air magic rippling through her fingers in quiet preparation. Alex walked alongside her, the lines of tension in her face mirrored by the tightly gripped hilt of her weapon. Celeste, flanked by the others, walked with a calmness that seemed forced, her gaze flitting from shadow to shadow as though expecting an ambush.

The deeper they went, the heavier the atmosphere became. It wasn't just the ruins that unsettled them; it was the sensation that the city itself was holding its breath, waiting. Shadows shifted in the corners of their vision, their movements too deliberate to be tricks of the light. The echo of whispers—inaudible, yet undeniably there—crawled along the edges of Ophelia's consciousness, setting her teeth on edge.

"We're being watched," she murmured.

Gabriel's head turned slightly, his dark eyes scanning the ruins ahead. "Keep moving," he said quietly. "Don't give it the satisfaction of knowing we feel it."

Ophelia nodded, though the unease gnawed at her. The Kala Ghanta's pull was stronger now, insistent and demanding. It wasn't just leading her; it was dragging her toward something, and whatever lay ahead promised to be anything but welcoming.

As they pressed forward, the ruins seemed to darken, the pale glow of Marisante's conjured light casting eerie shadows that stretched and twisted with each step. The path widened into a vast courtyard at the heart of the city. Ophelia's breath caught as her eyes fell on the figure standing in its center.

Eris.

She was framed by the decayed grandeur of the ancient city, crumbled arches and jagged spires rising around her. The luminescence of the glowing carvings reflected off her dark braid, her features severe and unforgiving. The energy radiating from her was undeniable—chaotic and unrestrained, it hummed in the air.

For a moment, Ophelia faltered. Her gaze locked on Eris, who stood as though she belonged here, her wild energy perfectly in tune with the broken beauty of Marisante. It was like staring into a mirror distorted by fury and grief, and the sight sent an icy ripple down Ophelia's spine.

Gabriel stepped closer. His hand brushed hers briefly. "Careful. We're with you."

Ophelia nodded, her fingers tightening around the hilt of her dagger. Her steps were slow and measured as she moved forward, her magic a quiet hum beneath her skin, ready to ignite. Behind her, she could feel the resolve of her companions: Brisa's ironclad focus, Alex's quiet intensity, and Gabriel's unwavering strength. Even Celeste exuded a tense determination, though her energy was a turbulent undercurrent that Ophelia refused to analyze.

Eris's lips curved into a taunting smile as her gaze landed on Ophelia. The air seemed to thicken, pressing against them like an invisible hand.

"Well," Eris said, cutting through the silence like a blade. "Sister. You finally found me."

Ophelia's chest tightened at the word, but she refused to

let it show. "You're bold to face all of us alone," she said evenly, taking another step forward. "Or maybe just desperate."

Eris tilted her head, lips deepening into something colder, crueler. "Alone?" she echoed, the words dripping with disdain. "Oh, sister, I'm never alone." Her fingers flexed, and the energy surrounding her pulsed with dark intent. "But you are adorably predictable. So quick to underestimate me."

Ophelia's jaw tightened, her magic sparking at her fingertips. She loathed the way Eris hissed "sister," the word dripping with poison. "This ends here," Ophelia said. "Whatever you think you'll gain from the Kala Ghanta, it's not worth what you're doing."

Eris let out a low, bitter laugh that echoed through the courtyard. "Oh, Ophelia," she said, shaking her head. "You've barely scratched the surface of what's at stake. You still think this is about the Bell. About power." She stepped forward, the air around her rippling with her energy. "This is about setting things right."

Her words struck Ophelia like a cold wind, but she forced herself to stand her ground. "You call this right?" Ophelia demanded, gesturing to the desolation around them. "This destruction?"

Eris's smile vanished, her expression darkening. "You have no idea what destruction is," she said. "But you're about to learn."

Before Ophelia could respond, Eris raised her hands, chanting a chilling incantation. The ground beneath their feet trembled violently, and a deep, guttural sound filled the air. Cracks splintered through the cobblestones, and from the broken earth, they began to emerge.

The cracks widened, splitting the ground like fractured glass. The sound of stone grinding against stone filled the air as skeletal figures began clawing their way out of the earth.

Their forms were draped in tattered remnants of robes, their eye sockets glowing with a sickly green light. Ghostly shapes followed, their translucent forms hovering above the ground, their faces frozen in expressions of anguish.

Eris stepped back, her hands still raised as her incantation reverberated through the courtyard. The air grew colder, heavy with the oppressive energy of the dead. The horde gathered around her, an army of Marisante's fallen citizens awakened from their cursed slumber.

Ophelia's breath hitched as the enormity of the moment settled over her. The undead were endless, filling the courtyard like a tide of despair. Their eerie silence was almost worse than any battle cry.

Gabriel moved closer, his blade already drawn. "Well," he muttered, his tone wry but edged with tension, "she's certainly not alone anymore."

Brisa let out a low whistle, her air magic sparking at her fingertips. "This is bad," she said, voice tight. "Really bad."

Eris's cold smile widened as she lowered her arms, her gaze fixed on Ophelia. "Still underestimating me, sister?" she asked, cutting through the tense air.

Ophelia ignored the taunt, forcing her fear down as she summoned her magic. It coiled around her, a fiery contrast to the deathly chill emanating from the horde. She took a step forward, planting herself firmly in the center of her group.

Her eyes locked on Eris, burning with determination. "You're about to regret underestimating us."

Eris tilted her head, her expression almost bored. "Oh, I'm not underestimating you," she said smoothly. "I'll just enjoy watching your face when you realize you're already too late."

With a flick of her wrist, she commanded the undead to attack.

The silence shattered as the horde surged forward, their

guttural cries filling the air. The skeletal warriors moved with unsettling precision, their movements unnatural. Ghostly forms drifted through the melee, their hands reaching out like claws.

Ophelia raised her hands, her magic flaring to life in a burst of red and gold light. A barrier erupted around her and her allies, holding back the initial wave of the undead. But the effort was draining, and cracks began to form in the shimmering shield.

Gabriel stepped to her side, his blade ready. "Drop it," he said. "We fight better without it."

Ophelia hesitated, her magic wavering, then nodded. With a forceful exhale, she let the barrier fall. The undead surged forward, but the group was ready.

Gabriel moved with lethal precision, his blade cutting through skeletal warriors with ease. Brisa unleashed a powerful gust of wind, scattering a cluster of the undead. Alex stepped forward, her hands glowing with dual magic—one hand radiating life, the other decay. Her powers rippled through the horde, reducing their forms to ash.

But for every enemy they felled, more seemed to rise.

"These things just keep coming!" Brisa shouted through clenched teeth, forcing another gust of wind toward the advancing horde. "We need to stop the source!"

Ophelia's eyes darted toward Eris, who stood at the center of the carnage, her arms outstretched as she continued her incantation. The dark energy radiating from her was suffocating, bending the air around her. Her eyes met Ophelia's, and her smile deepened in a wicked, triumphant curve.

"She's sustaining them!" Celeste called with urgency. A wall of fire sprang up before her, cutting off a wave of spectral warriors. "We have to take her down!"

Ophelia's magic flared in response, her frustration boiling

over. "You want me, Eris?" she shouted, stepping forward, her power crackling in the air around her. "Come and get me!"

Eris's laughter rang out, scathing and cold. "Oh, I don't need to come to you, sister. You'll come to me."

The ground beneath Ophelia trembled, and the skeletal horde parted as something massive began to rise. A hulking figure clawed its way out of the earth, its form a grotesque amalgamation of bone and dark energy. Its glowing eyes locked on Ophelia with predatory intent, and a low, rumbling growl emanated from its chest.

"Ophelia, move!" Gabriel shouted, darting toward her.

But before he could reach her, the beast lunged. Ophelia barely had time to raise a shield, the creature's claws slamming into it with bone-rattling force. She staggered backward, her arms trembling as the impact reverberated through her.

Gabriel reached her side, his blade flashing as he struck at the creature. Alex and Brisa joined the fight, their powers combining in a coordinated attack. They forced the beast back, but it fought with rabid fury, its claws tearing through the air in deadly arcs.

Ophelia regained her footing, her magic surging as she unleashed a blast of energy that struck the creature square in the chest. The combined efforts of the group finally brought it down, its massive form crumbling to dust.

But the victory was short-lived.

Eris raised her arms, lips moving faster now as the air thickened with power. The undead surged forward with renewed ferocity, their snarls rising in a chorus as sheer numbers pressed in from all sides.

Ophelia's chest tightened. They couldn't keep this up. Not like this.

"Focus on Eris!" she shouted, urgency rippling through every word. "She's the key!"

The group nodded, their determination hardening as they pushed forward. The resistance thickened, but so did their resolve.

As Ophelia fought her way forward, her eyes locked on Eris. She channeled every ounce of her energy into the fight, her magic crackling and flaring as it cut through the endless onslaught of undead warriors that blocked her path. Gabriel stayed close by her side, his blade moving in a deadly rhythm, slicing through the spectral figures that lunged at them.

"Ophelia!" Alex's voice pierced the cacophony, panic lacing her tone. Ophelia turned just in time to see her friend overwhelmed, spectral claws tearing at her as she struggled to fend them off. A surge of protectiveness rose within Ophelia, burning like fire through her veins. With a fierce yell, she unleashed a wave of magic that rippled outward, obliterating the creatures swarming Alex in a burst of golden light.

Alex retreated, her silver hair plastered to her face with sweat. She looked at Ophelia with wide, grateful eyes. "Thanks," she gasped, lifting her hands as another wave of the undead closed in. Her magic flared, sending a pulse of decay that crumbled a group of skeletons into ash. "We're running out of time!"

"Keep moving!" Brisa's voice rang out from behind, her tone crisp and commanding. She was at the rear of the group, her air power howling as it swept through the enemy ranks, again scattering the undead like dried leaves. "I'll cover the back!"

Ophelia nodded, her determination hardening. They pressed forward, the resistance thinning as they pushed closer to the heart of the ruins where Eris waited. The air around them grew thicker, saturated with magic that prickled against Ophelia's skin and made it hard to breathe. The closer they came, the more she felt the Bell's presence, a deep, thrumming vibration in her very bones. It called to her, its ancient power a siren song that made her head spin.

They were close.

"You can't win this, Eris!" Ophelia shouted, hoarse from the battle, but her spine straight and defiant. Her eyes locked on her sister's, blazing with determination. "Even if you destroy us, you won't hold onto that power. It'll consume you."

Eris threw her head back and laughed, the sound grating. "Oh, sister, you still don't understand. This isn't about power. I am the answer to the imbalance our family created," she said.

"What are you talking about?" Ophelia demanded, faltering for a moment as confusion flickered across her face.

Eris sneered, her gaze flicking toward the edge of the battlefield where Celeste was locked in a desperate struggle against a spectral attacker. "Ask Mother, if she survives."

Ophelia's fists clenched, her resolve hardening. "It doesn't matter what happened in the past. You're hurting people, Eris. This has to stop."

"Stop?" Eris asked, the single word laced with taunting sweetness. "I have no intention of stopping." She raised her arms, voice reverberating with a dark incantation. "You think you can stop me? Let's see how you fare against the ancestors of Marisante!"

The ground trembled violently, and the ruins seemed to awaken with sudden energy. From the broken streets and shattered buildings, the dead of Marisante began to rise. These were no mere skeletons. These forms were more intact, their ghostly faces twisted with anguish and rage. Their eyes glowed with unnatural light as they took up spectral weapons, their movements precise and purposeful.

Alex gasped, her hands glowing as she unleashed a wave of life magic that halted a small group of spectral warriors in their tracks. "We can't take them all!" she cried, her breath catching as she threw a glance over her shoulder, eyes wide with fear.

"Then we take her," Gabriel said, stepping forward, his blade gleaming in the eerie light. His voice was steady, his resolve unshakable.

Eris grinned, her hands weaving an intricate pattern in the air as she summoned more of the undead to her side. The ghosts surged forward like a tide, and the battle became a desperate struggle for survival. Ophelia's magic flared wildly as she fought, her control slipping under the strain of exhaustion. She caught fleeting glimpses of her family: Brisa, her winds a calibrated force that hurled enemies aside; Alex, her bursts of decay crumbling the spectral forms to ash; Gabriel, a blur of precision and deadly efficiency as he cut down anything in his path. Celeste, a whirlwind of fire and fury.

But it wasn't enough. Eris's power was overwhelming, her control over the dead unyielding. For every undead they defeated, two more rose in its place. Ophelia pushed forward, her magic carving a path through the fray as she forced herself closer to her sister. She could see the strain on Eris's face now, the effort it took to maintain her hold on the army she commanded. It was a small crack in her seemingly impenetrable armor, but Ophelia knew it wasn't enough.

"Eris!" Ophelia yelled, cutting through the din. She raised her hands, her magic crackling with raw energy. "This ends now!"

Eris turned to face her, her smile faltering for the first time. "You're right," she said, low and dangerous. "It does."

Before Ophelia could react, Eris unleashed a blast of dark magic that struck her like a hammer. The force sent her flying backward, her body slamming into the ground with a bone-jarring impact. Pain lanced through her, and for a moment, her vision swam. She struggled to get up, her limbs heavy and unresponsive.

Eris advanced, her steps deliberate and unhurried. "You've fought well, sister," she said, with something disturbingly close to admiration. "But you're not strong enough."

Ophelia's heart pounded in her chest as she watched Eris raise her hands, dark energy churning around her, alive with menace. She braced herself, knowing she couldn't stop what was coming.

Then, out of nowhere, Celeste appeared.

Her magic blazed like the sun, golden and fierce, as she threw herself between her daughters. The blast struck her full force, and Celeste cried out in pain as she was flung backward. Her body crumpled to the ground, motionless.

Eris took a stumbling step back, her expression flickering with something that might have been regret.

Alex rushed to Celeste, but Ophelia couldn't focus on them.

She used the momentary surprise to unleash all she had on her sister, sending a blast of power at Eris. Eris flew back, landing against a spire and losing control of the undead army instantaneously. The battlefield fell silent, the undead collapsing into dust as the magic animating them dissipated. The air was heavy with the scent of dust and ash.

Ophelia stumbled to her feet, drained but ready to end this.

Eris raised her hands, clearly trying to summon that army around her. She failed, over and over, nearly drained of power. She let loose a guttural scream, eyeing Ophelia and her allies. She seemed to know she couldn't win against them all.

"This isn't over, Ophelia," she said, cold and unyielding. With a flourish of dark energy, she vanished, leaving only the echoes of her power behind.

Ophelia rushed to Celeste's side, her hands trembling as she cradled her mother's face.

"Celeste. Mom," she whispered, voice ripping apart. "Stay with me. Please."

Alex worked next to Celeste, trying to summon healing energy. "My power is too depleted," she said. "We need to get her back to the surface."

Just then, a figure emerged from the shadows, as if the air itself had given birth to him. A shockwave of recognition rippled through her as her biological father stood before her, his expression grim and unreadable. His appearance was overwhelming, a force that shifted the air itself, steeped with the essence of millennia. He hadn't merely walked into the room, he'd threaded and materialized from the ether, a being so ancient and powerful that the laws of reality seemed to bend to his will.

"Leander," she said with a mix of awe and trepidation. Her mind raced to catch up with the moment. *Why was he here? How could he—a vampire, not a witch—thread?* But her questions went unasked as her eyes shifted to her mother and back to him.

His gaze settled on her, piercing yet strangely gentle, as though he could see straight through her façade. "Ophelia," he said, deep and deliberate, laced with an accent so ancient it seemed to echo from a forgotten era.

She was startled by his sudden appearance, yet something about him felt inevitable, as though he had always been there, lurking on the edges of her life.

Gabriel dipped his head toward Leander, a gesture of respect that Ophelia had never seen him offer anyone else. It was subtle but spoke volumes about the magnitude of the vampire before them.

Leander's eyes flicked briefly to Gabriel in acknowledgment, but his focus quickly returned to Ophelia. His movements were unhurried yet purposeful, commanding the space

without effort. "I'm sorry we don't have more time," he said, his words heavy, as if each syllable carried centuries of weight. "But there is work to be done, and my priority now is getting Celeste to safety."

His words snapped Ophelia out of her reverie. "Celeste—" she began, but Leander held up a hand, his gesture both gentle and firm.

"She is weak. I'm not sure if she can recover," he said, his tone brooking no argument. His gaze shifted briefly to Celeste, lying unconscious and pale, her chest rising and falling in shallow breaths. "I will transport her, along with Brisa and Alex, to safety. They cannot stay here. Their presence will only endanger them—and you—further."

Ophelia opened her mouth and closed it. She opened it again, ready to protest, but Gabriel's hand on her shoulder stopped her. "He's right," Gabriel said. "You and I need to find the Kala Ghanta and finish this."

Leander's eyes met hers again, and for the first time, she caught a flicker of something beyond the grim determination. Regret. "This is not a burden you should have to carry," he said softly, almost to himself. "But it is one you are capable of bearing, Ophelia."

Her throat tightened at his words, but she forced herself to focus. "What about you?" she asked, steadier than she felt.

Leander's lips curved into the faintest of smiles, one that didn't quite reach his eyes. "I will return," he said. "But for now, my priority is ensuring your mother and your allies survive. You and Gabriel must find the Kala Ghanta. Eris has been searching for it, but the Bell would not reveal itself to her. I believe it will show you the way."

She glanced at Gabriel, whose expression was unreadable but calm, as though he had already accepted what lay ahead.

Before Ophelia could ask him anything more, Leander

moved toward Celeste with a grace that seemed almost other-worldly. He knelt beside her, his hand brushing against her cheek with surprising tenderness. Brisa and Alex stood nearby, their expressions tense but resolute.

"Be ready," Leander said to them, voice low but commanding. "This will not be a pleasant journey."

Ophelia watched as he gathered them together, the air around him shimmering as his power surged. The ground seemed to hum with energy, and for a moment, everything was still. Then, with a burst of light, they were gone, leaving only an echo of magic in their wake.

The silence that followed was deafening. Ophelia stared at the spot where her father had stood, her emotions a tangled mess of awe, fear, and determination. She felt Gabriel step closer.

"He's right," Gabriel said quietly. "We don't have time to waste."

Ophelia nodded, her resolve hardening. Eris was waiting, and the fate of more than just their family hung in the balance.

"Let's finish this," she said.

Together, they turned and headed deeper into the ruins, the ancient city of Marisante watching silently.

TWENTY-EIGHT

The narrow corridors of Marisante twisted endlessly, their jagged walls covered in ancient etchings. Ophelia moved beside Gabriel, her breath shallow and her heart pounding in her chest. The air grew thicker with every step, pressing down on her like a living thing, and she couldn't shake the sensation of being watched.

Gabriel's movements were fluid, purposeful, but even he seemed on edge. His sharp eyes scanned every shadow, and the soft scrape of his boots on the stone floor was the only sound breaking the inescapable silence.

"I can feel it," Ophelia whispered, almost inaudible against the pressure of the atmosphere. Her magic stirred within her, drawn toward something she couldn't yet see. "It's close. The Kala Ghanta is close."

Gabriel glanced at her, his expression unreadable but his tone steady. "Let it guide you. We're too deep in this labyrinth to rely on sight alone."

She nodded, closing her eyes for a moment to center herself. The pull of the Bell was unmistakable now, a thrumming sensation that seemed to echo in her very bones. It wasn't a sound, but a vibration, a resonance that called to her bloodline like a siren's song. She could feel it growing stronger, more insistent, with each step forward.

As they turned another corner, the walls around them began to change. The jagged, rough stone gave way to smooth, carved surfaces, their intricate patterns glowing with a silvery-blue light. Ophelia ran her fingers over one of the carvings, the grooves warm under her touch.

When they entered the final chamber, Ophelia froze, drawing in a ragged breath. It was immense, the kind of space that made her feel both insignificant and connected to something far greater than herself. The images etched into the walls depicted scenes of power and sacrifice: witches weaving complex spells, fae channeling raw power, and vampires standing solemnly in ritual circles, offering their blood. Each figure shifted subtly in the dim glow, their forms imbued with a strange, almost ethereal energy. At the heart of it all was the Bell of Time, depicted as a radiant, otherworldly object, its power the axis around which everything else revolved.

"This place," Gabriel murmured. "It's more than a chamber. It's a sanctum."

Ophelia felt the truth of his words in her core. This wasn't just a room—it was a place of convergence, where power and history collided. The carvings seemed to ripple in response to her, the light growing brighter as her magic stirred.

The pull of the Bell grew almost unbearable. The air around them pulsed, heavy with an ancient energy that thrummed in time with her heartbeat. Each step she took seemed to echo endlessly, as though the space ahead refused to be filled by sound.

A shiver ran through Ophelia. This was the heart of Marisante, the place where all the threads of history converged. Her gaze moved to the center of the room, drawn by the same magnetic pull she'd felt since entering the city.

The altar stood there, silent and commanding, its intricate base carved with runes and symbols that glowed in the chamber's light. But the pedestal at its apex was empty.

The absence hit her like a physical blow. Ophelia's stomach twisted, her breath rushing out in a sharp exhale. Her magic surged in confusion and anger, coiling tightly within her as though seeking an outlet.

"It's gone," she whispered, the words bitter on her tongue. She stepped closer to the altar, her boots crunching softly against what might have been offerings once—withered petals, brittle leaves, and fine dust that disintegrated underfoot.

She stared at the barren pedestal, her mind racing. The pull of the Kala Ghanta still thrummed within her, a maddening contradiction to its absence. She placed her hands on the cold stone, her fingers tracing the ancient runes. "This doesn't make sense. I can feel it—its power—it's close."

Gabriel crouched near the pedestal, examining the floor. His hands skimmed over scorch marks and the remnants of a protective sigil that had long since faded. "Someone was here before us. Recently."

"Eris," Ophelia said, the name tightening her throat. "She must have tried to take it and failed. That's why she's been so desperate."

"Desperate enough to risk everything." Gabriel's voice was laced with disdain as he stood, brushing dust from his hands. "But if she couldn't find it, how do you plan to?"

The chamber seemed to answer them with a deep, resonant hum. The air grew heavier, the silence imposing on them. Ophelia closed her eyes, letting her magic flow outward, seeking any trace of the Bell. Her fingers twitched as she caught echoes of its power, subtle and distant, pulling her attention toward a shadowed corner of the room.

"There," she said, heart pounding as she turned her gaze and pointed to the carvings on the walls, where the glow had dimmed almost entirely. The glowing depictions of the Bell flickered, the light within them dimming before flaring to life again, as if reacting to them.

Gabriel moved ahead of her, his movements deliberate and silent. The closer they got, the colder the air became, the tangy scent of ozone pricking at Ophelia's senses. As they reached the wall, Gabriel ran his fingers over the carvings, his brow furrowing.

"Magic residue," he muttered. "Whoever was here, they used this to activate something."

Ophelia's magic surged in response, her hands moving instinctively over the carvings. The etched lines pulsed under her touch, their glow strengthening as her power intertwined with them. Images flickered to life on the wall, showing flashes of the Bell, its radiant form carried by shadowed figures, its glow fading as it disappeared into darkness.

"They moved it," Ophelia murmured. "They used this place to transport it." She tilted her head as a delicate hum reached her ears. It was soft, almost imperceptible, but it resonated in her bones, pulling at her magic like a gentle tide.

"There," she said, pointing toward a dark archway carved into the far wall.

Gabriel followed her gaze, his expression hardening. "I don't hear anything."

"You wouldn't," she replied, voice distant. She took a step toward the archway, the hum growing slightly louder with each movement. "It's not sound. It's magic. And it's calling me."

Gabriel hesitated for a moment, then fell into step behind her. "It might be a trap."

"Maybe," Ophelia said, glancing over her shoulder. A flicker of determination flashed in her eyes. "But we don't have a choice."

The archway loomed before them, its edges lined with dimly glowing symbols. The carvings seemed to watch them as they stepped through, history lingering around them like an oppressive force.

"Stay close," Gabriel murmured, his hand brushing against the hilt of the dagger at his belt.

"I wasn't planning to wander off," Ophelia replied dryly, though her focus was already fixed ahead.

As they disappeared into the darkness of the passageway, the empty chamber behind them seemed to exhale.

The narrow passage stretched on, the air growing cooler and denser with each step. Faint luminescent veins of magic threaded through the stone, illuminating their path in eerie blues and greens. Ophelia's pulse quickened, the pull of the Bell's magic growing stronger, thrumming in time with her own.

"I don't like this," Gabriel muttered. "It's too quiet. Too deliberate."

"It's leading me," Ophelia said, sharper than she intended. She slowed, glancing back at him with a softer expression. "I don't think it's trying to hurt me."

"You don't know that."

"Maybe not," she admitted, "but it feels ancient. Intentional. Like it wants to be found, but only by someone it chooses."

Gabriel's brow furrowed, his mistrust evident. Still, he didn't argue, and they continued deeper into the labyrinthine corridor.

The hum intensified as they emerged into another chamber, smaller than the first but no less striking. The floor was smooth, polished obsidian that reflected the glowing sigils on the walls. A shallow pool of water dominated the center of the room, its surface rippling with unseen movement.

Ophelia approached the pool cautiously, the Bell's magic vibrating within her like an unanswered question. She knelt at the edge, peering into the dark water.

"What do you see?" Gabriel asked, staying a few paces behind her.

"Nothing," she replied, frowning. "But I can feel it. It's below."

Gabriel's eyes swept the room, his posture tense. "We're not alone."

Ophelia froze, her heart pounding as she extended her magic outward. Gabriel was right. There was something else in the chamber, subtle but undeniable.

"It's not Eris," she whispered.

"Then what is it?"

Before she could answer, the water began to churn, the ripples growing into violent waves that lapped against the edges of the pool. A low, resonant hum filled the room, reverberating through the air.

Ophelia staggered back as a column of light shot up from the pool, illuminating the chamber with blinding intensity. Shielding her eyes, her magic flared instinctively in response.

When the light dimmed, the pool had transformed. The edges were now crystalline, revealing an intricate network of carvings etched into its depths. At the center, submerged just beneath the surface, was the Kala Ghanta.

Ophelia's hand hovered above the water, trembling as though caught between an irresistible pull and a forceful push. The Bell's magic surged in response, its energy coiling around her. It wasn't just power—it was intent. The sensation was strange and invasive, like fingers threading through her mind, prying open her thoughts. It whispered in an unfamiliar language, one her soul recognized but her mind couldn't grasp.

Her fingers twitched as the pull intensified, an unrelenting tide drawing her closer. The cool air of the chamber seemed to press against her chest, amplifying the heat radiating from the Bell. Her magic stirred in response, crackling gently around her fingertips, reaching out as if it, too, sought to connect with the artifact. She closed her eyes, letting the sensation wash over her, both comforting and suffocating.

"It wants me to take it," she murmured, as if saying it aloud might break her.

Gabriel was at her side in an instant. His strong hand clamped around her wrist with an urgency that sent a jolt through her, anchoring her before she could move further. "And what happens when you do?" he demanded, his dark eyes shining with a potent mix of anger and fear. His grip was firm but not harsh, as if afraid she might break under its weight.

Ophelia turned to him, her eyes locking on to his with a fiery intensity. Determination and trepidation waged war within her, but her resolve ultimately won out. "We find out," she said simply.

Gabriel's fingers tightened slightly around her wrist, his jaw clenching as he studied her. His concern etched deep lines into his face, and his dark eyes searched hers for a flicker of hesitation. "You can't just grab it, Ophelia," he said, his tone low and measured, each word carrying the heaviness of his apprehension. "You have no idea what this thing will do to you."

"I don't think I have a choice," she replied, the words resolute yet tinged with vulnerability. The Bell's pull was undeniable, a thrumming in her very bones that made it impossible to turn away. Her magic responded to it like a moth to a flame, melding with the artifact's energy in a symphony that only she could hear. "It's calling to me, Gabriel. I can feel it. Deep in my core."

He hesitated, his gaze unwavering as he tried to read her. The silence stretched taut between them, heavy with unspoken fears. Finally, his voice softened, though the tension in his posture did not. "If it hurts you—"

"Then you'll save me," she interrupted, a flicker of a smile breaking through the tension. It was small and fleeting, but it carried an intimacy that made his grip falter for just a moment.

Gabriel exhaled forcefully, his dark eyes narrowing as he released her wrist. The intensity in his gaze remained steadfast, even as he took a reluctant step back. "Be careful, Cinis," he said.

Ophelia turned back to the water, her heart pounding in time with the Bell's hum. Every nerve in her body screamed with anticipation and dread as she reached out again. Her magic surged instinctively, intertwining with the Bell's energy as if reconnecting with an old companion. The water was cool against her skin, a jarring contrast to the heat emanating from the artifact.

The moment her fingers brushed its surface, a deep shudder rippled through the air, vibrating in her chest like the resonance of a struck bell. The runes etched into the Kala Ghanta flared, their glow illuminating the room in pulses that mimicked a heartbeat. The Bell rose above the surface, hovering as if suspended by invisible threads, as the rest of the pool crystallized.

Ophelia gasped as the artifact's magic surged through her, a torrent of raw power and ancient memory that threatened to drown her.

She was no longer in the chamber.

Instead, she stood amidst a circle of witches, their faces illuminated by the fiery glow of molten gold and obsidian. They chanted in unison, their voices weaving an intricate web of magic that shimmered in the air around them. Blood spilled freely from their palms, mixing with molten materials as the Bell took shape. Ophelia could feel their desperation, their need to create something powerful enough to protect and destroy, to control and unleash. But as the Kala Ghanta solidified, she also felt their fear. It was more than they had bargained for.

The vision shifted. Time moved like sand slipping through her fingers, fragments of moments cascading past her. She saw the Bell used in rituals, its toll echoing across worlds and unraveling threads of time. She felt its hunger, its insatiable need for more—more power, more sacrifice, more of everything. And then she felt their regret, haunting and heavy, as they realized the cost of what they had wrought.

"Ophelia!" Gabriel's voice cut through like a lifeline, pulling her back.

She gasped, her eyes snapping open as the vision ruptured.

"It's so powerful. Sentient," she said. The words felt insufficient to describe the magnitude of what she had just experienced.

Gabriel stepped closer, his movements deliberate and measured. His eyes narrowed as he studied the artifact, his expression unreadable. "What do you mean, sentient?" he asked, voice cautious but tinged with curiosity.

Ophelia struggled to articulate the enormity of what she felt. "It has intent," she said slowly, searching for the right words. "A will of its own. And it's waiting."

"For what?" Gabriel's voice was low, his unease evident in the tension of his posture.

Ophelia shook her head, her gaze dropping to the Bell. Its runes shifted, their patterns hypnotic and ever-changing. "For something or someone. I'm not sure," she murmured.

But she knew. The realization came to her suddenly, unbidden, like a jagged shard of ice penetrating her chest. The Bell demanded balance, and balance always came with a cost. One of them would have to die. She hadn't believed that the first time she heard it. But, now, the knowledge struck her like a physical blow.

"Ophelia?" Gabriel's voice cut through the haze that clouded her mind. He was at her side in an instant, his hands steadying her shoulders. His eyes searched hers, dark and filled with worry. "What's wrong?"

She opened her mouth, the words caught in her throat like

a suffocating knot. Finally, she forced them out. "One of us," she choked. "One of us has to die. The scribes were right."

Gabriel's expression darkened, his jaw clenching as his hands tightened on her shoulders. "You don't know that. There has to be another way. That was only one interpretation," he said.

"I do," she insisted with a desperate edge. "I can feel it, Gabriel. It's in the magic. It's in the pull of the Bell. It won't stop until it gets what it wants. It demands a life in exchange for its destruction. That's the price."

Gabriel's gaze hardened, and his grip on her shoulders became almost painful. "Then it'll be me."

"No!" The word burst from her like a scream, raw and filled with anguish. She pushed away from him, shaking her head as tears burned in her eyes. "You can't. I won't let you."

His expression softened, though his resolve remained unshaken. "Ophelia, listen to me," he said. "This is bigger than us. If it takes my life to end this, then so be it. You've already given up so much—"

"And so have you!" she interrupted, breaking under the strain of emotions. "You've fought for me, sacrificed for me. Don't you dare act like your life is any less valuable than mine."

Gabriel's hands dropped to his sides, his dark eyes locking onto hers with an intensity that made her breath falter. "And I'd do it all again," he said softly, voice carrying an unyielding strength. "Without hesitation."

The words pierced through her, breaking something deep inside. She shook her head, her tears flowing freely now. "There has to be another way," she whispered, trembling.

"Maybe there is," Gabriel admitted, tone heavy with resignation. "But we don't have time to find it."

As he turned toward the Bell, Ophelia's heart shattered. But she knew he was right. Eris could return at any moment to use the Kala Ghanta. Or, possibly worse, someone else could already be closing in. If they didn't act now, they might lose their only chance to stop it from falling into the wrong hands.

The hum of the artifact grew louder, its energy crackling in the air, volatile and untamed. Gabriel stepped forward, his movements steady, his resolve like iron.

"Gabriel," she pleaded. She reached for him, but her limbs felt leaden, weighed down by the paralyzing magic of the Bell. As if it wanted Gabriel and not her. She fought against it, but she couldn't move. "Don't do this. Please," she begged.

He paused, just for a moment, his head turning slightly as if he wanted to look back at her. But he didn't. "You'll understand one day, Cinis," he said, barely audible. "You were always meant for more."

The Bell's light flared, the runes along its surface glowing with a blinding intensity that forced Ophelia to shield her eyes. The hum grew into a deafening roar, shaking the chamber and sending fissures splintering across the walls. The air vibrated with energy, and an electric charge filled the space, making her skin prickle.

"No!" Ophelia screamed. The sound ripped from her as the light consumed everything.

She felt the Bell's power surge, a force so overwhelming it drowned out every other sensation. The last thing she saw was Gabriel's silhouette, his figure standing tall and resolute as he reached for the artifact.

And then, silence.

CHAPTER

THIRTY

"No! No! No! No! No!" Ophelia's scream echoed through the chamber, raw and guttural. She fell to her knees, tears spilling freely down her face. Her fingers dug into the cold stone floor as grief ripped through her.

The light dimmed, leaving the chamber shrouded in a strange, otherworldly glow. The Bell hovered, its runes pulsing as though it were catching its breath. The hum of its power was softer now, but it lingered, an ominous reminder that it was far from dormant. The chamber felt emptier, colder, as though the Bell had not only consumed Gabriel but also drained the very air around her. The silence that followed was deafening.

Ophelia blinked, her vision blurry from the tears and the searing brightness of the Bell's light. She stumbled forward, her heart pounding in her chest. "Gabriel?" she called, her voice cracking. "Gabriel, where are you?"

The chamber echoed with her words, but no answer came.

Her gaze darted around the room, searching desperately.

The space where he had stood was empty, the air heavy with a stillness that felt wrong. Her chest tightened as panic clawed at her throat. "Gabriel!" she screamed, raw with desperation.

The Bell hummed softly, its runes flickering as if in response to her anguish. Ophelia turned to it, her fists clenched as a surge of anger and grief overtook her. "What did you do?" she demanded, shaking with rage. "Where is he?"

But the Bell remained silent, enigmatic and unyielding. Ophelia fell to her knees, her hands gripping the cold stone floor.

"Why did you do it?" she whispered. "Why did you leave me just when I found you?"

His absence crushed her. She bowed her head, her tears falling onto the stone, her body shaking with each ragged breath. He was gone.

Just as the despair threatened to consume her entirely, a low, resonant hum broke the silence. The Kala Ghanta glowed, its light pulsing like a heartbeat. Ophelia froze, her tear-streaked face snapping up to look at it.

The energy gathered, swirling within the Bell, until it expelled something with a forceful burst. A figure tumbled to the ground before her, limp and motionless.

"Gabriel!"

Ophelia scrambled forward, her hands shaking as she turned him over. His skin was pale, his body eerily still, but he was there. Her heart raced as she leaned closer, desperate to find any sign of life.

"Come on, Gabriel," she whispered, voice thick with tears. "Live. Please."

For a terrifying moment, nothing happened. Then his chest rose with a shallow gasp, and his dark eyes fluttered open.

"Ophelia," he rasped, weak but alive. "You want to try CPR again?" he asked.

Relief crashed over her like a wave, and a huff of laughter escaped her. She clutched him tightly, tears soaking into his shirt. "I thought I lost you," she sobbed. "I thought you were gone."

Gabriel managed the ghost of a smile, his hand coming up to weakly brush her hair back. "It didn't want me," he murmured.

She pulled back slightly, her eyes wide with disbelief. "What?"

"The Bell," he said. "It rejected me. It wouldn't take me as the sacrifice."

Her stomach twisted as his words sank in. The Bell hadn't just rejected him—it had chosen to spare him, leaving the question of whom it would accept painfully unresolved. Yet clear.

Ophelia's gaze flicked to the Kala Ghanta, its light still glowing, its pull stronger than ever. She swallowed hard, her resolve hardening.

"Then it's me," she said, voice steady despite the terror raging inside her.

"No," Gabriel said immediately, his grip on her arm tightening despite his weakened state. "You can't—"

"I have to," she interrupted, her tone leaving no room for argument. She rose to her feet, her eyes alight with determination. "It won't stop until it gets what it wants. And I can't let anyone else pay that price."

"Ophelia, please," Gabriel pleaded, voice cracking. "There has to be another way." He tried to stand, but he was too weak.

She turned to him, her expression softening. "We don't have time to find another way," she said, faltering mid-sentence. "You said so yourself. And if I don't do this, it'll keep consuming us until there's nothing left."

Gabriel finally struggled to his feet, his legs shaky beneath him, but he was frozen in place just as she'd been. "You don't know what it'll do to you. You can't just give yourself to it."

"I don't have a choice," she said, tears spilling down her cheeks. She reached out, cupping his face in her hands. "I need you to trust me, Gabriel. I need you to let me do this."

His hands covered hers, his dark eyes searching hers desperately. "I can't lose you," he whispered.

Her heart ached at the raw vulnerability in his voice, but she forced herself to step back out of his reach, her gaze lingering on him for a moment longer before she turned toward the Kala Ghanta.

As she approached, the Bell's light intensified, its magic reaching out to her like an eager embrace. The Kala Ghanta seemed to sense her intent, its energy surging in anticipation. Its power pressed against her chest, but she didn't falter.

"Ophelia, don't!" Gabriel's voice rang out behind her, filled with desperation.

She closed her eyes, tears streaming down her face as she whispered, "I'm sorry. I love you."

Her hand hovered over the Bell, the magic thrumming in time with her heartbeat. And then, just as she was about to make contact, a different voice cut through the tension.

"Stop!"

Ophelia froze, her eyes snapping open.

Leander strode into the chamber, his steps purposeful, the glow of the Kala Ghanta reflecting off his sculpted features, his eyes locked on her. The tension in the room shifted immediately, the Bell's thrumming energy seeming to react to his arrival.

"Leander," Gabriel rasped, still unsteady on his feet but pulling himself upright. His hand instinctively hovered near his weapon, though he didn't draw it. "What are you doing here?"

Leander's gaze flickered briefly to Gabriel before settling on Ophelia. "I'm here to do what must be done," he said, his tone steady but heavy with meaning. "Step away from the Bell, Ophelia."

Her hands hovered above the artifact as the pull of its magic grew almost unbearable. "No," she said. "I have to do this. It's the only way to end this."

Leander shook his head, his expression softening as he took a step closer. "You're wrong. This isn't your burden to bear."

Tears streaked down Ophelia's face as she turned to him, her magic flickering wildly with emotion. "Then whose burden is it? Yours? You can't just show up now and act like you know what's best for me."

"I'm not acting," Leander said, his voice filled with an unshakable resolve. "I've lived long enough to understand the price of power like this. And I won't let it take you."

Leander's eyes never left Ophelia's as he continued. "You're being driven by guilt and desperation. I won't let you sacrifice yourself for something you don't fully understand."

The words hit her like a blow, her chest tightening as she stared at him. "You don't know me," she said. "You've been a shadow my entire life. And now you want to tell me what I can and can't do?"

Leander's expression faltered, a flicker of regret passing over his face. "You're right. I haven't been there for you. And for that, I'm sorry. But that doesn't mean I'll stand by and let you throw your life away. I've lived for centuries. It's your turn to live."

The Kala Ghanta's glow intensified, its energy pulsating through the chamber as if responding to their argument. The air grew heavier, charged with the artifact's magic, enveloping them in its overwhelming presence.

"You don't understand!" Ophelia shouted, her magic surging around her in a wave of heat and light. "I can feel it, Leander! It's calling to me. It needs me."

"And that's exactly why you can't give in to it," he said, stepping closer. His voice softened, filled with a strange mixture of urgency and affection threading through his words. "The Kala Ghanta is a manipulator. It knows your weaknesses, your fears. It's using them against you. *All* it needs is a supernatural to go back to the time of its creation. *Not you.* Once that happens, the Bell will be rendered powerless, an object without purpose. It can never be used again."

Doubt and resolve warred within her, her fingers curling into fists as her mind raced. "If I don't stop it, who will?" she asked, the question a whisper.

Leander's expression hardened, and for the first time, the weight of centuries etched clearly on his face. "I will."

"No!" Ophelia's voice broke as she reached for him, but he caught her wrist gently, his touch firm but comforting.

"I've lived a very long life, Ophelia. I've made countless mistakes. This is my chance—my duty even—to finally make things right."

Gabriel stepped forward, his face a mask of barely contained emotion. "What about Eris? What about the war we're fighting?"

"The war isn't over. It's just beginning. And you don't need me for that. But this," Leander said, gesturing toward the Bell, "is a battle I can end. Right here, right now."

Ophelia's tears fell freely as she shook her head. "Leander, please."

"You're strong, Ophelia," Leander said, putting his hands on her shoulders. "Stronger than I ever could have imagined. But you have a greater role to play, and it's not here."

Her knees buckled, her heart splintering. "I'm not ready," she whispered. "I just met you."

"You don't have to be ready," he said, a single tear slipping down his face. "You just have to be willing to keep going. To fight for what's right."

He released her and turned toward the Bell, its glow now almost blinding. The artifact seemed to hum with recognition, its energy crackling in the air as Leander approached.

Gabriel reached for him with a growl of frustration. "Leander, stop. There's no guarantee this will work."

"There are no guarantees in war," Leander replied, his tone calm but resolute. "Only choices. And this is mine."

Ophelia stepped toward him, her magic sparking wildly around her as she tried to grab his arm. "Don't do this! Please!"

He turned back one last time, his gaze locking on to hers. "Ophelia, listen to me. You're going to face trials that will test everything you are—your strength, your resolve, your heart. But you'll endure. Because you're my daughter, and you are meant for more than this."

The words struck her like a lightning bolt, stealing her breath as she watched him turn away. The Kala Ghanta pulsed brighter, its magic swirling around him like a tempest as he reached out and placed his hands on its surface.

Light erupted from the Bell, a golden blaze that consumed Leander in an instant. Ophelia screamed, her body lurching forward, but Gabriel caught her, holding her back as the chamber filled with blinding radiance.

"Leander!" she cried.

The light swelled, a final burst of energy that seemed to shake the foundations of the world, and then it was gone. The chamber fell into an eerie silence, the Bell's glow extinguished. Leander was gone.

Ophelia sank to her knees, her chest heaving with sobs as the reality of what had just happened began to settle over her. The chamber was deathly still, the Kala Ghanta silent and inert, its once-vivid runes now dim and lifeless. The Bell had accepted the sacrifice. There was no question. Leander was gone, and the absence of him felt like a gaping wound in the air around them.

But it wasn't just Leander who had been lost. As Mo had warned, the sacrifice had unraveled the Kala Ghanta's very essence, severing it from the threads of time and magic that once fueled it. Ophelia felt deep within her that the ancient object—once powerful enough to reshape reality—was now nothing more than a hollow relic. Leander's selfless act had ensured that the Bell could never again be used, not by anyone, for any purpose.

Gabriel crouched beside her, his expression etched with grief and exhaustion. His hand rested gently on her shoulder, but his touch couldn't pierce through the anguish inside her.

"He's really gone," she said, voice unsteady. "He didn't even hesitate."

Gabriel's jaw tightened, his own grief evident in his movements. "He knew what he was doing, Ophelia."

Her fingers curled into the cold stone beneath her, her nails scraping against the surface as she tried to ground herself. "But why? Why did it have to be him? I just learned he was my father. I have so many unanswered questions."

Gabriel didn't respond immediately. Instead, he rose to his feet, his gaze fixed on the dormant Bell. "Because he understood what we're up against. He knew the stakes better than anyone."

Ophelia followed his gaze, standing next to him as her stomach twisted at the sight of the artifact.

"We carry his sacrifice with us," Gabriel said softly, his

hand brushing hers. "But we don't let it stop us. We honor it by moving forward."

She nodded, the pain in her chest dulling, for now, to a quiet ache.

"This isn't over. Whatever he saw coming, we'll be ready for it," he said, dark eyes holding hers, steady and resolute.

"Then let's start by getting out of here. There's nothing left for us here," she said.

THIRTY-ONE

The ruins of Marisante stretched endlessly around them, a maze of jagged spires and crumbling arches as they wound their way out of the chamber. Ophelia's steps slowed as an unsettling sensation crept over her, crawling across her skin like static electricity. She stopped abruptly, her head tilting as she tried to pinpoint the source of the strange energy.

"Ophelia?" Gabriel's voice was low, questioning. He followed her gaze as she scanned the desolate expanse, eyes unfocused.

"There's someone nearby," she murmured. Her magic stirred restlessly, reacting to the foreign entity like an animal sensing a predator.

Gabriel tensed beside her, his hand instinctively moving to the hilt of his dagger. "Are you sure? We've cleared most of the city. Unless Eris is still here," he said.

"It's not her," Ophelia said, shaking her head. "This is different. Stronger. Older." She frowned, frustration flickering across her face as she struggled to describe the sensation. "It's pulling at me. Like it wants me to find it."

Gabriel's eyes narrowed, his jaw tightening. "It could be a trap."

"Maybe," Ophelia admitted. "But I don't think so. I can't ignore it. It's too deliberate."

Without waiting for his reply, she started moving, her steps quick and purposeful. Gabriel followed, his movements cautious, eyes darting to every shadow and crevice as they navigated the ruins.

The sensation grew stronger as they walked, a pulsing energy that thrummed in Ophelia's chest and tugged at her magic. It led her away from the main thoroughfares, down narrow alleyways and crumbled staircases, until the ruins gave way to a sheer cliff face. The entrance to a cave yawned before them, dark and foreboding, the air around it humming with latent power.

Gabriel stepped in front of her, his expression grim. "If something's waiting in there, we're not going in blind."

Ophelia reached out, placing a hand on his arm. "It's not hostile," she said, her voice steady but laced with uncertainty. "At least, it doesn't feel that way."

Gabriel gave her a skeptical look but didn't argue. "Fine. But I'm going first."

"No," she said firmly, stepping around him. "It's calling to me, Gabriel. Whatever's in there, it's for me to face."

He hesitated, his protective instincts warring with his respect for her judgment. "Stay close," he said finally, his tone brooking no argument. He grabbed a flameless torch near them and held it out to her to light with fire magic.

Together, they stepped into the cave. The descent felt endless, each step heavier than the last. The temperature dropped immediately, the air cool and damp against their skin. Luminescent veins of magic threaded through the stone walls, casting an eerie blue-green glow that illuminated their path.

The presence grew stronger with every step, pressing against Ophelia's senses until it felt like a second heartbeat in her chest. Her breath quickened as they reached a widening in the cave, the space opening into a cavern filled with shimmering crystal formations.

The magnetic pull in Ophelia's chest deepened, its intensity matching the frantic beat of her heart. She pressed a hand to her ribs, as though she could steady the chaos within. Beside her, Gabriel moved with a hunter's precision, the flickering torchlight throwing jagged shadows on the slick, damp walls. The air between them felt charged.

"Do you feel it?" Ophelia whispered, barely more than a breath.

Gabriel nodded once, his jaw tight. "It's close. Whatever it is."

A shiver raced down her spine. The pull felt wrong now—not just powerful, but deeply, unnervingly personal. Something here wasn't just calling to her. It was waiting for her.

They passed through a narrow corridor, the walls so close they scraped her shoulders. The passage finally widened, opening into a cavern that seemed to consume the torchlight entirely. The air reeked of damp earth and iron, and the muted sound of dripping water echoed endlessly.

Ophelia paused, her magic flickering at her fingertips. "It's here," she whispered.

Gabriel stepped ahead of her, scanning the cavern with wary precision. "Stay close," he ordered. "We don't know what we're walking into."

Ophelia's gaze darted around the cavern. Iron bars lined

the walls, forming a series of cells, their doors warped and hanging open. Most were empty, but the darkened corners hinted at something worse—bones, broken chains, and stains that spoke of long-forgotten violence. She swallowed hard, her stomach churning.

"Gabriel, what is this place?"

He didn't answer, but the tension in his shoulders told her enough. Whatever this was, it wasn't just a prison; it was a graveyard.

They moved deeper into the cavern, their footsteps echoing ominously. At the far end of the space stood a heavy wooden door, its surface engraved with glowing runes. The pull within Ophelia surged, almost painful now, as if something on the other side was clawing at her soul.

"It's behind there," she said, voice tight.

Gabriel placed a hand on the door, his brow furrowing. "These runes...they're wards. Whoever put this here wanted to keep something—or someone—contained."

"Or protected," Ophelia countered. Her hand hovered next to his, trembling with the effort it took to hold back the magic surging within her. "We have to open it."

Gabriel hesitated, his eyes searching hers. Whatever he saw there made him nod grimly. He stepped back and gestured for her to proceed.

Ophelia pressed her palm to the door. The runes flared to life, a blistering heat against her skin. She flinched but held steady, channeling her magic into the barrier. The runes dimmed, flickered, and finally extinguished with a stuttering hiss. The door groaned as it creaked open.

Inside, the room was small, dimly lit by a single torch mounted on the wall. Shadows danced across the stone floor, pooling at the edges of the chamber. And in the center, bound by thick iron chains, was a figure slumped forward, head bowed.

Ophelia froze. The pull she had felt—the magic that had dragged her here—was radiating from this figure. Her muscles tensed, a cold spike of adrenaline rushing through her as her gaze locked on the pale form. She stepped inside, her movements hesitant.

Gabriel followed close behind, his hand on the hilt of his dagger. "Who—?" he began, but the words died on his lips as the form stirred.

The chains clinked as the figure shifted, lifting its head slowly. Pale skin, gaunt features, and hair that hung in dark, matted strands. But it was the eyes that stopped her heart. Emerald green, painfully familiar, eyes.

"No," Ophelia said, voice barely audible. She stumbled forward, her knees threatening to give out. "No, it can't be."

The figure's gaze locked on hers, and recognition flickered in those hauntingly familiar eyes. "Ophelia?" he croaked, his voice hoarse and raw, but unmistakable.

The room spun as the world tilted on its axis. She couldn't breathe, couldn't think. She had watched him die—felt the crushing finality of his absence—and yet, here he was.

Gabriel stepped forward, his expression dark and disbelieving. "It can't be. You're dead," he said, his voice low and icy.

The man—vampire—before them managed a bitter, broken laugh. "Not dead, yet," he rasped, his lips twisting into a humorless smile. "But there were times I wished for death."

Ophelia dropped to her knees, her hands hovering over the chains binding him. Tears blurred her vision, spilling over as she choked on a sob. "This isn't real," she whispered. "It can't be real."

"It's real," he said, heavy with exhaustion and pain. "I'm here, Ophelia. I've always been here."

The room seemed to shrink around her, his words crashing down on her. She reached out, her fingertips brushing against his skin—cold and fragile, but undeniably alive.

She whispered his name, her voice cracking, "Luka?"

Order Book 3 of The Wildes Witch Trilogy: Flames of Fury

ALSO BY CARRIE VIXENHART

THE WILDES WITCH TRILOGY

Eye of Fire, Book 1

Out of Ashes, Book 2

Flames of Fury, Book 3

AUTHOR'S NOTE

Thank you for diving into Ophelia's world of magic, mystery, and untamed passion. If you enjoyed this journey, I'd love to stay connected.

JOIN MY NEWSLETTER

 Want exclusive sneak peeks, updates on future books, blog posts, and behind-the-scenes content? Please visit my website and sign up for my newsletter! www.vixenhart.com

SOCIAL MEDIA

Let's keep the conversation going! Follow me on social media for updates and a glimpse into my writing life. @carrievixenhart

ACKNOWLEDGMENTS

This book would not exist without the many incredible people who supported me along the way. First and foremost, thank you to my daughters. Your brilliance and creativity inspire me. I promise Ophelia isn't my favorite daughter, no matter what you think.

To my family, thank you for being loud, outlandish, and unapologetically boisterous. You all are the bedrock of a rich and beautifully layered life. And for that, I'm endlessly grateful.

To my friends and the best thing I ever discovered on the internet: Thank you for cheering me on during this wild ride, being my hype squad, and graciously supporting me as I relentlessly chased my overly ambitious, self-imposed deadlines.

A special shoutout to my early readers for your honest feedback and sharp critiques: Alison, Amy, Brigette, Elayna, Kelly, Keri, Lara, Lindsey, Lynn, Mary, Melissa, Rebekah, Tara, Toni, and Wendy. You made this book better (and occasionally humbled me in the best way possible).

To my phenomenal editors—Alex Harpp, Leanne Rabesa, and Jamie Ryter—thank you for helping me shape this book into something I'm immensely proud of. To Sarah Hansen of Okay Creations, your cover art is everything I dreamed of and more.

To my yoga community, thank you for keeping me balanced, both on and off the mat. To my sailing community,

I'm sorry about that one time with the heat exhaustion and feeding the fish. Let's never talk about it again.

To my Shelf Love crew: Your enthusiasm, support, and shared passion for spicy stories and over-the-top plot twists lift me up in ways I'll always cherish.

Books are woven from lived experiences, shared connections, and the stories we carry. Thank you for being part of mine.

About the Author

A free spirit at heart, Carrie Vixenhart's passion for life has carried her across the globe. She delights in sharing new wonders with her daughters, both through travel and the magic of books. Carrie is perpetually drawn to the ocean, where she feels most at peace. A dedicated yogi and aspiring sailor, she dreams of one day exploring the world by water. Fueled by a bottomless coffee cup, she weaves high-suspense urban fantasy packed with steamy romance and supernatural drama.

instagram.com/carrievixenhart
tiktok.com/@carrievixenhart
amazon.com/author/carrievixenhart